Sensible Shoes

by

Cindy Causey

Sensible Shoes

Cover Art by *Teddi Black*

The Wild Rose Press, Inc.
PO Box 708
Adams Basin, NY 14410-0708
Visit us at www.thewildrosepress.com

Publishing History
First Edition, 2025
Trade Paperback ISBN 978-1-5092-5946-5
Digital ISBN 978-1-5092-5947-2

Published in the United States of America

Dedication

To Ted, Carol, and Leigh Ann, who are past fifty, but
still fabulous

Chapter One

"Tess, can you come here a second? I have an opportunity to discuss with you."

Lord, help me. An opportunity. Those are never good.

Heaving a huge sigh, I left my gray cubicle at the *Dallas Tribune* and rounded the corner, entering my boss' slightly bigger gray cubicle.

"You bellowed?" I asked, comfortable enough with our boss-sycophant relationship to tease her a little.

Ruth Wiseman grimaced as she did often. She was short and stocky, with a shock of over-dyed red hair and huge black glasses perched on her generously proportioned nose. The lack of a cigar hanging from her lips was the only thing distinguishing her from a mob boss. New Jersey-born and bred, she was all about the newspaper, but in spite of her gruff exterior, she had the proverbial heart of gold.

I liked to think of Ruth as a burnt marshmallow—hard and crusty on the outside with a gooey, sweet center.

She would have hated the comparison.

"Tess, sit down."

Yet another bad sign. Sitting means explanations. Explanations mean convincing. Convincing means bad news.

"What's up?" I ventured.

"Well, I'm sure you heard Sylvia is leaving."

"Yes, getting married. Again." Sylvia wrote the fashion column for the paper. She was flashy and buff and sexy and fell in love with all the wrong men.

"Right, and Bruno wants to take her back to Brazil to meet his family. She'll be gone several months."

A creeping dread spread throughout my nervous system. "And?"

"And I want you to take over her column until she gets back."

The creeping dread wrapped its tentacles around my throat and squeezed really hard.

"You want me to write the fashion column?" I squeaked. "What about the Home & Garden column? I'm starting the series on grubworm eradication."

"Summer's almost over, Tess. This is the perfect time for your column to take a little hiatus." Ruth smiled as if she were handing a sucker to a small child.

"And just skip the fall Harvest Season? We always do a big story on the many ways to use gourds. You want me to ignore that?" I implored, clutching at editorial straws.

"If you're worried, we can rerun last year's columns for a while. Not much changes from year to year."

"My God, Ruth, have you completely forgotten about the pumpkin shortage last fall? I was working day and night."

The look she gave me made it clear she saw through my lame argument. She was right; the Home & Garden column almost wrote itself. I even had enough free time recently to put notes together for a book on environmental gardening. Although I'd probably never write it, the idea nudged me once in a while. But to walk away from gourd season for fashion? No one could ever think that was my career path.

I leaned in a little closer to Ruth, trying for intimacy and understanding on a woman-to-woman level. "You must be kidding. I can't write the fashion column. Look at me."

When the paper had loosened its dress code years earlier, I switched from shorter skirts with jackets and three-inch heels to longer skirts with tunics and comfy crepe-soled shoes. Since then, I had eased into comfier leggings and long, boxy tunics in an array of reliable colors. But lately I noticed everyone wearing short, summery dresses and strappy sandals showcasing painted toenails and tiny toe rings.

I sighed and glanced down at my unadorned feet, ensconced in sturdy red flats that made a patriotic picture with my navy leggings and flag-waving white tunic. The only person in the building who was less a fashionista than I was Ruth, who now leaned back in her chair, fingers tented in front of her scowling face.

"Tess, Tess, I'm not expecting you to write like Sylvia. I'm not even expecting you to write about fashion. What I have in mind is a column to women, for women, about women. Real women. Like one of those influencers on the Internet. You know…funny, wise, poignant, and… relevant."

The creeping dread, now fully formed, tossed a grenade into my stomach. She might as well have asked me to write like Shakespeare. "You want me to be funny, wise, and poignant and…relevant? Are you insane?"

Okay, I may have stepped over the line with that last bit, because Ruth's face twisted a little in the ominous way I had seen so often just before she pounded her fist on the desk. "Just write the damn thing, Tess. I don't care if you're funny, wise, poignant, or what was the other thing?"

"Relevant," I murmured.

"Relevant, for God's sake. Just do it. I need a column for the women's page starting next week, and you're it. Write about what you know. Family. Food. The laundry. A library book. You've got family. You've got laundry. It'll be a cinch."

"But—"

"No buts. Just do it. It'll be good for you. You need to get out of your rut." She turned her attention to her computer screen.

As if in a trance, I rose from the chair and turned to leave.

"Oh, Tess?" She said, without looking at me.

"Yes?" *Maybe she's changed her mind; she saw my outfit, and she changed her mind.*

"Happy birthday."

****

I just wanted a quiet birthday—nothing too big or too flashy—nothing that would call attention to the fact that I was fifty years old and looked every minute of it— nothing too loud, too hot, too crowded, too messy, or too tiring.

Too bad.

I was supposed to come home from work at the usual time, feed the cat, and go to dinner somewhere quiet with my kids. Another uneventful, boring, mundane year gone by.

While my boss had derailed my thinking and caused me to face a weekend of worrying and fretting, fretting and worrying, I still had my birthday. She couldn't take that away. It would be calm and simple and quiet.

That was the plan.

I pulled into the driveway of my suburban Dallas home, stepped out of the car, and was slammed by the sizzling Texas heat. I didn't notice, though, since I was sweating like a marathon runner despite the frigid air conditioning blowing in my face the whole way home.

Surely, women had died of menopause. Simply self-combusted while brushing their teeth or watching a cooking show or typing a report or pumping gas. I hated the idea of dying all flushed and damp, collapsed at the office coffee pot as if I'd just played a round of tennis.

I made my way past the wilting hanging baskets to the back door, chiding myself for not watering before I left for work that morning. *No one will see them. No one will know you are a fraud...a pathetic gardener with a brown thumb.*

Once inside, I fed Tuxedo the cat, although the animal was so huge, he could have lived off stored fat for months. Then I went into the bedroom to freshen up. I glanced in the mirror, slicked on some lipstick, ran a brush through my stick-straight brown hair, made more limp by the oppressive Texas humidity, and sighed again.

Oh well, it was just dinner with the kids.

It was our tradition since the divorce that my son and daughter and I celebrated my birthday solo. No other friends or relations.

On Saturday, I would celebrate in another way by going to the theatre with Sam Winborn, the man I'd been seeing for almost a year. I hated the word "boyfriend" for someone my age, and "friend" didn't seem important enough, so I avoided any label at all. Which was the way

Sam and I approached everything.

His wife was in a nursing home with early-onset Alzheimer's and hadn't recognized him in over a year, but he was fiercely faithful to her, visiting every day. Our relationship had started out as one lonely person spending time with another, and it hadn't progressed much past that, which was okay with me. I liked my life orderly, predictable, and stress-free.

At least until today when Ruth dropped her bombshell. Influencer, indeed!

In the den, I watched a few minutes of the news and snacked on stale chips and salsa before the front door flew open, and my children bounded in, all smiles and full of birthday salutations.

It was odd they arrived together. Normally, they would straggle in from the far-flung nether regions of the Dallas Metroplex. They came from work, racing in at the last minute. This time, they were a good ten minutes early.

Another missed omen.

They stopped in the middle of the room and stared at me.

"Is that what you're wearing?" Whitney asked, her eyes wide in astonishment.

Whitney and Sydney were twins, named by their father. I should have known then he was gay.

"Yes, I'm wearing this," I answered. We had this discussion every time we were together. I dressed like a frump; Whitney told me so. It was part of our family dynamic.

She came up behind me and fluffed my hair. "Can't we do something with this?"

"Look, my dear," I said, shaking her hand off my

head and facing her, hands on hips. "This is how I look, get used to it. Now, where are we going to eat? I'm hungry."

Her brother, Sydney, plopped down on the sofa and changed the channel on the television. "We have to watch something on TV before we go."

"What?" I stared at him and then at Whitney, who hurried over to sit next to him.

"Yeah, Mom, we need to see this episode, it's the one where Ross—"

I interrupted. "You want to watch a rerun of an old sitcom?"

They ignored my question, staring at the screen like their lives depended on it.

"Syd? What are you doing? You don't even like that show!"

He looked up at me, eyes wide, "Sure I do, Mom. And I've never seen this episode. It's the one where Ross—"

"I don't care what Ross does! I just want to go eat!"

Sydney, who was older than Whitney by one minute and, therefore, considered himself more mature, cooed, "Patience is a virtue, Mom."

Too mentally exhausted from my quasi-confrontation with Ruth to argue, I squeezed onto the sofa between them, my purse perched on my lap, and watched the episode where Ross—

The doorbell chimed, and before I could struggle off the sofa to answer it, my ex-husband, Jack Marston, and his current lover, the very honed personal trainer, Tad, bustled in, carrying all sorts of foil-covered pots and platters.

"Jack, we were just leaving for dinner. What are you

doing here?" I asked as they headed straight for the kitchen, where they uncovered trays of food and unpacked bags filled with garnishes.

They were grinning like the cat that ate the canary, and so were the kids.

"Oh, God! You didn't!" I exclaimed, horrified as realization dawned in my fevered brain.

"Happy birthday, Mom," the twins squealed, jumping off the sofa and grabbing me in a bear hug.

Jack, a stockbroker turned restaurateur, flashed me with his still-adorable grin. "Happy birthday, sweetie."

"Don't sweetie me. What are you doing? Who put you up to this?"

"Well, we're making Mexican food. And you can thank your offspring and mine for the surprise party."

Before I could confront my offspring and his, my parents came in with a cooler, kissed me on both cheeks, and joined Jack and Tad in the kitchen.

"You, too?" I asked, certain now that we were in for the long haul—one of the never-ending Thomason birthday parties. An evening of food, fellowship, and frivolity, not what I had wanted on my birthday.

"Well, of course, dear," my mother said. "Now go put on some makeup. You look tired."

"I am tired, Mom, and I'm not prepared for a party."

"Yes, well, your children wanted to do something special for your fiftieth, and you should be grateful they love you that much." She turned her attention back to filling glasses with ice, muttering under her breath, "My children never gave me a surprise party."

"Geez, Mom, you threatened us with pain of death if we ever surprised you. You said you didn't want to be caught without your face on."

"Yes, well, mothers are supposed to say things they don't mean."

"Daddy, help," I pleaded.

My father began ignoring my mother twenty years earlier when he retired and had to spend entire days with her. It had been the key to keeping the marriage happy all these years.

"What, Chicken?" he asked, oblivious to the conversation. Chicken was his pet name for me. My sister, Lennie, was Lambkin, and my brother, Paul, was Piglet. I would have preferred being the soft and cuddly little lamb, but being the Chicken was much better than the Pig.

I sighed, as usual, unable to understand my parents at fifty any more than I understood them at eighteen. "Never mind, Daddy."

I headed to the bedroom to put on some makeup as instructed but was interrupted by the arrival of nephews Matt and Jason, twelve-year-old twins (yes, twins ran in the family), who muttered their greetings and headed for the den, laptop in tow. Within sixty seconds, they were arguing over which video game to play. Their parents, Piglet Paul and his wife, the perfectly coiffed Donna, breezed in, carrying several beautifully wrapped presents and a covered tray.

Lambkin Lennie was unmarried and lived in Wisconsin but spent her time traveling the globe as a producer for the Nature's Vision television network. She had called the night before to wish me happy birthday and tell me about her vacation in Venice with Paolo, a wildlife videographer. I had always hated Lennie.

While Paul talked with Dad about the Fed's latest move, Donna, removing the lid with a flourish, revealed a tray of the most beautiful hors d'oeuvres I had ever seen.

"Mmm, did you make these?" I asked, savoring some delectable tidbit.

"God, no," Donna laughed. "Paul insists we get them at that little place on Oak Lawn. He told me long ago that my cooking wasn't very good, so I shouldn't bother." She slipped one into her mouth with a wink. "They are good, aren't they? You know, I never eat this stuff. Paul is so aware of my weight. If I gain an ounce, he knows it."

"Good grief, Donna. Why don't you tell him to go to hell?"

"Oh, I couldn't, Tess. He's so good to me and the boys. He gives us everything. Keeping the house, entertaining his friends, and looking my best are the least I can do for him." She patted her hair with one manicured hand.

I continued my trek to the bedroom, glad I wasn't married to my brother and silently congratulating Lambkin Lennie on her choice to remain unencumbered.

I put on more lipstick, fluffed my hair, watched it sink to its original level, and surveyed myself in the mirror.

Fifty years old. Half a century. Oh, well, no one ignored me, and no one told me every move to make. My children were grown. And although I had wanted a quiet evening, I did have people who loved me enough to invade my house. At least they brought dinner…and presents.

I came out of the bedroom and said hello to Mark Horton, Whitney's most recent serious boyfriend. He was slight and bookish with narrow black glasses and narrow black pants, and just the right amount of beard to be considered hip. Whitney called him "brilliant," and I wondered what that meant, but I was glad she had moved on from athletic, empty-headed Bryan, who had sucked up every morsel of food in my house like a vacuum cleaner.

Right behind Mark was my friend, Sam, who had let himself and a huge balloon bouquet in the front door. "Is this where the party is?" he asked with a knowing grin.

"So, you were in on this, too?" I accused him, brushing a kiss across his cheek and tying the balloons to a table leg.

"Heck, yeah, Whitney called me last week. I almost gave it away the other night, though."

"Well, I didn't catch on. I was caught completely off guard." I grabbed his hand and pulled him into the den.

He was hijacked into the economic discussion with my dad and Paul. I made a mental note to rescue him in a few minutes.

Sam could hold his own with them, of course, as a banking loan officer, but I hated for him to be poked and prodded for his opinion as the expert in the room. Dressed as usual in a button-down shirt and creased khakis, he was impeccable, intelligent, polite, and thoughtful. And comfortable and boring and predictable. *Ah, perfection.*

"Hey, Daddy, when's dinner?" Whitney called from the den, switching off the TV.

"In just a minute. We have to let the cheese melt on the—" Jack was interrupted by the loud *bang* of a balloon popping.

Tuxedo flew under the sofa. Matt, apparently bored by the video game and turning to other pastimes, stood

11

chuckling with a balloon carcass dangling from his fingers. His brother, Jason, tossed him another balloon, barely missing the whirling ceiling fan. Matt popped it, much to his own delight.

"Boys, that's enough. Sit still until dinner, please," Donna commanded.

Paul intervened, his arm around Jason's shoulder, "It's all right. I'm sure Aunt Tess doesn't mind, now do you, Tess? They're not hurting anything."

Before I could tell him yes, I minded, and those were my balloons, and why didn't he control his little demon children? Donna said, "The balloons were a gift from Sam, and they could have broken something, Paul."

"It's all just cheap crap. They can't hurt it."

Donna's horrified expression spoke volumes, but she didn't come to the defense of my cheap crap. I decided killing Paul would have to wait until later.

Just in the nick of time, Jack, with his more-than-able-bodied assistant, Tad, served a dinner of specialties from his restaurant Habanera, new-wave Mexican food that made tears come to my eyes; it was so spicy and sinful.

While everyone ate, Paul and Dad argued about the virtues and pitfalls of day trading, demanding an opinion pro or con from poor Sam. Donna monopolized Tad throughout the meal with a discussion about her problem thighs. Jack looked amused. Whitney and Sydney rolled their eyes at each other, but mostly, Whitney and Mark had their heads together, talking in stealthy whispers. Young love.

The boys said the food was "yuck" and went back to their abandoned video game. My mother chattered non-stop to the room in general about funerals they had attended that week. Daddy dug into his meal as if it were his last.

When the plates were piled in the sink, the group gathered around so I could open the mound of gaily-wrapped presents stacked on the hearth. I sat in the straight-back "Chair of Honor" as Whitney called it.

The doorbell rang, but before anyone could answer it, Lucy Trevain breezed in. A flamboyant redhead, Lucy wore linen shorts, thong sandals, a toe ring, and a sleeveless shirt that showed her ample bosom to full advantage. Her makeup did little to hide the tiny lines that crinkled around her emerald-green eyes when she laughed, which she did often. Lucy had been my best friend since third grade, and I idolized her.

She set her present, in The White Tiger gift bag, on the hearth and carried another sack to the kitchen. She came back and sat down next to me, air-kissing me on both cheeks.

"I'm glad you're here," I whispered.

"Wouldn't miss it," she assured me.

One by one, I unwrapped each package, discovering an array of gag gifts worthy of Rodney Dangerfield. Among the assembled treasures were laxatives, orthopedic socks, melatonin, and a fake bottle of male hormone pills from Jack.

"It never hurts to be prepared." He grinned. Sam blushed four shades of red. I glared at Jack, but he just laughed and slid closer to Tad.

Next, I opened a pair of reading glasses, which I actually needed, a sinfully soft throw, face cream guaranteed "to reduce wrinkles and make you look ten years younger," and a membership to an over-fifty club from my parents.

"You'll love the discounts if you don't mind eating at 4:30," Daddy promised.

In The White Tiger bag, wrapped in layers of white tissue, was a bright red teddy from Lucy. When I held it up, a waterfall of silky nylon cascaded from my fingertips, and I cocked my eyebrow at her. She laughed. "You've got to be ready, Teddy." Sam blushed again.

I laughed at each gift until there were no more packages left.

"Thank you all so much. This was so fun. Such cute presents. You're all so clever." I began gathering the trash accumulated at my feet.

"Wait, Mom, there's one more," Sydney said and pulled an envelope out from behind a potted plant on the hearth. "This is from everybody."

The envelope was creamy and smooth, with the heft of an elaborate wedding invitation. On the front was my name in flowing script. I opened it with care, reluctant to mar its beauty, and slipped a greeting card out.

Tucked inside was a stack of gift cards. The first was to Patchouli, a very nice spa where they did trendy makeovers: hair, nails, facials, pedicures, and removal of body hair from places I didn't even want to think about. The next was to The White Tiger, an exclusive clothing store that sold one-of-a-kind outfits to thin, wealthy women. Plus, a membership to Weight Magic, known for its high success rate in problem obesity cases, and a six-month membership to Body Sculptors, the health club in our neighborhood where Tad worked.

The card said, "Because we love you and want you to be as beautiful outside as you are inside." It was signed by everyone in the room, except Sam and Lucy.

I looked up, tears in my eyes. I knew they would

think I was crying from joyous gratitude, so I ran with it. "Thank you all so much. This is the sweetest gift. I just can't thank you enough for the wonderful party, all the fun presents, and the delicious food."

Lucy, apparently sensing my discomfort, announced, "Let's have cake. I saw Jack's creation in the kitchen."

Jack hurried to help Lucy cover for me. "It's my special Italian Cream Cake." He smiled as I swiped the tears away with the back of my hand. Whatever had passed between me and Jack since he declared he was gay, quit his job, and moved in with a podiatrist, I knew he still loved me.

"Hmm, you are a culinary god." I smiled back.

"I brought ice cream," Lucy added as they headed for the kitchen.

A few moments later a short processional emerged from the kitchen, Jack in front, carrying a huge, three-layer cake, studded with what looked like two-hundred candles. Lucy wielded a fireplace lighter and within seconds the candles, only fifty of them as it turned out, went up in a blaze of glory unseen since Jack decided to ignite a couple of chicken breasts with a generous dousing of my favorite Merlot. The fiery spectacle was then followed by oohs and ahs usually reserved for Fourth of July fireworks displays.

I tried to extinguish all the candles in one breath but huffed and puffed for thirty seconds before the last one sputtered out.

Jack put a platonic arm around my shoulder and kissed my hair. "Happy birthday, sweetie," he murmured before moving into Tad's well-muscled embrace.

Sam walked over to stand next to me, lacing his

fingers with mine. "Happy birthday, Tess. You'll have to wait until tomorrow night for your present from me, though."

"I'll look forward to it." I turned my face up to his, expecting a birthday kiss. Instead, his cell phone rang, and he squeezed my fingers, let go of my hand, and eased away to take the call.

More congratulatory kisses and hugs followed all couched in a certain kind of sympathy, I thought. And a measure of relief. Those who were younger than I were no doubt thanking God they still had years, some of them decades, to go before they hit the big five-O. Others were thanking God they were past that awkward stage in their lives.

"Cut the cake, Mom," Sydney demanded.

"I'll scoop the ice cream," Lucy offered, digging into my favorite flavor, Banana Split.

"For heaven's sake, Luce. Banana Split? That's going to clash with my Italian Cream," Jack exclaimed with the look of horror he reserved for pattern-mixing and white shoes after Labor Day.

Never one to mince words, Lucy retorted, "Get over it, darling. When it's your birthday, I'll bring Double Latté Espresso Cappuccino."

Jack shot her a withering look. She smiled sweetly at him. I picked up the cake server and cut into the towering fantasy.

"Here, hon, let me do that. You always make a mess." Mom swept the server from my hand and cut perfect pieces from the cake, sliding them onto paper plates.

I melted back through the throng huddled around the cake until I stood in the doorway to the living room, surveying the scene.

My family. It was like most families, I supposed, with some innocuous skeletons in the closet, a smattering of obnoxious characters, but mostly normal, middle-class, suburban folks. Celebrating a family milestone. Marking a rite of passage.

Passage to what? Not middle age. I'd been middle-aged for about a decade. Old age? Hell, no! But a passage, nonetheless. Into the second half of life. Sure, I could live another fifty years. I didn't smoke or drink…much. I got plenty of sleep and ate roughage. I might have as much life left in me as I'd already lived.

We were celebrating a rebirth. The first day of the second half of my life. Fifty more years.

If I didn't burn up first, I thought, fanning myself with a copy of *Senior Living* magazine Mom and Dad had included with their gift.

"Hot, honey?" Dad asked, coming up behind me.

"No, I'm okay," I answered but continued to fan my perspiring face.

"I'll adjust the thermostat."

"No, Dad, it's okay. It's just me. It will pass."

He looked at me for a moment. "Oh," he said slowly, nodding. "The Change was bad for your mother, too, Chicken. She couldn't remember a damned thing and nearly stripped naked four or five times a day." He shook his head, then said, as if to himself, "No interest in sex, either."

"Well, Dad, I'm hoping it will be better for me."

He looked over at Sam, still talking on the phone, then back at me, smiling. "At least you don't have to worry about the sex."

Chapter Two

Sam clicked his cell off and hurried over. "That was the nursing home. Julia's had a spell, and they need me to come over and calm her down. I better go." Without waiting for a response, he brushed a kiss across my forehead and walked to the front door.

I opened the door just in time for him to rush through it. "I'll see you tomorrow night, then," I called after him.

"Right, pick you up at seven o'clock."

I joined Donna in the kitchen to finish loading the dishwasher. Her boys were arguing in the den over who had won *Super Smash-Up*.

Paul came in and ordered, "Let's go. Get the boys. I'll be in the car."

Without hesitation, Donna dried her hands on a dishtowel and turned to her sons. "Get your stuff, boys, let's go." When they didn't move, she added, "Dad's waiting in the car." They retrieved their laptop and headed obediently out the door, muttering goodbyes as they went.

Donna hugged me. "Happy birthday, Tess. It was a very nice party."

I thought she looked a little wistful.

Mom and Dad followed, he with his hand under her elbow. They'd been married fifty-five years and still loved each other. I tried to picture them having sex, then thought better of it.

Whitney, Mark, and Syd left for a party of their own; after all, their evening didn't begin until I was watching the ten o'clock news. Jack and Tad packed up their pots and platters and headed for the car.

"Thanks, Jack. Dinner was delicious. And, Tad, thank you, too, for helping."

Tad smiled and waved as he disappeared into their hulking SUV. I hadn't heard him say four words all night.

"He's the strong, silent type," Jack said, lingering for a moment on the porch.

"Is that what he is?" I asked, teasing.

"Oh, stop it, Tess." Jack chuckled. "He's fun and gorgeous and not particularly demanding."

I feigned outrage. "Was I demanding, then?"

"You had your moments, sweetie." He waved as he sauntered down the sidewalk, then stopped and said, "I almost forgot. There's someone I want you to meet. I'll call you to find out when we can hook up."

Oh, Lord, not again. Jack was forever bringing men to my doorstep, the way a cat brings home birds. They were what I called "Guilt Men," possible future husbands for me, to assuage Jack's responsibility for the failure of our marriage. Each and every one had been an unmitigated disaster, from the engineer who spent the evening telling me in detail how to kill and dress a deer to the pharmaceutical rep who scheduled every aspect of our date right down to inking in a time for me to go to the bathroom.

"I'm with Sam," I said, hoping that would deflect his incoming volley.

"No, no, this is different," he argued.

"Yeah, that's what you always say. And guess what?

19

They're different, all right."

He laughed. "No, I mean that this one is for me, not you. He's helping me expand the restaurant, maybe catering or franchises. He's going to be my business partner. I just want you to meet him."

A glance at Tad, sitting sullenly in the passenger seat, told me he wasn't very pleased that his cozy ménage now numbered trois. Jack slid into the seat next to him, and they drove off, leaving Lucy and me alone on the sidewalk.

We looped our arms around each other's waists and headed back into the house. I couldn't help noticing that Lucy's arm didn't go quite as far around me as mine did around her.

"Well, thank God that's over," I muttered as we gathered debris from around the living room.

"I thought it was a nice party," she said. She picked up the envelope with the gift cards sticking out of it and waved it at me. "Fabulous present."

"Yeah, there's nothing nicer than being told you're fat, wrinkled, and hairy."

"They mean well."

"They mean to mold me into their image."

"Maybe they have other motives in mind. Don't be so cynical."

I collapsed on the sofa, crepe paper dangling from my fingers. "Here's what I think, Luce. They think I'm unattractive. And I think they think I'm unhappy."

"I think you're wrong."

"About which part? That I'm unattractive or that I'm unhappy?

"Neither. Or both. Look, this is just about your family loving you and wanting you to do something for yourself. They think you've quit thinking about yourself, that you don't love yourself enough to look your best."

I stared at my beautiful, vibrant friend and tried—really hard—to hear what she was saying without prejudice. And somehow, it started to make sense.

I had taken the easy road up to now, at least as far as my appearance was concerned. I had used my age as an excuse for giving up. After all, if my husband left me for another man, what difference did it make if I were beautiful? It wouldn't have saved my relationship with Jack. And Sam, because he was married, was safe and didn't require seduction, just a strong shoulder.

"Also," Lucy continued, cutting through my musings, "I think they're afraid of losing you."

"What?"

"There's something scary about having someone you love hit fifty. Your children want you to be with them for a long time. They don't want you getting diabetes or cancer or heart disease. This," she said, waving the envelope in front of me, "is their way of ensuring your future, of guaranteeing you'll be around to see your grandchildren and maybe even your great-grandchildren."

Tears burned my eyes, and I blinked them back. I hadn't given much thought to grandchildren, much less great-grandchildren.

"This," she said again, tossing the envelope into my lap, "is all about love. And you should be grateful. Not everyone has a family like yours."

Lucy knew what she was talking about. Her family had disintegrated years ago, ravaged by divorce and drinking and poor choices. Her relationship with her witchy mother was complicated and painful. She had an aunt she saw on holidays, but that was about it.

Suddenly, I felt ashamed. My family loved me enough to hurt my feelings. I should be grateful. Lucy was right.

I hugged her. "Thanks."

"You're welcome."

We carried the trash into the kitchen. I wiped off the counters while she poured two glasses of wine.

"So," she said, handing one to me, "are you going to do it?"

"Do what?" I let the pale liquid glide down my throat and wished I had some crackers and cheese.

"Cash in the gift cards."

"Do I have a choice?"

"No." Lucy grinned. "Oh, you could lie and say you went to all these places. But I know you. You'd feel guilty and never be able to keep the secret. It would come out eventually, and then you'd be sorry and embarrassed. Do yourself a favor, Tess. Save us all the misery of your conscience."

I laughed at my friend's accurate assessment of my over-active guilt response. "Okay, but on one condition."

"What's that?" She took a sip of wine, and her red lipstick stained the rim of the glass.

"You have to do it with me."

Lucy grinned again, and her perfect teeth nearly blinded me. "Chicken!"

"So, I've been called." I giggled. "Come on. It'll be fun."

She drained her glass in one swallow. "Sorry, friend. This is one thing you need to do for yourself, with yourself, and by yourself. Besides, I'm going to be out of pocket for the next few weeks. I'll just slow you down."

"Traveling again, huh?"

She set her glass in the dishwasher, picked up her purse, and headed toward the front door. "Yeah, sort of."

I watched her get into the red sports car at the curb. Her father had invented some widget used in every computer in the country, and despite his early and devastating suicide, had left her wealthy beyond anything I could imagine. She'd been driving fabulous cars and wearing fabulous clothes for as long as I could remember. Family was the only thing she had ever lacked.

It was something I had in spades.

I turned back into the house and headed toward the bedroom, stopping to pick up the envelope stuffed with gift cards. It weighed heavy in my hand.

The truth, as I was willing to admit it, was that I *was* unhappy. My relationship with Sam, while easy, was less than fulfilling. I had companionship in a limited way. A phone call every other day, Mexican food on Wednesday, a date on Saturday night. What was missing? Did I want someone to share my other days and nights with, someone to talk to over coffee, to travel with, to complain to, to hug, to kiss, to get naked with? Yes, I did. Did I have that with Sam? No, I did not.

I dropped the envelope on the dresser, turned the ceiling fan on high, and shed my clothes as fast as possible, feeling the heat rise inside me until I was flushed and damp.

I lay back on the bed in my underwear, letting the cool air flow over my hot body.

As much as I wanted to get naked with a man, the thought of taking off my clothes in front of another human being terrified me. My laundry list of physical flaws was a long one, beginning with cottage cheese thighs and ending with a second chin. It wasn't a list I wanted discovered by someone I was trying to seduce. Maybe that was why Sam and I remained comfortably platonic. As long as we didn't have sex, he wasn't cheating on his wife, and I didn't have to let him see the real me. A win-win for both of us.

But if I embarked on this extreme makeover, what would happen then? I could become beautiful and sexy. I could seduce poor Sam and turn him into an adulterer. And I would be the "other woman."

Not the kind of Influencer Ruth had in mind, I'm sure.

Then, horrified, a worse thought occurred to me: what if none of the remedies these places offered did the trick? What if when I stripped away my fat, lazy, hairy outer layers and worked my way down to my essential core, I wasn't gorgeous?

A mistress or a frump. Were these the choices I had been reduced to?

I glanced at the envelope. I could ignore the cards. Slip them into a drawer and forget about them. But Lucy was right. I'd know, and if the truth came out, everyone would hate me.

A mistress, a frump, or a liar.

I groaned aloud and hauled myself off the bed. I would have to decide. And soon.

But first, I would go back to the kitchen and grab a teeny piece of Italian cream cake and a glass of milk.

****

I rarely stood naked in front of the full-length mirror mounted on my closet door. Okay, I *never* stood naked in front of it. I bustled right past, eager to become fully clothed as quickly as possible, lest it get a good look at me.

The mirror had been my enemy for as long as I could remember. Pointing out my shortcomings, mocking my chubbiness, taking inventory of my numerous flaws. No, my mirror was not my friend, and I gave it the cold shoulder as often as possible, stopping by long enough for a perfunctory once-over on my way out of the room in the morning.

But naked, for longer than it took to wrap my fuzzy fleece robe around me and slip on some warm socks at night? No, I didn't think so.

Which was why, as I stood there the next morning, birthday suit freshly scrubbed from the shower, I felt as if I were looking at my body for the first time.

I should have checked on it sooner.

Starting at the top of my head, I dismissed my limp, string-straight hair as not my fault. It was my mother's hair, and her mother's before her. My hand-me-down hair had not held up well. I had tried every product out there: bodybuilders, fluffers, thickeners, and volumizers. Sprays, spritzes, and gels. Leave-ins and rinse-outs. I had even stripped all the color out of it once because someone said it would give it body. I ended up with limp, string-straight *blonde* hair. Within four months, I had looked like an aging rock star.

That led to my short-hair period. I cut it off in stages until it was so short I was frequently mistaken for a man. That led to the current mid-length-hair period, often corralled in a clip to ward off the heat.

I had given up on my hair. I had learned to live in my hair. To be happy with the hair God gave me. And my mother and my grandmother.

My gaze traveled down to my face and rested on my eyes. They were deep hazel-green, nicely rounded, and fringed with thick lashes. I had always considered them the saving grace of my face, although recently, they had begun to betray me, wrinkling a little around the edges and having trouble focusing on anything within a three-foot radius. I had bought bookish black reading glasses at the drugstore, thinking they made me look hip and smart. In reality, they made me look old and presbyopic.

Making my way down my face, I noted chubby cheeks, splotchy skin tone, an okay nose, and full lips. After that, things got dismal.

I was pillowy. Soft and thick and squishy. From the front, I looked merely dimply, but from the side—oh, Lord! I looked six months pregnant!

Moving on as rapidly as possible, I came to my best feature, my legs. Even at my age, they were still well-shaped, thicker than they should have been, with the aforementioned cottage cheese thighs, but overall, not bad.

But not even my legs could help the fact I was round. Not the shape God or I intended. Things had gotten out of control while I was busy hurrying past the mirror.

The fat was hidden well enough on my five-foot-eight-inch frame. Spaced out so no one ever asked me if I might be pregnant, but showing enough so they might think it.

I wasn't sure which was worse: to be mistaken for a man or to have people think I was a fifty-year-old, presbyopic, unwed mother.

I pulled on comfy jeans with elastic in the waist, slipped on podiatrist-approved white running shoes, and slid a chambray shirt over a white tank top. I grabbed my purse and the envelope with the gift cards in it and headed for the car.

I'd show them presbyopic.

****

But first, I needed to think.

If I were to embark on this perilous journey of reawakening and discovery, I needed to consult my sweet muse, to experience the warmth of an old friend, to snuggle into the comfort of the familiar.

I needed a full caf, mocha hazelnut latte, with a double whip.

I pulled into a parking space near the entrance to my local coffee emporium, brimming with a Saturday morning crowd of sippers, hurriers, lap-toppers, and phone gazers. I slipped into line, ordered my coffee, with a larger than usual dollop of guilt, and settled myself at a table just big enough for a napkin.

The gift cards felt heavy in my bag, and I pulled them out, arranged them in a fan, then laid them on the table in a triangle, a square, a circle, and finally, alphabetically.

I leaned back in the chair, sipped on the sweet mocha froth, and sighed aloud.

"It can't be that bad." The sound of a rumbling male voice, laced with humor, made me turn to my right and stare at the man seated there, newspaper on the table in front of him.

"I beg your pardon?"

He leaned forward a little, and I could see traces of gray in his temples and laugh lines around his eyes. They were very nice brown eyes.

They went with his very nice face, which was

perfectly proportioned and just rugged enough to be interesting. His mouth quirked up a little at one corner as if he were slightly amused.

"Whatever those cards are, they seem to be upsetting you."

"They're gift cards."

"Mmm, don't you hate those?"

I chuckled. "Not normally, but these are particularly evil."

"Ah, gift cards for the seven deadly sins. You don't see those every day."

The guy was intriguing. A sense of humor. And those eyes.

"Only four of the seven: diet food, highlights, sit-ups, and maybe a silk blouse."

He laughed, a rich, robust, from-the-gut kind of laugh. "I'm afraid that's a list I'm unfamiliar with. Someone gave you sit-ups and diet food?"

"Yeah, I'm sure they did it out of love."

"Tough love. Are you sure you got the right cards?"

"Positive, why?"

"Because you don't need any of that stuff—except maybe the silk blouse." He smiled, and the lines around his eyes crinkled with warmth.

"Thanks," I murmured, stunned at the compliment and overwhelmed by regret that I hadn't put eye makeup on one of my few flattering features.

"Hi, I'm Roger Austin," he said, sticking out his hand.

I grasped it, allowing his slender fingers to fold over mine in a firm grip. "I'm Tess Thomason."

"Do you come here often?"

"More than I should, apparently," I grimaced and

gestured at the array of evidence in front of me.

"Yeah, I'm addicted to their latté," he said, patting his flat stomach.

"It's not fair that everything good is bad for you." I looked at my empty cup, willing myself not to go back for another.

"Not everything," he said, winking.

How cute was that? No one ever winked anymore. It was a lost art, like crewel embroidery or map making. I smiled at him. "It's been my experience that anything, and I mean anything, can get you into trouble."

"Don't you think that's a rather cynical approach to life?"

"I'd say realistic. How does the saying go? Anything in excess…"

"Well, there's got to be something wonderful that can't be abused in some way."

"Well, when you think of it, tell me." I laughed, "No, don't, because then I'll go out and become addicted to it!"

He laughed then, and the rumbling sound filled every crevice of the room. I loved to hear him laugh and felt myself wanting to say things to make him laugh again.

He rescued me from myself. "You strike me as someone with more self-discipline than that."

"Trust me, I could turn anything into a bad habit."

He looked at me with sincerity brimming in his brown eyes. "Some good things are incorruptible."

"Like what?" I challenged.

He checked his phone. "We'll have to go into that another time, I'm afraid. I have to go to work."

"Working on Saturday?"

"No rest for the weary. Or for the guy with a new job."

Roger picked up his paper and his coffee cup and stood up. He towered over me at about six-foot-four. The pale blue polo shirt skimmed his chest and made his arms seem tanner than they were. And his jeans molded every angle and plane of his long, lean legs. From my vantage point at thigh level, I had to crane my neck to see him smiling down at me.

"It's been nice meeting you, Tess Thomason."

He seemed to be testing the sound of my name in his head, tasting it on his tongue. A tingling sensation shot up my spine.

"I enjoyed meeting you, too, Roger Austin." I stopped short of saying I hoped to see him again. What was the point? He was probably married, although he wore no ring.

He gestured to the gift cards on the table. "Good luck with those. Maybe they'll surprise you. Especially The White Tiger. They have some very nice silk blouses."

As I stared after him, he disappeared out the door, down the walk, and around the corner of the shopping center.

He knows about The White Tiger? In my experience, most men were not into fashion. Most men did not know about The White Tiger. Most men wouldn't care. Sam wouldn't care.

Yeah, Roger Austin is married, and he's bought silk blouses for his wife at The White Tiger. I would have an interesting conversation with a married man who buys great gifts. Just my luck.

I railed silently at the love gods, then shifted my

gaze back to the array of offerings on the table. I rearranged the cards again, this time from ugliest to prettiest.

What would an influencer do?

Then, as if the Internet cloud opened and a host of heavenly bloggers began singing, I knew what to do. I'd write a column about it. About how I got the damn cards and struggled with them and decided to go to these places and write about what happened afterward. I would write to women, for women, about what women were doing. Women of a certain age. I would become a senior influencer!

And by then Sylvia would be back from Brazil in time for my annual article on Winterizing Your Shrubbery.

It would work. I could do it.

****

Fashionista

By Sylvia Bernstein

The first thing you need to know is I'm not Sylvia Bernstein. That will become evident in a moment, but I thought I would warn you upfront. We are celebrating Sylvia's nuptials and her extended honeymoon in Brazil, which means Fashionista is without its namesake. I will be filling this space with something a little different— okay, a lot different. A column not about fashion, which anyone around here will tell you is not my forte, but about women, for women, and to women.

Women of a certain age. Women like me. Women like you.

You may not be that different from me. Maybe you're lonely; maybe you're in a dead-end job; maybe your life seems boring and predictable. Maybe you're unhappy with what you see in the mirror.

Guess what? Me, too!

I just turned fifty, and for my birthday, I got a drugstore full of gag gifts and some gift cards hinting that I am fat, hairy, and badly dressed. This hit a little too close to home, and hurt my feelings for a minute, then I decided what the heck! Maybe I can use these insulting cards to go on a journey of self-discovery.

Look, I'm no more qualified to write this column than you are. But I promise to write what I know. I know about aging kids and aging parents. Ex-husbands and new boyfriends. Hot flashes and cold pizza. I know about being a woman. And so do you.

Maybe we could go on this journey together, you and me. We'll explore new territory, examine the obstacles ahead, and try new paths. We'll laugh a lot, cry a little, and lean on each other for strength. Traveling is tough, especially with the kind of baggage we're carrying, but we can make it. Together.

First, get comfortable. Get out of those six-inch heels. They're not the kind of shoes you need where we're going. Ease your feet into a pair of colorful slip-ons. Doesn't that feel better?

And now. A new name for the column—at least until Sylvia salsa dances her way back from Brazil. Let's call it…

Sensible Shoes
By Tess Thomason

Chapter Three

As I walked to the car, I dug in my purse for the cell phone, hoping to stop its insistent ringing. My ability to multi-task had burned to ash in my first hot flash, and since then I tried not to talk on the phone while walking, driving, or anything else for that matter. But who could ignore a ringing phone? It might be one of the kids desperate for solace amidst their relationship crisis du jour.

So, I scrambled for the phone, unlocked the car, and realized when I excavated the thing from the depths of my purse that I had punched it off.

Damn technology.

I hated my cell phone. I liked having some solitude during the day, and I enjoyed my incommunicado status when I was reading or watching TV. No one could reach me, interrupt my thoughts, disturb my music or my muse.

But that was before cell phones, and now, here I was, my muse so much fodder for every Syd, Jack, and Whitney who wanted to reach me.

I sighed.

Now, I would have to figure out who had called, which involved looking at the tiny screen and pressing the tiny buttons. Now I would need my glasses. Which were in my purse.

"Lucy, it's me. Did you call?" I asked when I finally determined it was my sweet friend who had been trying to reach me.

"Yeah, what did you decide?" she asked.

"I'm doing it. I think I can work it into the column Ruth wants me to write. I'm approaching them in a non-stressful fashion. I'm on my way now to check out Weight Magic."

"Good girl. What have you got to lose?"

"About thirty pounds, I think."

"Old joke," Lucy said with the slightest amusement in her voice.

"What about you? What are you doing today?"

The line was quiet for so long that I thought I'd lost the connection. "Luce? Are you there?"

"Yeah, sorry, got distracted by the cattle truck changing lanes in front of me. I'm running some errands, is all." She paused again. "Are you going to be home later?"

"Sure, around lunchtime. You want to come over? I'll make something low fat, low cal, and low carb."

"Mmm, yummy. Noon?"

"Yeah, see you then."

I hung up, unable to shake the feeling something was odd about Lucy, and I felt vaguely apprehensive about seeing her at lunch. Last night at the party, she had been herself, for the most part, but somehow introspective and more serious than usual afterward when we were cleaning up. Not as carefree and off the wall as I counted on her being.

After all, she was the fun one, the devil-may-care girl I never could be. She was the one who took the risks, lived on the edge, and did the things I didn't dream of doing but was envious of, nonetheless. She was the me I would have been were I not an avowed coward.

Today, she seemed distracted and had a sense of urgency in her voice I hadn't heard since her father's death.

I dismissed the feelings as my normal over-the-top mothering instinct and concentrated on the first of my four new challenges.

****

The banner over the door at Weight Magic warned, "Only You Can Make It Happen."

If it's all up to me, then what do I need them for?

I opened the gleaming silver door and stepped inside.

"You Are What You Eat," proclaimed a gold-embossed card on the receptionist's mahogany desk. I pictured myself as a giant double mocha latte with a whip.

The receptionist was rail-thin, sporting a mauve suit and the blondest hair and pinkest lips I had seen this side of the twenty-something barista at my coffee shop.

She handed me a brief questionnaire and after I filled it in, I handed it back to her. She scanned it, looked up at me, and smiled. "If you'll follow me, we'll get started."

She ushered me into a dressing room and gave me a hibiscus-covered muumuu to wear with comfy little terrycloth socks. If they wanted to remind me of my current state of largeness, one look in the three-hundred-sixty-degree mirrors did just that, reinforcing my resolve with metaphorical steel bars.

A pert, young woman in a pink lab coat took me into a tiny room filled with women dressed in muumuus like mine. We were like the parade of body shapes you might see in a medical textbook. Tall, short, obese, thin, top-heavy, and pear-shaped. The one remaining shape was reserved for me, reduced to my most geometric simplicity: round.

One at a time, we were taken through a cadre of tests: measured, quizzed, and profiled, keeping the attendant clipboard carefully concealed from my prying eyes. Each technician was cuter, perkier, and more solicitous than the last. I felt as if I'd taken a bath in honey.

Everywhere I turned, another adage spurred me on, buoyed me up, and lifted my sagging spirits (not to mention my rear end.)

At last, I was led into a beautifully appointed office with a pristine desk, brass lamp, and Queen Anne chairs upholstered in raw silk. A woman in her late thirties stood to greet me, manicured hand extended. She wore a rose-colored suit, similar in hue to the stripe on the chairs and a shade darker than the wall.

Altogether, she and the room were the epitome of the serenity, peace, and beauty one would surely obtain if one were to become a disciple of the Weight Magic philosophy.

I wanted to believe, truly I did.

"Hello, Tess, won't you sit down?" she murmured, gesturing to one of the chairs.

How did she know my name, I wondered, noting the desk was clear of any file folders or scrap of paper that would have given her my identity. *She's an angel, a clairvoyant, a prophet sent by God to help me lose weight!* I was hypnotized by the soothing pink room and the soothing pink woman speaking in hushed tones.

"So, do you have any questions?" she asked, folding her hands on the desk.

"No," I replied, stifling a drowsy yawn.

"That's lovely."

I thought so, too. Lovely.

"We've prepared this menu plan for you, Tess," she said, and a pink folder appeared in her hand. She glanced through it, then looked up at me. "The meals you need for one month will be at the front desk when you leave."

I looked at her and nodded.

"That is if you are going to become one of us."

The few, the proud, the thin.

"Oh, yes. I want to." I murmured, struck with the notion that I somehow wasn't worthy to be one of them. I somehow wasn't pink enough.

"Excellent," she said, smiling the beatific smile of a saint. "That will be six hundred dollars."

"Six hundred dollars?" I repeated, entranced by white teeth and rosy lips.

"Yes, the consultation and profile are our gift to you. The food is twenty dollars a day. So, for one month, that's six hundred dollars."

"I have a gift certificate." I handed over the card.

"Excellent, Tess, excellent. Let's see…" She perused the card. "Yes, you can give me a check for the difference."

"The difference?"

"Yes, the card is for one hundred dollars. So, we'll need a check for five hundred dollars."

For the first time, I noticed a little sign on the desk that said Invest in Yourself.

Turns out Weight Magic was all about motivation.

And expensive food.

****

Sensible Shoes

By Tess Thomason

We've all heard nearly two-thirds of Americans are overweight. And I am no exception.

I would like to be in the thinner third; really, I would. I'm terrified I am going to end up on the nightly news, walking down the street, videotaped from the rear, neck down, hips undulating like a hammock full of puppies, the example du jour of obesity.

There's a word we hate, right? Overweight, chubby, even fat is better than obese which has the clinical sound of a death knell attached to it.

So, I trekked to my nearby weight management emporium, determined to start a new chapter in my food-loving life. And now my freezer is stocked with boxes of European-inspired entrees, tiny, decadent desserts, and even yummy snacks, although I don't see how you can freeze chips, peanut butter, or Cheese Twisters.

I wrote the weight loss people a ginormous check for one month's worth of food, calculating how much more than my normal food budget I was spending. Turns out healthy, smaller portions cost a lot more than boatloads of food full of carbs and trans fats.

And because I need continuous motivation, I took the aphorisms splashed around their offices and posted them on sticky notes all over my house.

I'm ready to go now. Fired up and determined. Ready to "take responsibility for my own choices."

But first, I'll finish the Cheese Twisters.

****

I was right about Lucy. Something was wrong.

She was on time.

That only happened when the event involved a handsome man—not the case today, so when I spotted her red Mercedes in front of my house, I checked my watch to see how late I was.

She'd had a key since the day I'd locked myself out of the house in my bathrobe ten years earlier. The day the kids were in middle school, Jack was in New York, and my parents had gone to Cleveland. The day I bashed in the bedroom window with the lug wrench from my car. The day I made five sets of keys, stashed them in fake rocks all around the house, and handed one to Lucy on a tiny red ribbon.

Today I found her sitting on a barstool at the kitchen counter, drinking a diet soda, and cradling Tuxedo in her lap.

"Hey, what's up with you?" I asked, setting the Weight Magic bags on the counter. Boxes of frozen entrees, snack bars, and cans of shakes spilled out.

She examined one of the delicious, perfectly balanced, nutritious dinners. "Wow, this looks serious."

"What an experience that place was," I exclaimed, shoving the food into the freezer.

She sipped her soda, distracted, and stared at the refrigerator magnet from Pizza Palace. "So, you're doing it?"

"Yeah, I guess so. I'll start tonight with…" I studied the last box, then tossed it into the freezer. "Tuscan chicken."

"Well, that doesn't sound too bad." Lucy paused and looked at me. "I'm proud of you, Tess. Glad you're doing something to take care of yourself. Put yourself first. That's important." Her voice was heavy with drama as her eyes dropped to the drink can in her hand.

"Okay, that's it!" I barked, slamming the freezer door. Tuxedo leaped to the floor and dashed out of the room. "What the hell is wrong with you?"

Her head jerked up in surprise. Emotional outbursts were not my stock in trade. "What do you mean?"

"I mean you've been acting weird for twenty-four hours. Way too serious, off in another world. What's going on, Luce?"

She sighed, slid off the barstool, and began pacing around the kitchen. "Well, I was showering the other day."

"Yeah, that makes me crazy every time."

She shot me a withering, shut-up-and-listen look.

"Okay, sorry, please continue."

"I…I found a lump in my breast."

A fist closed around my heart. "Oh, God."

"Yeah."

"So, what did you do?"

"I worried about it for a few days."

"A few days? How many days?"

"Ninety or so."

"Damn, Lucy! Are you kidding me? Why didn't you say something? Why didn't you go to the doctor? This could be serious!" I screamed, panic rising in my throat, chasing my voice to a higher pitch.

"I hoped it was my imagination. I guess I thought if I ignored it, it would go away." Her eyes filled with tears, and her voice fell. "But it didn't."

"Why didn't you tell me? I would have made you go."

Looking up at me through watery eyes, she smiled a wan, defeated kind of smile. "That's why I didn't tell you."

I sank onto a stool, collapsing under the weight of guilt. My nagging might have caused my friend to avoid confiding in me. "Aw, Luce."

She put her arm around me, leaning her head on my shoulder.

"So, you went to the doctor?"

"Yes, I made the appointment last week, telling myself it was still nothing, but needing to know for sure. I went yesterday."

"Yesterday? You didn't say anything."

"Well, I didn't want you to worry. And I didn't want to spoil the party. But that's why I was late."

She had arrived at the party long after doctor's office hours. I cocked my head in question. "The doctor saw you in the evening?"

She shook her head. "The mammogram was scheduled for four o'clock."

I winced. "I hate those. It's like having your chest closed in a refrigerator door."

"Right. That torturous machine could only have been invented by a man. Anyway, they did the mammogram. You know how they make you wait while they read the film? Well, I'm sitting there in the little cape, struggling to do some paperwork without flashing the whole waiting room, and the nurse comes in and says they need additional views."

"Additional views? What does that mean?" How many views could they take? We were talking about a breast, not Mt. Denali. My hysterical mind conjured pictures of the left face, right face, the glacial crevasse.

"It means they either couldn't read part of the film or they found something suspicious. Anyway, they took me back in and took more pictures of my right breast."

"More pictures?" I asked, unable to do more than repeat phrases as questions. Warning bells clanged in my head. This didn't sound good. Not good at all.

"You know…this way, that way, closer, more compressed—if that's possible. At one point I thought, if there is something in there, they'll smash it to smithereens for sure. Then, of course, I had this picture of a big bag full of cancer breaking open and spilling out, running rampant all over my chest."

The breath caught in my throat. "Stop thinking like that. I'm sure it's nothing. They said it's nothing, right?"

Oh, God, Lucy. Cancer.

"Actually, they read the second set of films and decided to do an ultrasound."

"Like they do with pregnant women?"

"Right. They led me into another room, all dark and quiet, and did the ultrasound as if my right breast were about four months along."

"And?"

She didn't say anything, didn't look at me for a few seconds. "Well, they saw a mass."

"A mass of what?"

"God knows. They just called it a mass."

My heart beat hard against my chest. I retrieved a cold can of diet soda from the fridge and held it in both hands, willing myself to calm down. Lucy didn't need me to be a basket case. She needed me to be strong. "So, what then?"

"Well, by then, it was late, so they scheduled me for a biopsy on Monday, and I came to the party."

"Why didn't you say anything? All that stupid conversation about the stupid gift cards. You must have been worried sick."

"I needed the diversion. The party was fun. I liked concentrating on your dilemma."

I hugged my friend close. "You should have told me. We could have talked about it. You could have stayed with me. You didn't need to be alone with this."

"That's why I called you this morning. I needed to share with someone. You're the only person who knows."

"What about your mom?"

She laughed derisively, as she usually did when I mentioned her mother. "She'd be the last person I'd tell."

"Maybe she'd surprise you," I said, knowing better but needing to suggest it.

"Are you kidding? She'd give me hell about it, and you know it. I don't need her lectures or her help. It always comes with way too many strings attached."

That much was true. Edith Trevain was a judgmental manipulator disguised in wealthy benefactor clothing. I think Lucy blamed her overbearing, mean-spirited mother for her father's suicide. She hated her mother for it and wanted no part of her.

"Well, then," I said with false cheerfulness, "I guess you're stuck with me. I'll go with you on Monday, and then we'll deal with what comes next. Together."

I needed to be busy, so I jumped off the stool, grabbed several packages from the pantry, and gave Lucy the fixings for tuna sandwiches. While she slathered bread with mayonnaise, I put a can of soup on the stove and then handed her a pint of ice cream.

"Nothing's so bad that it can't be solved by a wholesome lunch, starting with dessert," I philosophized, digging into my Cherries Nirvana.

She toasted me with her container of Chunky Hunky. "We who are about to die salute you."

"Not funny," I reprimanded.

"I don't think so either," she replied.

I turned away to stir the soup so she wouldn't see the tears sliding onto my cheeks.

****

My mother taught me years ago not to "borrow trouble." Ironic since she was the consummate worrier, taking it to levels an Olympic athlete would envy. It was easy for me to grow up without learning to worry; Mother was worrying enough for everyone.

So, my immediate response to Lucy's news was to shove it out of the way, put on a happy face, and get on with things. My emotions about my best friend possibly having cancer simmered on the back burner of my mind. If they ever boiled over, I knew I would fall apart. Not what she needed, not what I needed, not what anyone needed.

So, I phoned my mom, told her about Lucy, and passed the torch of worry to her. Then, as I did when one person I loved was in trouble, I called all the others to check on them.

That was a mistake.

It was best to let sleeping children lie.

I dialed Whitney and when she didn't answer, I left a cheerful message thanking her for the party and telling her I loved her. I was unable to resist mentioning she should get regular checkups, take a multi-vitamin every day, and drink plenty of water.

When I called Syd's cell, he answered.

"Hi, honey," I chirped. "I wanted to tell you what a good time I had last night, and thank you so much for all the gift cards. I actually went to Weight Magic today and got—"

He interrupted, "Mom, can I call you back? I'm

talking to this girl about moving with her to California in a couple of weeks."

"Moving to California?" I felt a lead weight hit the pit of my stomach.

"Yeah, her name's Bridget and she's in a band. They're going to tour the West Coast and try to get on a label."

A jumble of questions filled my head. I plucked one off the top. "So, when are you going?"

"We have to be out there in two weeks—middle of September. Mom, I still have Bridget on the line. Can I call you back?"

"Sure, honey, call me back."

I sank into the sofa and punched off the phone, clutching it to my bosom as if it were my firstborn.

Syd moving to California. He couldn't move to California; he was only twenty-three. Twenty-three-year-olds didn't suddenly move to a city thousands of miles away. He had recently graduated from the University of North Texas. He had big plans to get on with one of the companies headquartered in the Dallas area. I didn't even know he was dating this musician girl.

Syd had always been a gutsy kid: physical, headstrong, and courageous to the point of foolhardiness. He constantly had a bandage on some part of his anatomy, giving way to casts, slings, and braces as he got older and started playing football, going on ski trips, and riding bikes on stair rails.

Jack and I used to look at each other and shrug in confusion, unable to fathom which of our distant ancestors this hell-for-leather kid took after. Certainly, it was neither of us.

As I sat there stewing over Syd embarking on yet

another risky adventure, a cloud of heat welled up inside me, filling my chest, expanding to my fingertips and toes, then shooting out my ears. I fanned myself with the phone.

Then I called my mother and, without even the slightest twinge of guilt, told her Syd was moving to California.

****

"Moving to California? Well, well, hmm," Jack said later that night when I mentioned Syd's plans to him on the phone. "It wouldn't surprise me, I guess. He hasn't gotten a job. He's young. He's got a degree. The timing is probably right."

"The timing is probably right?" I exploded. "That's crazy! He can't pick up and leave Dallas. California is too…warm," I muttered, not wanting to share my true feelings. California was just too damn far away.

"Too warm?" Jack chuckled. "I'm not sure that's a good enough reason."

"It's a mother's reason," I confessed.

"He's a big boy, Tess; it's time he spread his wings a little. Don't say anything yet. The whole thing could fall apart anyway."

"I hate it when you're logical."

"I know. That makes it all worthwhile." Jack hung up after promising he'd talk to Syd and let me know what was up.

With a sigh, I wandered into the bedroom to get ready for my date with Sam. By the time the doorbell rang, I was sweating and had changed clothes twelve times before putting on the same thing I had worn when he took me to see *Wicked* a few weeks before. Season tickets to the musicals were wreaking havoc with my less-than-adequate evening wardrobe.

"Ready?" Sam asked when I answered the door. He stood there looking cool and collected in his blue suit.

I felt tendrils of hair sticking to the back of my neck as we walked to his car.

It was an omen of things to come.

For the first time in forever, or so the manager told us from the stage, the air conditioner at the Dallas Music Hall was on the fritz. No problem, he promised; they had brought in giant fans to cool down the stifling auditorium. The show would go on.

Packed like sardines in the ancient seating, we sweated through the first act, for not a single soul opted out of seeing *Phantom of the Opera* on the historic stage. We had, after all, shelled out a pretty penny for the privilege of sticking shoulder to thigh to the person on either side of us.

Personally, I couldn't tell where my hot flash ended and normal sweltering began.

At intermission, everyone stood in unison, broke their attachment to the human chain with a *thwack,* and melted into the open areas, gladly accepting bottles of chilled water handed out by ushers at the doors.

When the lights flickered, we filed back in with a sigh, took our seats, and struggled to hear the final strains of "Music of the Night," drowned out by a dozen huge fans.

On the drive home, Sam and I took an inventory: two actors had fainted on stage, three patrons had succumbed in the audience, an usher collapsed in an aisle, and the chandelier, blown off course by the giant fans, had nearly decapitated the cellist.

We all deserved a standing ovation for surviving the

evening.

I was glad when Sam dropped me at home without suggesting we go anywhere afterward. I wanted to take a cool shower, curl up with Tuxedo on the sofa, eat a bowl of banana split ice cream, and go to bed.

No wonder my kids gave me a makeover, I thought, staring at my reflection in the mirror twenty minutes later. Fresh from the shower, I was wearing a faded red nightshirt with a fluffy dog's head appliquéd on the front and the wagging tail on the back, a gift from my mother five years earlier.

Forgoing the ice cream, I snuggled under the quilt on my bed, kicked it off, and made a mental note to throw the nightshirt away in the morning. After all, a new me deserved new nighties.

Without warning, the red teddy Lucy gave me for my birthday called to me from the drawer. Climbing out of bed, I retrieved it and let the silk slide through my fingers. I held the fabric up to my face and glanced in the mirror. The rosy hue made my complexion glow somehow and my eyes sparkle. In an instant, I had shrugged off the offensive doggy nightshirt and into the sexy, slinky teddy.

One look in the mirror told me there was good news and bad news. The amazing color made me rethink all the browns and grays in my closet. And the length showed my legs to their best advantage. I looked like a thoroughbred prancing around my bedroom.

But there the magic ended. Sitting atop those long stems was a big, round, lumpy red apple. The silk stretched enough to fit, but the look was anything but the sexy seductress I envisioned. I wriggled out of the teddy and shoved it back into the drawer.

With a sigh, I walked naked into the bathroom, stepped on the scales, and maneuvered into a position I felt was accurate without giving the heinous device any advantage. A tinny, computerized voice announced my weight.

"Two hundred four pounds."

Gasp. That couldn't be right. No woman should weigh two hundred pounds. I stepped off and back on again.

The voice repeated, "Two hundred four pounds."

I wanted to clamp my hand over its computerized mouth in case someone else could hear.

I had always been tall, so it didn't seem like I weighed that much. No one would have thought I weighed that much, but *my* knowing it filled me with self-loathing of monumental proportions—which was appropriate considering I was as big as Mt. Rushmore!

I took a breath, then stepped off the scales. So, two hundred four would be my benchmark weight. And that damn teddy would be my benchmark garment. I would lose forty pounds. It would cost me a fortune in Weight Magic TV dinners, sweat, and tears, but I would do it.

With new resolve, I shrugged back into the doggy nightshirt, switched on the ceiling fan in my bedroom, a hedge against the inevitable night sweats to come, crawled into bed, and pulled the quilt up under my chin.

Lucy had announced her upcoming biopsy. I refused to think about the consequences of whatever news she might receive on Monday. I would be there for her no matter what. Then I would call my mother and let her do the worrying.

Syd had disclosed his intentions of moving across country. He had never called back, of course, so I was still full of speculation, but I was determined not to get upset about his leaving until the reality of it hit me in the face like the Santa Ana wind.

Okay, so there were two big checkmarks in the denial column of my life, but what the hell? I had boldly embarked on a journey of self-improvement and made positive steps in the direction of reaching my goal: a thinner, more beautiful, and healthier me.

I drifted off to sleep, dreaming of Syd, decked out in a cape and mask, devouring the Weight Magic dinners in my freezer.

Chapter Four

It was a tradition. Sort of an unspoken, unbroken law of the Thomason clan that Sunday was a day for faith, family, football, and food. At least that's what my dad always said. Raised a northern Baptist, he was never fond of the formalized worship service, so we only went to Sunday School, but did it religiously.

After church, we gathered around the big family table at my parents' house for a roast of some sort, left to cook to a succulent turn while we were gone. Dad considered the Sabbath a day of rest, but his love of food won out over his need for observation of ancient Jewish custom, so he banished Mother from the kitchen and cooked. She shouldn't have to commit a sin because he wanted a pork roast.

He did, however, enlist help from me and Donna. I suppose we were somehow immune from sin.

While we were in the kitchen, Mother held court in the den. Paul poured wine for anyone who wanted it, mostly for himself. His sons wrestled unnoticed in front of the TV.

Sam spent Sunday with his wife, Julia, at the nursing home, reading to her, feeding her, talking to her unresponsive face about his week, omitting time spent with me, I was sure. I didn't mind he wasn't with me on Sunday. It was right he be with Julia that day. Sunday was for family.

You'd think since we had all seen each other at the infamous birthday bash on Friday night, my family would forgo the gathering on Sunday, but no, the two were not connected. The birthday party was a crass, bacchanalian celebration; Sundays were sacred.

By twelve fifteen, everyone had arrived, pots in hand, and platters were passed, family style.

"So, Syd, what's this about California?" my brother asked.

"How'd you know about that?" Syd asked, his question muffled by a mouth full of mashed potatoes.

Paul thought for a moment. "Your grandmother told me."

Wow, that's fast work, even for Mother.

"What about California?" Donna, sitting to my right, asked.

"Well, my friend Bridget's brother lives there. He said we could stay with him while we tour the state with her band."

"Who is this Bridget?" I asked, suspicious of this woman who held sway over my son.

"You know, Mom, you and Whit met her a couple weeks ago. She's the one who waited on us at Burger Shack."

A picture of red-tipped hair, tattoos, and multiple piercings flashed through my head. She had looked a little like an off-duty superhero.

Whitney nodded. "Oh, that Bridget. Of course. She seemed nice. How do you know her?"

"She was in my chemistry class last year." He speared a piece of broccoli and continued, "She's cool. She set fire to a university dumpster because they refused to switch to cleaner-burning propane."

"Ah, she's an activist," Donna muttered.

"No, she's a musician," Syd corrected.

"She's an arsonist," Paul added, challenging my motherhood with a raised eyebrow.

"So, honey," I said, changing the subject before anyone else chimed in. "Tell us about the band. What kind of music do they play?"

"Celtic music."

I immediately heard strains of bagpipes and flutes drifting through my head. I loved Celtic music. Maybe this wasn't so bad. How much of an anarchist could a Celtic musician be?

"Yeah," Syd continued, his face animated with enthusiasm. "They play normal music, but also this incredible experimental music on things you find in a kitchen."

I had let my guard down too soon. My kitchen wasn't particularly musical. "In a kitchen?"

"They take appliances or kitchen gadgets or pots and pans and make music. It sounds like that singer you love, Mom—Envy, Aunty?"

A deafening silence filled the room as everyone stared at Sydney. The last thing I could conjure was the ethereal sounds of my Celtic music goddess emanating from a crockpot.

Familiar heat flowered in my chest. "What about your degree in accounting?" I asked, fanning myself with a pickle I had taken from the relish tray.

"That's the beauty of it, Mom. I'll be the accountant for the band during the day and a member of their tech crew at night."

"A roadie? You're going to be a roadie?" Whitney squealed, seemingly delighted at her brother's jettisoned corporate career.

He shot her a withering glance. "Whit, we're called the tech crew now."

I sighed. I knew I'd lost him when he said "we're."

My mother had been silent to this point. "What instrument are you going to play in the band, Sydney?"

"No, Grandma, I'm not playing in the band. I'm going to do other things for them," he corrected, steering away from confusing particulars already discussed and misunderstood.

"You played the bassoon in junior high," she reminded him.

"Mom, he hasn't played for years," I interjected. "He said he was going to be their accountant, not a musician."

"That's a relief," she said, smiling. "You were a terrible musician."

"Thanks, Grams," Syd replied, rolling his eyes.

"Oh, it's not your fault, dear. Your mother is tone deaf."

****

Sunday afternoons at the Thomason's were pretty predictable. After we'd eaten our fill, the women cleaned the kitchen while the men went to the den to watch football. No one ever mentioned the disparity of this arrangement to Daddy, Paul, or Syd. Men didn't do dishes, especially on the Sabbath.

Donna and I found ourselves alone in the kitchen. My kids had to be at work waiting tables at Habanera by three o'clock, and Mom had excused herself for a nap.

"So, what have you been up to?" I asked Donna.

"The usual, I guess."

"What's the usual?" I asked, curious about what my

sister-in-law did all day. Paul hadn't allowed her to work since the boys were born, and now that they were in school, I wondered how she spent her day.

She gave me a sidelong glance, either suspicious of my line of questioning or surprised anyone cared to ask. "Well, after I drop the boys at school, I run errands or supervise the maid or the yard crew. Before I know it, it's time to pick them up."

"What about you? Do you do anything for you?"

She stopped drying the huge roaster. "Not really. I used to belong to some clubs and charity groups, but Paul complained they took too much time away from the boys and the house."

"Does Paul belong to any clubs?"

"Oh sure, tons." She ticked them off on her fingers. "The country club, Kiwanis, Rotary. He says they help business."

"Do you get to do anything for yourself?"

She slid the roaster into the cupboard under the stove, and straightened, pushing a strand of hair from her face. She was pretty in a porcelain doll sort of way with dark, wavy hair and creamy skin. But her eyes always looked sad to me.

"Well, of course. I get my hair and nails done and get a facial twice a month. I take a yoga class and play tennis once a week at the club to stay in shape. I shop for clothes, of course. I'm also busy planning dinner parties at the house for Paul's work associates." She flashed me a big smile as if that were the end of the conversation.

I felt a little guilty for pushing her to talk as if I were passing judgment on her situation. Although, that's exactly what I was doing. Like my situation was perfect. "You know what, we should go to a movie sometime.

Just the two of us."

She brightened like a little child. "That would be so fun." Then her face fell. "But I could never leave the house at night or on the weekend."

"Why not?" I asked, although I already knew the answer.

"Because Paul would say no, that I need to stay home with him and the boys."

"Why? Can't he take the boys for one night while you have an evening out with me?"

"It's not the way it works at our house."

"So, you never go out at night or on the weekends?"

She laughed a little. "Of course, I go out. Paul and I take the boys to the movie or rollerblading or to the skateboard park or to their soccer games or—" Her voice trailed off.

"Do you and Paul ever go out alone? You know, get a sitter, go to dinner, or to a play?" I asked, realizing the turn our conversation was taking.

"Not really. We have sitters come to watch the boys when we entertain, but we don't ever go out. There's not much time for that sort of thing."

I tossed the dishtowel on the counter. "Well, I think we need to have a date. You and I. Dinner and a movie. How about Tuesday?"

"Oh, I don't know, Tuesday is so soon." Her eyes widened with a mixture of fear and excitement. I felt like I was asking her to sneak out of the house to go to a wild high-school party.

"Let's go talk to Paul right now." I grabbed her by the hand and hustled her into the den.

"No, no, Tess, he won't like it. I can't."

"Can't what? Paul asked, without looking away

from the television set.

"I want Donna to join me for a movie and dinner on Tuesday. A girls' night out. You can watch the boys, can't you?"

He looked up then and right at Donna. "You know that's my handball night at the club."

Donna shrank a little behind me. "Of course, I forgot."

"What about Thursday?" I ventured, wondering what kind of man would keep his wife captive at home and alarmed that it might be my brother.

"Thursday is dinner with the Wingfields. Really, Tess, this isn't a good week."

"How about next week?" I pushed, sensing Donna shiver beside me.

Paul stared at me, his lips quirked in the slightest of smiles. "How about if we get back to you? We'll look at our calendar and see what will work. Donna's a busy woman, aren't you, honey?"

"Yes, I am busy," she hurried to answer. "I don't think it's going to work out, Tess. I appreciate the invitation, but you can see my schedule is packed."

"But…" I murmured as she moved away to sit next to Paul on the sofa. He put a protective arm around her shoulder.

"Really, Tess, forget it." She looked away.

I went back into the kitchen, folded the dishtowel, and hung it on the rack to dry, said goodbye to no one in particular, and drove home, wondering what kind of Pandora's box I had peeked into.

****

"Can This Marriage Be Saved?" the magazine article asked and then proceeded to tell me the story of

Josh and Linda and their marital woes. Josh was a spendthrift, and Linda was a slob. Somehow, their disputes over bank accounts and dust bunnies paled in comparison to my concern about why Lucy's biopsy was taking so long.

The Women's Imaging Center waiting room of the hospital was obviously designed to provide a comforting experience for those who lingered there: brocade walls and matching upholstered chairs, huge urns filled with silk flower arrangements, and paintings framed in gilt.

I checked my watch. Two hours. I set the magazine on top of the stack I had already finished reading and looked around the room. After such a long wait, I had soaked in all the lavish décor I cared for and just wanted to hear about my friend.

As I was about to lunge for the door that led to the treatment rooms, Lucy came out, looking apologetic.

"Hi, sorry it took so long."

"It's okay. Are you through?" I stood to greet her.

"Yes, let's go eat." She swept past me and headed to the parking lot.

All the way to the restaurant, she sat in the passenger seat with her eyes closed. I couldn't tell if she were sleeping or exhausted from the procedure. I didn't dare bother her with all the questions welling up inside me.

She roused when I stopped the car. I asked, "Are you sure you want to eat? I'll take you home so you can nap if you want."

"Are you kidding? I'm hungry."

After we ordered, I leaned across the table, "Okay, so what did they say?"

"Well, of course, they won't know for a few days. But they weren't very reassuring. None of that 'Oh, this looks like nothing' or 'that looks perfectly normal.' No, they were very noncommittal, dammit."

"They don't want to say anything and then be wrong, so they're trained to be completely unemotional. They're inscrutable. Like Zen masters."

"And car mechanics."

Our salads came, and as we ate, Lucy recounted the events of the morning.

"It was a little like drilling for ore. They used a gun kind of thing and shot a hollow shaft into the mass, then brought out part of it. They did that a couple of times, then it was over."

"It took so long, I figured they were giving you a full body scan or something."

"Well, they did have to do an ultrasound and then wait for the area to numb. I guess that took a while. I'm sorry."

"It's okay. I was just worried."

"Well, it's over now. Except the waiting."

"And the dessert."

"You can't eat dessert. You're doing Weight Magic!"

"Party pooper! I'd be willing to sacrifice my diet for my best friend's happiness. Dessert would make you feel better, wouldn't it?"

"No, I will not be an enabler for you."

If Lucy could go through what she was facing, then I could dig down deep and find some modicum of willpower. "Right. I can do this. No problem. Let's go to Coffee Heaven and get a fat-free latté. Race you to the car!"

"Oh no," Lucy replied dramatically, hand to her bandaged breast. "I can't do that. I'm an invalid, you know. I require special treatment. I require…a head start!"

She went scooting out of the restaurant, leaving me to rummage in my purse for my keys and hustle out after her. When I reached the car, she was laughing. "Thought you wanted to race."

I glared at her. "No, you big cheater. You will get no more special treatment from me."

She stuck out her bottom lip in an exaggerated pout.

"And don't give me any of your lip."

****

On Wednesday, I stared at the computer screen in my office, watching the cursor mock me with its expectant stillness.

"Come on, wimp," it said. "You call yourself a writer. Show me what you got."

My first two columns had come to me easily over the weekend, fueled by the adrenaline rush of events surrounding me. I had turned them in to Ruth and received her normal, "Hmm, thanks."

But the next one escaped me, and I had started and stopped a dozen times over the last two days. Either I had lost touch with my feminine side already, or this was harder than I thought.

My mind wandered. The events of the past several days played over and over, careening from one to the other like a pinball machine, taking turns firing rockets of worry into my stomach. Things were a little out of control in Tess World, and I didn't like it one bit.

Why couldn't things stay the way they were? I was comfortable in my boring dumpiness, my kids were safely ensconced near home, my friend was her healthy, decadent, and exciting self, and I didn't have to write this stupid column.

What could I possibly say to other women that they didn't already know? I couldn't counsel anyone. I could only wring my hands and rail against my own fate.

Okay, that's what I'd do. After all, misery loves company.

Sensible Shoes

By Tess Thomason

Change isn't what it's cracked up to be. You hear all the time, "Change is Good," "Embrace Change," but I'm here to tell you that's a pile of poo.

Most of us hate change. It marches into the middle of our well-ordered lives and tosses everything into the air, letting the pieces fall helter-skelter around us. Change gets us off schedule, screws up our five-year plan, makes a mess, and then saunters off to leave us holding a bag of the aforementioned poo.

I know whereof I speak (yeah, I know nobody says "whereof" anymore, but I like how it sounds and it's my column, so…) In the last few days, I have been whacked in the face by three huge, life-changing pieces of news.

Here they are, in no particular order.

I hit a milestone birthday and as a result took stock of my less-than-healthy lifestyle, replacing my love of cream cheese with a freezer full of low-cal dinners.

My twenty-three-year-old son announced his plans to move to California with his rocker girlfriend. I thought he wanted to be an accountant.

And my best friend may have breast cancer.

Any one of these things would throw my life into a tailspin, but all three at once are a little overwhelming, so the feelings of pandemonium I have are normal. At least I tell myself that as I scramble away from the ledge.

What I'm wondering is whether my roiling insides will calm down. I mean, I'm not going to quit being old, overweight, and out of shape without doing something about it. My son is going to the west coast for a while until he meets someone who wants to be a marine biologist in, oh, I don't know, maybe Maine. And while I will pray for my darling friend, she and I both know this doesn't look good, and she will have a hard road of surgery and recovery ahead.

Change. Yeah, the truth is, it sucks.

I'd like my life to go back to the way it was last week, thank you very much.

I'd like to return to my comfort zone.

Now, please.

Chapter Five

As I heated up a Weight Magic Viennese Chicken dinner that evening, my phone rang.

"The doctor's office called," Lucy announced, after I said hello.

The microwave dinged, and I pulled the plastic-covered tray out by the corner, cradling the phone to my ear. "What did they say?"

"It's cancer," Lucy said it as if the delivery of a new sofa had been put off a week. It was like her to be upset in a very matter-of-fact sort of way.

But the stone of apprehension sinking into the pit of *my* stomach squashed my appetite. I left the food on the counter, walked into the den, and sat down on the couch as if I weighed a ton. "Oh, God."

"They want to see me tomorrow to talk about options."

"Do you want me to go with you?"

"No, you have to work. But could you meet me for lunch after?"

"Sure," I paused, waiting for her to respond. When she didn't, I prodded, "Lucy?"

"Yes?"

"Don't worry. It's going to be okay."

"I know. I'm just so pissed off."

"At what?"

"At myself."

"Why?"

"Ninety days, Tess. I waited ninety days."

"I know."

"It was smaller then. They said it's a rather large mass, now."

"What does that mean?"

"Well, they can't do a lumpectomy. They already said so."

"Oh, God."

"You keep saying that."

"Sorry, I seem to have left my smart mouth in my other purse. Maybe it won't be as bad as we're thinking."

"I just hope it's not worse than we're thinking." She paused. "Ninety days, Tess. I could kill myself for waiting."

Oh, God.

****

Lucy and I lunched the next day at The Stables, a trendy little place near a horse farm in far North Dallas. She arrived looking gorgeous as usual, wearing a nubby white sweater, tailored black pants, and little black booties. Her hair grazed her shoulders at a fashionable length. But I could make out the dark circles under her eyes and the attempt to conceal them with foundation.

We ordered giant salads, the luncheon food of choice for women pretending to watch their weight. Secretly, we all know Caesar dressing tops the list of faux diet foods.

After the peach tea arrived, I asked about the surgery.

"They're going to do a mastectomy," Lucy answered, avoiding my gaze. "But not the kind with the lymph nodes, so that's a good thing."

"Yeah, that's a good thing," I agreed, thinking it sounded anything but good.

"And they'll do reconstructive surgery right then, so I won't be disfigured. That's a good thing."

"Yeah, that's a good thing." My complete lack of witty banter made me feel idiotic, but the thought of my beautiful friend having to undergo such a radical procedure was devastating. "So, that will be the end of it, then?"

She looked at me, her face ashen, "No, I'll have radiation and chemo after. Just to be sure."

"Of course, they want to be sure." I shoved the image of Lucy, sick and bald, from my mind and tried to force an upbeat note into my voice. "So, how long before the surgery? A week? Two?"

"Monday."

"Oh, that soon, huh?" I stammered, stunned with the urgency of this whole thing.

Lucy leaned across the table and put her hand on mine. "I have a favor to ask you, Tess."

"What, you need a kidney?"

She smiled a little. "Cute. I was wondering if you would be there for the surgery?"

"Sure, but what about your mother? You have to tell her."

She removed her hand from my arm and picked up her fork, spearing a piece of lettuce. "I'll tell her, of course, for all the good it'll do. She'll be busy playing bridge or something that day."

She imitated Edith Trevain's haughty, nasal tone, "Lucy, darling, how dreadful for you. It's the worst, but I can't be there. South of France, you know. Scheduled for months. So sorry, darling. I'm sure everything will be fine. Call Dr. Truett. He does everyone who's anyone."

Lucy finished her performance and bowed as I clapped. "And she'll follow the whole thing up with a giant fruit basket, timed to arrive in my room right after the surgery."

I giggled at the accuracy of the portrayal, noticing Edith never seemed to utter a complete sentence, but all the while, my heart broke for Lucy. My own mother would have walked over hot coals to be with me in such a dire time.

Her expression sobered. "So could you come, please. The doctor needs someone to talk to afterward."

I squeezed her hand. "Of course, I'll drive you over and stay with you the whole time." Then I added, desperate to lighten the somber moment, "I'll sit in your room during the day and watch soap operas, and at night, I'll curl up next to you in the bed. I'll never leave your side. Everyone will think we're lesbians. You'll beg the doctors to make me go home."

She grimaced, and we both laughed out loud at the picture of me snuggled up next to her in the hospital bed with a soap opera blaring out of the TV on the wall.

But then Lucy bowed her head to study her salad. When she raised it a moment later, tears shimmered in her eyes. "Thanks."

****

By Saturday I was a nervous wreck thinking about Lucy, and I had to get out of the house. With a renewed appreciation for my physical health, and armed with a six-month membership to Body Sculptors, I shoe-horned my cellulite into some old yoga pants and tank top. One glance in the mirror sent me running for the biggest T-shirt I owned. I pulled on slouchy athletic socks and my white running shoes.

I checked back in the mirror, sure I would now look like a cool dancer from the eighties.

Not exactly.

I grabbed a threadbare beach towel, and with a sigh, headed out the door.

First stop was Coffee Heaven. I needed fortification if I were to spend the morning grunting and sweating.

I was proud of myself, though, because I ordered a latté with skim milk. No point in undoing all the progress Weight Magic had made in the last week.

I turned from the register and ran headlong into Roger Austin, looking gorgeous in jeans and a pale yellow golf shirt.

"Oh, hi!"

"Tess," he said, grinning down at me. "Used any of those gift cards yet?"

"As a matter of fact, I have. And I'm on my way to sit-ups as we speak." I realized then that I was wearing my Dancer-Wanna-Be ensemble and tugged the T-shirt farther down over my spandex-encased derriere.

"Well, good for you!"

"That's the idea, I think." I felt the blush of embarrassment spread from my face to my toes. Eager to shift the conversation away from me, I asked, "Where are you off to?"

"I have a meeting with my new business partner."

"Oh, yeah, you mentioned a new job last time I saw you. So, it's a new business venture, huh, that's exciting."

"I am excited. This is a new venue for me." He motioned to a table, and we both took a seat. "What about you? What do you do when you're not up to your eyebrows in self-improvement?"

"I write a gardening column for the *Dallas Tribune*."

"So, you've probably got a huge garden, hedges, and mazes. No, wait, vegetables, herbs, fruit trees. No," he mused, hand to chin, studying me. "Flowers. Perennials, biennials…all the, uh, ennials."

I laughed. "Nothing quite so…floral. I'm more of a shrub person."

He leaned back in his chair. "Ah, shrubs. I have a brown thumb, myself. I've left a trail of dead plants everywhere I've lived. I gave up trying to grow things. Mother Earth heaved a sigh of relief, I'm sure."

"I'm sure. So, where have you lived?"

He gazed at the ceiling and began to tick them off on his fingers one by one. "Kentucky, Rio, Bermuda, Tokyo, New York City."

"Wow, what were you doing in all those places? Were you in the service? Are you an international spy?"

He laughed. "Nothing so clandestine. I move around for business."

"What kind of business takes you to all those places?"

"I'm an investor. So, I'm involved in lots of different businesses."

"You give money to people who want to start new ventures? Like what?"

"Oh, real estate, thoroughbred horse racing, hotel management, among others. But I got my start in the music business."

"The music business?" I repeated. "My son is going off to California with some weird band that plays Celtic kitchen music."

Roger cocked his head in question.

"Don't ask," I answered with a wave of my hand. "He'll be home soon. He's got a degree in accounting, for God's sake."

"Don't underestimate the pull of the music business on kids. It's pretty powerful."

"Were you in a band?"

"Sure, every kid of the eighties was in a band. We were terrible, of course, but we kept it up. We even cut a record and went on tour. That's what got me into the music business."

I laughed, trying to picture mature, graying, preppy Roger with a mullet and a guitar. "Were you called something offbeat and unfathomable?"

"Well, yeah, it was the eighties."

"What? Tell me."

"Okay, but don't laugh."

"Cross my heart." I followed the verbal promise with the appropriate gesture.

"Green Cheese."

I choked back the laugh that threatened to betray me. "Why?"

"No reason except that my friend Buddy thought it sounded offbeat and unfathomable."

I laughed out loud then, remembering my friends and myself in the eighties. I thought about my kids now and how there's a universal need to be different and yet the same somehow.

Roger laughed, too, and I gladly would have frozen the moment: sipping lattés with this interesting man and feeling young again.

"Did you ever have any girls in your band?" I asked, fishing for more information. Maybe I could get him to mention his wife.

"One, Olivia, she was our version of a rock icon."

"She must have been beautiful."

He looked a little wistful. "Yeah, she was."

Suddenly, I felt fatter and more unattractive than ever and wanted to escape to Body Sculptors and become as beautiful as Olivia. "I have to go," I said and nearly knocked over the table when I stood.

Roger stood, too. "I enjoyed our conversation. Maybe I'll see you here again."

"Oh, I doubt it," I answered, my flight mechanism in full throttle. "I'm taking a break from Coffee Heaven for a while. This was my farewell latté."

I hurried into the bright September sun, acutely aware of him staring after me and cursing the yoga pants that jiggled all the way to the car.

****

Body Sculptors, the trendy new fitness center, had opened last year. I had friends who went there, stay-at-home moms from the neighborhood who already looked like dancers or tennis pros.

But I was not going to be intimidated by hard bodies. On the drive over, I convinced myself hard bodies were often accompanied by mushy minds. That theory was reinforced when the first person I ran into in the reception area was Jack's lover, Tad.

There was no harder body than Tad's, whose abs were ripped, stripped, and stacked up like a six-pack of soda. No muscle had been left unhoned. A translucent sheen of oil shimmered on his skin, highlighting every curve and sinew. His black hair was slicked back from his chiseled face, curling slightly on the nape of his neck. In one hand, he held a clipboard, poised as if to write something of import.

He looked for all the world like a Greek God, the modern equivalent of Perseus, a seeker of truth and justice, the embodiment of all things good and righteous.

Then he spoke, and I remembered it was all a myth.

"Yo, Tess, what's up?" He grinned at me, displaying an array of straight white teeth.

"Hi, Tad. I wasn't sure you'd be here."

"They asked me to start a new program for women, such as yourself, who may need to lose a few extra pounds and firm up those batwing arms and other, uh, problem areas."

He looked right at my stomach. So, of course, I sucked it in, which increased the size of my breasts by a couple inches but did little to help the stomach situation. "Ah, perfect. So how does that work?" I said, exhaling slowly, lest the spandex give way.

"Well, three times a week, you come in and rotate through a series of stations. The program is designed to work your whole body, get your heart rate going, and firm you up all over."

That didn't sound too bad. Sensible, moderate, slow progress toward the eighties dance icon I knew lurked inside my giant T-shirt.

"Okay," I said, handing over the appropriate gift card. "Sign me up."

Tad took the card and had me fill out several forms, then he led me from the chrome and glass reception area to the chrome and steel dressing area.

"You can put your stuff in one of the lockers, then take the key with you." He jangled a similar key hanging from the waistband of his tiny shorts.

I opened a yellow locker, stuck my bag and towel

into it, closed the door, and took the key. But since my waistband was buried beneath rolls of fat, I looped the coil over my wrist instead and let the key dangle against my palm like a giant charm.

Tad led me through a short hallway lined with mirrors, and I wondered what kind of perverse mind would think that was in any way helpful. We stopped in a small room that held very little except a doctor's scale.

The breath caught in my throat. It was one thing to let Jack's young stud fantasize about what lay beneath my giant T-shirt and something much different to let him have actual knowledge of just how out of shape I was. My palms began to sweat.

"Okay, Tess, jump up onto the scale."

"Why? I already know how much I weigh."

"We need a benchmark weight for a couple of reasons. One is so we can track your progress, and the other is so I can tailor a workout program for you." He emphasized the words "for you" as if that were a selling feature. Which, for some people, it would have been. But for me, the idea was anonymity. Give me the workout regimen for the masses. Let me blend in with the teeming, sweaty hordes. Don't single me out to be poked, prodded, and, for God's sake, weighed.

After all I had just heard the truth in no uncertain terms from my own scale at home. I didn't need the bad news to be reinforced in front of Tad, who could kiss and tell all my bulging secrets to my ex-husband whenever they needed to ratchet up their pillow talk.

"Okay." I stepped on the scale. Short of running from the building, what else could I do?

I just had to hope Tad's handsome body held a heart that wouldn't betray me.

I held my breath as he moved the sliders around until the bubble stayed in the center of the crosspiece.

"Two ten," he practically shouted, guaranteeing the next person I saw would know how much I weighed.

"That can't be right," I argued. "I only weigh two hundred four at home."

He waved a dismissive hand. "Home scales are often off by about five pounds. This scale is a lot more accurate."

Six more pounds. It might as well be six hundred. How I longed for the days of ignorant bliss when I thought I weighed two hundred four.

Could this day get any worse?

Tad wrote my weight down on the clipboard, opened a drawer, and pulled out a pair of calipers. "Okay, now let's measure your body fat."

****

During the torturous morning I spent at Body Sculptors, I learned two things.

First, working out with Tad, while debilitating to my ego, might do me some good. He had, after all, come up with some sound ideas, seemed knowledgeable about working out in relation to fat and age, and was encouraging and enthusiastic rather than tyrannical and snobbish.

After a brief run-through on the machines, every muscle in my body ached, and my legs were less al dente than the vermicelli in the Weight Magic Napoli Chicken dinner I had the night before. But I felt good as if I were doing something positive for myself, taking a step forward.

I suppose in the back of my mind, I worried that if something terrible could happen to someone like Lucy, who was in great shape, then I was doomed. I wasn't ready to be doomed, and so, I renewed my resolve to reinvent myself.

I was, after all, footloose and fancy-free. I had spent the last five years since the divorce in limbo unless you counted my platonic relationship with Sam, who seemed somehow more like a maiden aunt than a boyfriend. All this time, I waited for the rest of my life to start. I survived the numbing fear and loneliness that comes with finding yourself solo after twenty years of marriage. But then what? Was I waiting for Jack to come back; announce he wasn't gay after all; it had all been a mistake?

Not likely.

Jack loved his new life. He had left me to move in with his podiatrist. That lasted a year until the podiatrist took off with their collection of Lalique and a stock portfolio Jack had babied along for him.

Granted, I had gloated for a while, glad Jack was experiencing some of the misery I felt. But he picked himself up, quit his job at the brokerage firm, and signed up for culinary school. Upon graduation, he opened Habanera.

It was there he met Tad, a personal trainer who moonlighted as a bartender. They'd been together ever since. I thought Jack felt a certain security in knowing he had it over Tad in the brains department. Maybe he believed a brawny young man would stick around longer than the doctor had.

Which brought me to the second thing I learned while working out with Tad.

Jack's new partner in the restaurant business—a hunky older guy (according to Tad)—was "just ruining everything."

The guy wasn't a chef but a businessman who was taking over all of Jack's time, introducing him to new people and taking him out to places where everyone wore designer clothes and drank designer cocktails. The idea was to build a catering business and expand the restaurant and Jack's persona to a blog, cookbooks, and maybe even television.

"He says the point is to get Jack's name out in circles of people who can put Habanera on the map and get him social media exposure," Tad grumbled to me. "But I'm thinking it's more Jack himself he's after." His voice shook with jealousy and insecurity, and it struck me for the first time Tad really loved Jack.

I don't think it had ever dawned on me that the emotions they would feel for each other would be similar to my own when Jack and I were young and in love. The realization made me feel a warmth and affection for Tad that was new to me.

It also made me feel an instant dislike toward Hunky Older Guy (HOG). Without ever meeting him, I knew he was one of those slick, suit-wearing, smooth-talking, pretty homosexuals who left broken hearts in their wake.

In that instant, the Earth Mother within me rose up to protect pure hearts like Tad's and vulnerable ones like Jack's from predators like HOG.

"I'm sure Jack loves you, Tad," I encouraged. "I doubt the wily ways of this man will come between you." I hoped my voice and expression held more reassurance than I felt.

As I left the health club, I promised myself I would find a way to meet Jack's new business partner.

****

Sunday lunch at my parents' had ended in time for the noon football kickoff. Donna and I packaged up the leftovers in various plastic containers, grumbling that the men had wolfed down their meal so as not to miss a moment of the game. We contemplated sending out for pizza the next time but worried it would violate the principle of One-Man-One-Roast on Sundays.

We sat at the table, visiting over coffee, me being careful not to stir up any trouble between Donna and Paul until we heard a commotion from the den.

"Mom! Aunt Donna! Come out here!" Whitney yelled. "Grandma, wake up and come in the den!"

Donna and I scurried out of the kitchen.

Whitney and Mark stood in the center of the den, halftime commentary blaring from the TV. "What's wrong?" I demanded, picking up the remote from my dad's lap and turning down the volume.

My mother shuffled in from her nap in the living room. "What in the blazes is going on? I was dreaming about Brad Pitt and me and a handful of…well, never mind."

Whitney and Mark grinned from ear to ear, hands clutched tightly. A wave of nausea washed over me, and I grabbed Donna's arm to steady myself.

Whitney squealed, "We have an announcement to make."

Please God, no, not now.

She looked at Mark, who cleared his throat, then spoke in a shaky voice. "Whitney has agreed to be my wife. We're getting married at Christmas. And we want you all to be there."

Whitney squealed again, only louder, and leaped into Mark's arms. I sank into the nearest vacant chair and watched as pandemonium erupted in the den. The rush to congratulate the couple rivaled any blitz a front line could have mustered, and Whitney and Mark were nearly knocked backward by the well-wishers.

When the dust settled, I made my way to Whitney, hugged her, and whispered, "Congratulations, sweetie. This is a surprise."

Without shifting in my embrace, Whitney whispered back, "I know, I'll talk to you later, okay?"

"Okay," I said and released her, letting her slide back into Mark's embrace, but not before I took note of the tears threatening to spill down her cheeks.

Please God, no, not now.

****

Later that afternoon I called Jack. "Did you hear about your daughter?"

"Yes, I did. Great news, isn't it?"

"Great news? How can you say that? She's just a child. She's too young to get married. And I think there's something fishy about the whole thing."

"Good grief, Tess! Didn't we just have this conversation about Syd? Are you ever going to realize your kids are grown now, and they have lives to live that may not involve being surgically attached to you?"

"I don't want them attached to me. I just want them to be ready for these big life-changing events. I don't want them to make mistakes like we did."

He was quiet for a long time. "You think we were a mistake?"

"Well, yeah, don't you? I mean we got a divorce, didn't we?"

"Yeah, but it wasn't like it was a mistake. I loved you, and we made two great children."

"Children who are going to be the death of me."

"Come on, wasn't there anything good about us?"

It was my turn to be quiet. "That's the problem, Jack. Everything was great with us. I was crazy about you. We had a good life. We never argued. The kids were perfect, our house was perfect, our lives were perfect. At least mine was. Your life, as it turned out, was a little less than perfect."

"It's not my fault I'm gay."

"Yeah, I know it's not your fault, and I'm not holding that against you. I just wish you'd realized it before we were married, that's all."

"We never would have had the kids. They were worth it, weren't they?"

I thought about Syd going to California to play spoons in a band and Whitney marrying Mark, who was nearly a stranger. "No, I don't think so. I don't think so at all."

Jack laughed. We'd had this conversation a dozen times before, and it never changed anything. We still loved each other in a weird, familial sort of way, which involved a rare breed of intimacy shared only with people who had seen you birth babies.

"So, back to Whitney," I said.

"Right, I talked to her, and the reception will be at Habanera, so that's easy. They're still working on the rest of it, and I'm sure you'll be the go-to mom for everything else."

"Well, what do you want to do for the reception? Can we have the place to ourselves?"

"Oh, sure, of course. Tell you what. I'll have my new business partner call you. He's handling catering for me. This will give him a chance to get his feet wet with an actual event."

"He's not from the catering world?"

"No, he's really an entrepreneur. He knows how to get businesses going. I hooked up with him to build the catering business, possibly open a chain of restaurants, get to the next level, you know."

I thought about Tad, so distraught at the health club. "Yeah, I heard."

"What?"

"Never mind. I'll talk to Whitney, then we'll speak with your catering guy. I've been looking forward to meeting him."

I hung up, ready to plan my attack against Hunky Older Guy. But first, I would fortify myself with a Mediterranean Chicken Surprise.

Chapter Six

On Monday, Lucy and I got to the hospital at the crack of dawn. I checked her in, stayed with her for what seemed like hours, then waved cheerfully as they wheeled her away.

I brought books to read, magazines to peruse, and my laptop should the "Sensible Shoes" muse stumble in, but they all sat idle in my lap as I stared at a pastel picture of a meadow on the waiting room wall, not seeing it, seeing Lucy's face instead.

The face of resolute fear. As we drove to the hospital, checked in, and waited, it was the face she wore, bravely, stoically. She would get through the next weeks and months because she had no choice. But it was clear from her face she was not going easy.

And how would I have felt? What would my thoughts have been? Fear I might not survive the surgery. Worry about a long recovery without someone to share the burden. Apprehension about loss of income from work. And the heavy knowledge my body would never be whole again. The notion I might never have someone who would look past the scars to love me.

That had to weigh on Lucy's mind. I'm sure it had been a factor in her decision to have immediate reconstructive surgery. She was not the type of person to discount the importance of her appearance in maintaining the lifestyle she had come to appreciate.

"The doctors tell me they can make the scar insignificant so no one would notice." She had laughed then and added, "Unless they take a closer look, which, of course, is the point, right?"

I had laughed along with her but wondered whether I would have the same priorities given that situation. Or would I be more cautious, choosing instead to keep things simple in case the cancer came back and could be detected more easily.

The difference between Lucy and me was I had been married, had a partner who loved me, and had children I adored and was close to. I wasn't looking for a mate and, therefore, wouldn't have concerned myself as much with appearance as with eradicating the cancer once and for all.

I also wouldn't have waited ninety days.

Through the course of the morning everyone in my family called to check on Lucy's progress. I was able to tell them she was fine. At least that's what the nurse said, who came out midway through the surgery to talk to me.

Jack called, and when I finished telling him about Lucy's progress, he said, with an excitement in his voice I didn't understand, "I told my business partner about the wedding, and he wants to talk to you about it sometime soon."

"Okay, let me get Lucy settled. Then I'd love to meet with you both."

"Great. I'll tell him. He's anxious to start work on the reception. He wants to make it fabulous."

"Oh, God, Jack. Fabulous?" Alarm bells sounded in my head. "Does that mean everything draped in tulle, sort of like *Ode to a Grecian Urn*?"

Jack sighed, the deep, heavy sigh reserved for

people who just don't *get it*. "Could it be, darling, you are treading in an area you know nothing about? After all, Tess, your idea of a canapé is a cracker with spray cheese and a piece of pimiento."

I mimicked, "Could it be, darling, you're just intimidated by my fabulous sense of style and entertaining panache?"

"Oh, I doubt it," he teased. "But I'll let you take all the credit when I make you look good."

"I guess I'll have to live with that."

"Of course, you will. We'll set up a time to meet soon."

Jack clicked off before I could ask any pertinent questions about his partner. Like his name.

Shortly after my bland, institutional lunch in the hospital cafeteria, which, by the way made the Weight Magic Romana Chicken dinner from the night before seem gourmet by comparison, Edith Trevain wafted into the waiting room.

I say that because she sort of floated in on a cloud of perfume, all pink bouclé and pearls, and in soft focus somehow. At seventy-five, she was still a stunning woman.

"Tess, you're here, of course. Ever the faithful companion," she said when she spotted me across the empty waiting room.

"Hello, Edith," I answered, trying not to think of myself as some sort of collie lolling at the foot of its master's bed.

Edith took the seat next to me. "Have you heard anything yet?" she asked, checking her lipstick in an enameled compact.

I licked my lips, realizing I hadn't put any lipstick

on that morning, or any other time during the day for that matter.

"No," I answered. "The nurse came out earlier and said everything was going well."

She shook her head and sat down. "What a mess this is! I can't believe my daughter is in there right now, being mutilated." She sighed and picked an imaginary piece of lint off her skirt. "At least she's having the reconstruction done right away. It's been hard enough for her to get a husband. And now, this."

Lucy's mother reinforced my long-standing hatred of her every time she opened her mouth. Never had I known a woman so narrow-minded, so self-centered, so judgmental, and so damn mean.

We sat together in silence, punctuated by occasional small talk, usually in response to Edith's comments about what someone was wearing or how they did their hair. She alone would condemn people for fashion faux pas in the midst of hospital crises.

I caught myself wondering how best to kill her when Dr. Jacob Volmer, Lucy's surgeon, came into the room. An attractive man, in a darkly mysterious sort of way, with thick, wavy hair, a brushy mustache, and an athletic build, he exuded sexual confidence not unlike a Latin movie star.

"Are you here for Lucy Trevain?" he asked, without a Latin accent.

Edith and I both stood and answered "yes" at the same time.

"Well, we ran into a little trouble. The cancer was more advanced than we thought. There was some slight involvement in the lymph nodes, so we had to take more of the breast than we had planned. Reconstruction was too risky at this point."

Edith's intake of breath was audible.

"Later, we can discuss the options with Lucy. Otherwise, she's fine, in recovery, and should be wheeled to a room in a few minutes. You can meet her there. The receptionist will tell you where to go. I'll be in to check on her tomorrow."

He turned to go, but Edith stopped him with one well-manicured hand on his arm. It lingered there as she spoke.

"Doctor," she purred. "Won't you stay with us a little longer? We have so many questions." She paused, sighed, then said with as much drama as a daytime soap opera, "And this has been such an ordeal."

The handsome doctor had the good sense not to fall for these histrionics. He patted Edith's hand, then gently lifted it off his arm and dropped it. I wondered if Lucy had warned him about her mother or whether he was used to women hitting on him in the middle of the surgical waiting room.

"I'll be glad to answer any questions you might have, Mrs. Trevain. Why don't you write them down and give them to my nurse?" With a slight smile, he disappeared through the doorway.

I nodded after him. *Very smooth.*

Edith harrumphed her displeasure and sashayed over to the receptionist's desk. "Excuse me, where have they taken my daughter?"

The receptionist, dressed in her candy-striped volunteer uniform, looked up from a tattered copy of *Style*. "The patient's name, please?"

"The only patient you have," she fumed, gesturing to the empty room. "Lucy Trevain."

Unaffected by Edith's bad manners, the woman scribbled down a number, handed it to her, and told us how to get to the room. Her sunny disposition was apparently more than Edith could stand.

"Come, Tess," she commanded and flounced out of the waiting area, nose in the air, the taffeta lining of her skirt swishing angrily.

I hurried after her, not because she had ordered me to, but because I couldn't wait to see what a spectacle she would make of herself next, and also to make sure the first person Lucy saw when she awoke was not her mother.

I shouldn't have worried. Edith made herself scarce as soon as she found out I was staying the night at the hospital. Something about the ballet. Whatever it was, I rejoiced she was gone, and I wouldn't have to listen to her complain to the nurses that it was too cold, or too hot, or "what is that smell?"

As it was, I murmured reassurances to Lucy when she stirred and watched old reruns on TV. The volume on the remote was broken, but the fact the sound was down didn't bother me since I wanted Lucy to sleep, and I knew all the stories anyway.

That evening I had to eat dinner in the hospital cafeteria, and to my surprise, I missed the Sicilian Chicken in my freezer at home.

****

The next morning, I awoke to find Lucy grinning at me. That would have been fine had the grin not been accompanied by a lolling head and the most vacant eyes I'd ever seen.

Drugs. The girl was stoned. And while I had little or no experience with recreational drugs, it didn't take a narc to recognize high when it was lying in the bed in front of me.

"Hey, Luce, how are you, sweetie?"

"I'm good. I'm all in one piece." She giggled. "No, that's wrong. Part of me is gone, right?"

I nodded, trying not to laugh, worried I might cry.

"Well, then I'm only partly here, but that part seems to be doing jus' fine." She slurred the last part.

"What can I get you? Water?" The breakfast tray rested on the cantilevered bed table. "Breakfast?"

She smiled back at me in a lopsided way. "Sure, lemme think." She tried to tap her chin with her forefinger, but her hand slid out from under, and she lurched a little forward. "Eggs Benedict," she said as I caught her by the shoulders and laid her back against the pillow.

"Hmm, I'm guessing that isn't going to be on the menu this morning, madam." There were little plastic-covered containers on the tray, an array of liquid goodies sure to delight any toddler. "Can I interest you in some soup and a little fruit juice?"

"Sounds great," she said with a grimace. "Can you smuggle me a filet later?"

"I'll just check with the doctor about that, okay?"

"Party pooper," she pouted, sipping the juice through a straw as I held the cup.

She slurped a little broth but eventually plopped back on the pillows to nap until the nurse came in.

That's how it went most of the day. She roused for a moment, then drifted back into a blissful, healing sleep, unaware of the tubes running in and out of her body and the lumpy bandage on her chest.

Dr. Volmer came in later in the day. By then, Lucy

was awake enough to lock on to what he was saying.

"You didn't do the reconstruction? Why?" she exclaimed, her sunken eyes round and tinged with fear.

"As I explained to your family," Dr. Volmer said, in a voice I'm sure he reserved for small children, the elderly, and women who'd just lost their breasts. "The cancer affected some of the lymph nodes, and we had to take more of the breast than we thought. It doesn't rule out reconstruction later. But we felt it best to keep the area clear for the time being until we're sure all the cancer is eradicated."

"Eradicated." She repeated and turned to me to explain as if I had been living on Saturn. "That's the chemo and radiation I told you about."

Dr. Volmer winked at me. "That's right, Lucy. We'll let you heal from the surgery, then begin treatments. Your oncologist will be in to speak to you tomorrow. He'll set that up with you. In the meantime, relax, and let the nurses and your very nice friend here help you get better. You can go home at the end of the week if everything goes according to plan." He beamed at her as if nothing in the world could go wrong now.

I appreciated that in a doctor. We needed reassurance, Lucy and I, that our world wasn't rocketing out of control.

I walked him to the door and introduced myself.

"Call me if you need anything," he said. "My office can reach me day or night. The next few weeks will be rough. Will you be staying with her?"

"Well, no, er, we hadn't discussed it. I don't know."

"Miss Thomason. Tess," he repeated when I corrected him. "It's important someone be with Lucy as much as possible. Especially these first few days. We can arrange for a live-in nurse if no one is available."

"Oh, she'd hate that. No, I'm sure we can work something out," I assured him, the wheels clicking in my brain about how I was going to manage Lucy and work at the same time.

She lived across town from me and my job, in a tiny townhouse to boot. Her spare room was an office, and her bedroom was upstairs, on the third floor.

My house, on the other hand, was convenient to the hospital, my job, Whitney, and my mom, who could look after her during the day. There were four bedrooms, two vacant at the moment. And while all but the master bedroom were upstairs (only two floors, though), I felt sure we could manage.

"No problem, I know just the thing," I told Dr. Volmer as he left the room.

"Good. I hope to see you tomorrow, Tess," he answered with a smile, and I wondered if he made every woman he encountered weak in the knees.

****

"I can't impose on you that way," Lucy argued the next day when I came to see her. "I've got plenty of money. I'll hire some solid woman with big hands and a starched uniform to come in."

"You will not," I screeched, visions of sadistic nurses filling my head. "I'll take care of you. Whitney and Mom will help. It'll be fun, like a big slumber party."

Lucy cocked her head and stared at me.

"Okay, we won't toilet paper anyone's house, and I have to go to bed by ten, but otherwise, it'll be just the same."

She laughed a little and threw up her hands in capitulation. Well, she threw up one and grimaced when she moved the other. The anesthesia from the surgery had worn off, and the pain was left. She kept pushing the button on the morphine drip, and occasionally it would deliver more drugs through the IV snaking into her arm.

We hadn't talked much about the surgery or what was to come. There would be time for that when she could think about something other than the pain.

Sleep was solace. So, she napped often, waking for meals, walking with the nurse, or going to the bathroom. I went to work, came by at lunch, then again after dinner.

The second evening, a volunteer brought in a huge fruit basket. Lucy handed me the card with a wry smile.

It was pre-printed with the message "Get well soon, Edith Trevain."

"For heaven's sake." I shook my head, and then we both burst out laughing. "The fruit is much more personable than your mother," I quipped.

"And sweeter," she added, clutching her chest as she laughed.

"And so much more pink." I plowed ahead, enjoying the exchange at Edith's expense, but our levity ended abruptly when Dr. Volmer sauntered in.

He wasn't wearing scrubs but looked rugged and dashing in jeans and a crisp white shirt with the sleeves rolled up. He smiled at me. "Hi, Tess, how's our girl tonight."

"Fine, I think. She's awake but has some pain."

I stepped away from the bed so he could concentrate on Lucy. While I concentrated on him.

He chatted with Lucy, and she answered his questions, then asked some of her own, eager to get more information than she had gleaned in her drugged state the day before.

Dr. Volmer's bedside manner was professional, warm, disarming in its frankness, and thoroughly charming. "So, Lucy, what are your plans when you leave here? Have you two discussed that?" He looked back and forth between us, jarring me out of my reverie.

"We were just talking about it," I said, rushing to say it out loud before Lucy could veto the idea.

"You need to rest in a calm, caring environment," he told her. "Get up and moving. No lifting or stretching, of course. A therapist from rehab will stop by to set up home visits. And you'll get information about support groups in the area."

I looked over at my friend lying in the bed. She seemed pale and frailer than I'd ever seen her.

Dr. Volmer continued, "It's important that you talk about this experience with sympathetic listeners, Lucy. There's a grieving process that goes on as if someone has died. You'll have to work through it."

"I don't think I need a support group, doctor. I feel fine. And I'm not grieving as you suggested. I'm sore and tired from the surgery but not grief-stricken. As long as you got all the cancer, I'm perfectly fine about the whole thing." Lucy chattered on. I recognized firing squad bravado when I heard it. I figured the crash into despair would happen during the next week. When she got a good look at her chest.

I was sure Dr. Volmer had heard it all before. He listened to Lucy patiently, then said," I know it seems like everything will get back to normal now, but I encourage you to check out the support group, follow through with your therapy, and take Tess up on her offer to stay at her house during your recuperation. You'll need help, Lucy, and someone with a shoulder to cry on."

Lucy shook her head and smiled, "I agreed to stay at Tess' house, although I think it's unnecessary. And I'll do the therapy, but we'll have to see about the support group. I can't see myself sitting around with a bunch of other women whining about our lost boobs."

Dr. Volmer and I laughed. "Okay, okay," he said in mock surrender. "Suit yourself. I'll see you in two weeks at my office." He leaned over and pointed a finger in her face. "And that's not up for negotiation."

She flashed him her most dazzling smile, and I was reminded of all the men whose hearts had been broken by my friend. She was terrified at the idea of marriage, having seen her parents' colossal fall from matrimonial bliss, and was never able to maintain a relationship with any man once he spoke those three poisonous words: I love you.

Maybe Jacob Volmer was made of stouter stuff.

"I'll be there," she promised. "Wouldn't miss it."

I followed him out of the room and into the hallway after he said goodbye to Lucy. "You know she's full of hot air, right?" I asked.

"Of course, it's typical. She's high on the pain meds, for one thing. She's here in the cocoon of the hospital for another. Reality hasn't set in and won't until she's alone at home with the bandage off and chemo staring her in the face."

He took my hand. "Tess, that's why it's important you be there with her. She'll need your strength to get through the next few weeks."

I left my hand cradled in his. "I'll be there for her. My whole family will be. We love her, and we'll take care of her."

He released my hand, and it flopped lifeless to my

side, tingling clear up to the shoulder.

Then he smiled, and his teeth were white and straight beneath the mustache. "Good, then I won't worry about her. I'm sure she's in capable hands."

"Funny, I was thinking the same about you," I said in a rare moment of risky candor.

"Thank you," he said, looking a little embarrassed. "I'll come back around before Lucy is discharged."

I watched him walk to the elevator, the well-fitting jeans accentuating the animal magnetism that emanated from him. And I wondered what his story was because even in street clothes, he wasn't wearing a wedding ring.

****

"Divorced," Lucy informed me, with a gleam in her eye, when I asked her about Dr. Volmer the next day.

I didn't mean to be so obvious; it's just that I was dying of curiosity about the man. Older, I gathered; Jewish, I supposed; wealthy, I assumed, all these things I could discern or surmise. But his marital status eluded me.

A man who wore a ring was married, no doubt, no ambiguity. But there were men out there, my father being one, who, for reasons only they and their finger knew, did not wear a wedding band, although they might have been ensconced in the most passionate romance since Tristan and Isolde.

Sam wore a ring. I knew immediately he was married, albeit unhappily, but he was devoted to Julia and honored the symbol on his finger. It was a clear signal, and I appreciated it.

Jacob (as I had taken to calling him in my head) did me no such favor. I was left to guess and endure Lucy's uplifted eyebrow.

"I was curious, that's all," I exclaimed. "He's handsome, God knows, and very nice, but not my type at all."

"What, because he's Jewish?"

"Hell, no, because he's handsome and wealthy."

She looked at me as if I were an idiot. "And that's not your type?"

"No, you know my type, Luce."

When she cocked her head to one side in amusement, I continued, "Unattractive, no ambition, hates children and animals, spits in public, and abuses the waitstaff in restaurants."

She laughed, then sucked in her breath and grabbed her side. "You have never once had a relationship with that kind of a troll."

"Oh, that's right—my relationships have all been *gay*!"

She shook her head. It was an old conversation, and we both knew it would go nowhere, but we always played it out anyway.

She kept it going. "Only that *one*. And granted, it was a biggie. But that's no reason to condemn the entire male half of the species."

"What? You think I could get a guy like Jacob Volmer to look twice at me?"

She studied me for a moment, then said without a trace of humor, "Yes, I do."

"You're insane."

"And you're a chicken."

"I am not! I have low self-esteem, but I'm not a chicken!"

"Plock! Plock! Plock!"

"Oh, for God's sake. I'll show you. I'll ask Doctor-

Handsome-Wealthy-and-Jewish out on a date, and you watch how fast he turns me down." Completely flustered by the fact that I had fallen into Lucy's bait bucket head first, I gathered my bag and jacket.

"Where're you going?"

"I have to get back to work. My lunch hour is over."

I stopped short when I noticed how crestfallen she looked. "It's all right, I'll be back tonight. I'll bring you dessert."

"Okay, I didn't mean to make you mad," she pouted.

I dropped my stuff and plopped down on the bed beside her. "You didn't make me mad. You just pushed one of my buttons. That's all."

"Oh, which one?"

I thought for a second. Which one? I had so many lately. It seemed in the throes of menopause, things bothered me more than ever, some for no other reason than they existed. "I think it was the old I-don't-deserve-a-good-guy button. It sits right next to the I'm-fifty-and-my-husband-left-me-for-another-man button."

Lucy rolled her eyes. "Don't even talk to me about husbands. At least you had one long enough to get two fabulous kids out of the deal. He loved you for a long time. He still loves you a lot, you know."

"I know."

She looked out the window into the hospital parking lot. "I'll never have that now."

I had known this moment would come. Edith Trevain's voice would fill her head with nonsense as it always had. "Hey, hey, we're not going to think like that. There are a lot of intelligent, thoughtful, compassionate men out there who will not think twice about loving you, no matter what."

"Oh, yeah, right. Like, all of a sudden, they're going to come out of hiding? There haven't been any single men out there like that for a long time. They're not going to miraculously appear now. Especially now."

"Well, that does it." I stood up and planted my hands on my hips. "This little pity party is over. As of this minute, we are no longer going to think bad thoughts about ourselves. We are going to fill our minds with positive notions, the likes of which Weight Magic has never even seen. You're going to get through this. And you will be as beautiful and wonderful as you ever were. And I am not going to beat myself up anymore over a man who decided my vagina was not good enough for him."

I waited for her giggling, painful fit to subside before I continued my manifesto.

"As of this moment, I vow I will get a date with Jacob Volmer if it's the last thing I ever do. I am not a chicken."

I made a dramatic exit, leaving Lucy laughing. As I walked to my car in the parking lot, I thought about chickens and Weight Magic and wondered what I would have for dinner.

****

Okay, so I had just vowed to get a date with Jacob Volmer, even though I was in an erstwhile relationship, albeit a strange one, with Sam Winborn. Contradictory? Poo!

The fact I was involved with Sam meant nothing since he was a married man, not looking for love, but merely seeking friendship. Any feelings I might have would one day be dashed to pieces on the rocks of despair, so why waste time? I might as well play fast and loose with Jacob since I was convinced no amount of chasing on my part would ever result in trapping on his part.

I'll admit it was a little out of character for me to be interested in two men at the same time, but things had changed of late which led me to believe I better try for the brass ring while I could still reach it.

First, of course, was Lucy. But the second thing was my unmistakable weight loss. Already I could tell my clothes were less snug, my face less round. I had been eating the Weight Magic dinners for almost two weeks and working out at the gym every evening after I left the hospital.

As I looked in the mirror, I could see the difference, and I was pumped. A great journey lay ahead; I could feel it.

That's why I was so surprised when the brass ring whacked me in the face.

Chapter Seven

The phone jolted me awake at eleven thirty that night.

" 'Lo," I answered, groggy and disoriented from twenty minutes of sleep.

"Mom, it's Whitney. Did I wake you?"

"No, I was just lying here with my eyes closed."

"Cute, I need to talk to you. Can I come over?"

I sprang bolt upright in the bed, fully awake, every nerve ending shooting messages to my brain. Danger! Danger! "Okay, honey, is something wrong?" I asked, amazed at how calm I sounded.

"I'll tell you when I get there."

"Well, o—" The phone clicked dead before I could finish.

And I heard the front door open.

"Mom?" Whitney yelled.

"Coming." I slipped on my robe and shuffled into the den, where I saw my firstborn standing in the middle of the room, looking as if she might bolt and run any second. "Were you standing on the porch when you called?"

"I didn't think I should just burst in on you. You might have a gun or something."

"Yeah, I brandish weapons so often around here I can imagine you would be afraid of that."

"Well, when you hear what I have to say, you're

going to shoot me anyway."

"You're pregnant."

She sank into the nearest chair with a sigh big enough to topple a tree. "God, how do you do that?

"I'm your mother. You're getting married in two months to a guy you've known for a short while and about whom I haven't heard very much. Plus, my sweet daughter, you're putting on weight."

"Ooh!" She buried her head in her hands.

"I suspected, but I hoped I was wrong."

She looked up at me, swiping at her tear-streaked face. "I couldn't keep it from you any longer. I thought I would burst if I didn't tell you."

I motioned for her to join me, and we cuddled on the sofa like we did when she was little.

"So, when is the baby due?"

"February. Don't you want to know what happened?"

"I think I know what happened, sweetie."

It came out in a rush, then, the explanation and the excuses and the reasons, and I nodded through them all.

"So, do you love Mark?"

She was quiet for a moment, then said, "Yes, I do. It happened so fast, but he's amazing and smart and sweet and funny, and I think I do love him."

"And does he love you?"

"I'm not sure. He asked me to marry him right away when we found out. And he seems excited about the wedding and about the baby. But…"

"But what?"

"Well, he hasn't ever said 'I love you.' "

"Hmm," I said, trying to control the screaming in my head.

"Hmm? What does hmm mean? You think I'm a slut? You think this marriage is doomed? You hate Mark?"

That about covered it, except the slut part. I knew Whitney too well to think that of her. "No, honey. It's pointless to lecture you now on the dangers of sleeping with someone you barely know, someone you haven't committed to, and who hasn't committed to you. I thought we'd had that conversation, so I'm a little surprised."

"I'm sorry, Mom. I know you're disappointed." She stared into her lap, hands wringing.

I lifted her face with my hand cupped under her chin. "Whitney, it doesn't matter what I think now. You're a grown woman, and you're going to have a baby and be a wife. That's what's important here. We will turn this pile of lemons into lemonade because that is what we do."

"So, you don't hate me?" She looked so young and vulnerable it was all I could do not to weep. So, I just brushed a strand of hair out of her face.

"No, honey, I don't hate you. I can't hate you. It's impossible for me to hate you. In fact, I'm required by law and the Almighty to love you, no matter what."

She smiled a little.

"But I am a little pissed I'm going to be a grandmother so soon. I'll have to go out and buy a rocker and some support hose."

"Sorry, Mom." She smiled bigger. "Hey, if it's any consolation, I think you're the most beautiful and wise grandmother in the world."

"Yeah, yeah, I think you're required by the Almighty to say that, too."

Her face fell again, and a look of panic flickered in

her eyes. "What about Daddy? He's going to kill me."

I hugged her. "Oh, honey, Daddy will be okay. It's your grandmother you need to worry about."

****

Sensible Shoes
By Tess Thomason

I hate it when the phone rings late at night. It's never good news. Telemarketers don't call past nine. Friends don't call to chat after ten. My children don't call at all unless there's a problem. And their problems always happen after six p.m.

So, when the phone rings at eleven thirty, alarm bells sound in my head. I think about not answering it. If you don't know about a problem, it doesn't affect you, right? Some wise person once said, "Ignorance is bliss." "Out of sight, out of mind." "What you don't know won't hurt you." Truer words were never spoken.

But the image of the child hurt, bleeding, or stranded compels me to pick up the phone and brace myself for the bad news.

Just once, I wish they'd awaken me from a sound sleep to tell me they'd won the lottery, cured cancer, or invented a machine that carries groceries from the car to the kitchen.

But no, I get flat tires, drunken dates, and broken relationships. Doesn't anyone break up during the day?

All the milestones of our lives happen in the dark. And they all require a phone call to Mom and Dad.

I guess it would be worse if the phone never rang.

****

"He's just a puppy," Syd explained to me the next day when I was still trying to digest Whitney's news.

"Yes, I see that," I agreed as I peered into the

portable kennel he was holding. Inside, a hairy little ball bounced around, making yippy noises. "Why is he here?"

"I need to leave him here while I'm in California."

"This is *your* dog?" I asked, incredulous, since Syd had never cared about animals, had never been the boy who brought home strays. That was always Whitney's job.

"No, he's Bridget's, but she doesn't have any place to keep him, and we can't bring him with us. It would be wrong to have him cooped up all the time in his kennel."

Strains of "Born Free" played in my head.

"What about Whitney? Did you ask her to keep him?"

With that kind of "duh" look kids reserve for their parents, Syd answered, releasing the furball from its confinement. "Yeah, but she can't have more than two pets, and she has the cats already. Here, hold him. He's super soft."

"No!" I yelped and jumped back. "I won't touch him." Syd and I both knew that if I looked into the eyes of that animal, I would have to keep him.

"Oh, come on, Mom, he's so cute. Here, just hold him for a second." Syd thrust the furry ball into my face.

"No! No! I will not take this dog. I can't have a dog. I have Tuxedo, and I have Lucy coming."

Syd grinned. "No problem. Tuxedo won't care, and you know that dogs help sick people feel better. It's a fact."

"Fact, my ass."

"Mom, cursing in front of your child. Tsk, tsk."

"Child, my ass. You're the devil. And you've brought this cute dog here to seduce me." I took the dog from my son and nuzzled him into my neck.

It was a tiny shih-tzu with hair covering his eyes. Holding him was like cradling a furry bag of beans.

"His name is Slider, 'cause he runs down the hall and slides into the bathroom."

I handed Slider back to Satan. "He's very cute. I can't keep him."

"Mom, if you don't take him, he'll have to go to the pound."

"What about Bridget's parents, or are they kitchen Celts in Ireland?"

Syd grimaced. "Funny, Mom, really funny. No, they live in Cincinnati. We can't take him to Cincinnati."

I stood firm, hands on my hips. "Well, you can't leave him here. But you could stay here and keep Slider while Bridget is gone. You don't want to go to California, do you, honey?"

Like a long-suffering sage, Syd said, "Mom, we've been all through this. I'm leaving on Monday. And I'll be gone until after the first of the year."

"You'll miss the wedding. You'll miss Thanksgiving and Christmas. You'll miss turkey and dressing...*twice.*"

"I'm guessing they have turkey and dressing in California."

"Oh, yeah, tofu turkey and some kind of weird quinoa and bean sprout dressing. You'll hate it."

"Geez, Mom, Bridget's not vegan. She works at Burger Shack," he said as if that explained everything.

I threw my hands up in a gesture of surrender. "Okay, I give up. But not about the dog. No dogs. No, sirree. No dogs around here."

Still holding Slider, Syd dug in his pocket and

retrieved something in his clenched fist. Then he did the unforgivable. He secured the dog's bangs out of its eyes with a baby hair clip and held it up in front of me.

"Look at him, Mom. Do you want this innocent little animal to go to *the slaughter*? His blood will be on your hands."

I tried to look away, I did, but the little beanbag licked my face and squirmed so hard I had to reach out and take him from Sydney. "Dammit, that was unfair. You are going to owe me big time, mister."

My son grinned in triumph. "Yeah, I'll pay you back when the band hits it big."

"Right. I'll be waiting for that." I buried my nose in Slider's fur.

"But, first, Mom, we need to discuss your language."

****

The most important thing on the wedding to-do list, at least in Whitney's mind, was the dress. Ceremonies and receptions be damned, the wedding plans only officially commenced when the dress was chosen, fitted, and hung in my house.

So, Whitney and I and her maid of honor, Jennifer, met at the Bridal Barn to find a dress that wouldn't increase the national debt. After all Jack, Whitney, and I had discussed a budget whereby Whitney added the tips from her waitress job, I mortgaged my house, and Jack put up Habanera.

Okay, it wasn't that bad. We had raided our savings and intended to max some credit cards, but still, there was a budget, and it would be adhered to, by God.

While Ms. Barbeaux, the oh-so-French consultant at the store, took Jennifer to the bridesmaid dresses, I asked

Whitney how Mark was doing.

"He's fine, I guess. Excited and scared and feeling stupid, just like me." She paused and then grinned. "You know what he asked me about the dress?"

"No, what?"

"He wanted to know if I had to wear black or red or something."

"No kidding! What did you tell him?"

"That black is for women who are burying their husbands, and red is for former prostitutes or someone who stole someone else's boyfriend."

"Perfect, I love tradition."

"Then I told him that since we were pregnant, I would have to wear pink or blue."

"Good girl. It's important that you screw up his head right away, so he'll always be on his toes."

"I thought so."

"Miss Thomason, this way, *s'il vous plaît*. I have selected several gowns for you to try that I think you will love." Ms. Barbeaux led us to a bank of chairs facing a little stage with mirrors all around. I sat down, and Whitney followed her to a dressing area where Jennifer was trying on confections in the deep green family, Whitney's color selection for her winter wedding.

For the next hour, we oohed and ahhed over several choices, each more stunning than the next. Whit looked beautiful in them all, but in the back of my mind, I wondered how the dress would fit three months down the road.

I pulled her to one side. "Whitney, these Cinderella ball gowns with tight-fitting bodices are never going to work. You're going to be seven months pregnant at the wedding."

"They can be altered, Mom."

"Not that much. Have you told this woman you're pregnant?"

"No, it's none of her business." She seemed aghast that I would even think such a thing.

"Well, I think, for her to do a good job, she needs to know. And what about Jennifer?"

"Jennifer knows, geez, she's my best friend."

"Well, then, there's no reason not to tell this woman. She's a stranger. It won't matter. Otherwise, this is never going to work."

Jennifer, who had apparently overheard us from her place by the tiaras, piped up. "I agree, Whit, this is crazy. None of these dresses will fit by then."

I smiled at Jennifer, who had been Whitney's BFF since grade school. Her Lucy. I turned back to Whitney. "Come on, sweetie, let's find something beautiful with a nice elastic waist."

She glared at me. I smiled sweetly at her and said to Ms. Barbeaux. "I'm afraid we've been wasting your time. My daughter's pregnant and will be about seven months along by the time of the wedding. Do you have something that could be altered to fit?"

Ms. Barbeaux, who I'm sure had seen it all, beamed. "But of course, this way, *s'il vous plaît*. I have the perfect gown for you."

And she did. A long row of them. And amidst the luxurious beading and tulle overlays and appliquéd bodices we discovered the perfect gown for Whitney. Sleek jersey knit with long, pointed sleeves and a deeply draped neckline, but plunging dramatically in back to below the waist. And adding even more glamour, a short train swept the floor.

And, while it fit her like a glove now, the stretchy knit could be altered later, and since camouflaged pregnancies were no longer the order of the day, thank God, Whitney could float proudly down the aisle, knowing she was beautiful and stylish.

The best part—Mark would be so surprised. The dress was white.

****

Lucy seemed weak as a kitten and flinched every time she moved. Medication kept her groggy but pain-free, which was a blessing. Jacob had reassured us that she would feel better in a few days.

I put her in the guest room upstairs. It had a window that looked out into the backyard where the spreading sweet gum tree was dropping its brilliant fall foliage. I had packed away the Christmas décor bins that lived in that room and put it all in the attic earlier that week, then re-made the bed with fresh sheets, piling on the pillows.

The adjoining bathroom was scrubbed clean and softened with brand-new fluffy towels in soothing sage green. Lucy loved candles, so I had stocked up on sandalwood and vanilla, placing them strategically around the bedroom and bath, and providing a fireplace lighter to set the room ablaze.

I got her into bed and unpacked her suitcase into the empty dresser. Beautiful satins and silks made up her sickbed attire. Each piece was more exquisite than the one before: embroidered nightgowns, a lacy, silk peignoir ideal for the honeymoon she'd never had, the satin kimono with gold brocade dragon on the back she'd bought in Japan last year, and high heel mules with a marabou fluff just like Rita Hayworth wore in the forties.

The image of my doggy nightshirt in the trash

downstairs flashed into my mind. I prayed I would never have to recuperate at someone else's home.

Then I went to work setting up a bedside table laden with Lucy's cell phone, water carafe, notepad, and pen. When the room was dressed to my liking, I turned to find my friend dozing, so I tiptoed downstairs to start dinner.

Thirty minutes later, with a meatloaf in the oven, I sat down on the sofa with a glass of wine, Tuxedo nestled next to my thigh. Slider, jealous, I suppose, jumped into my lap and I startled, sloshing the red liquid down my white cotton shirt.

My life was officially out of control. The little, yippy dog, cute as he was, piled on top of the pregnant daughter, sick friend, and leaving son was the last straw. I needed a shoulder.

I called Jack.

Some divorces are sloppy and nasty and mean and cruel. Ours was sweet and loving and hugging and caring. Yeah, weird. But nice, and I didn't mind it. And because we shared children, it seemed logical for me to alert him that the last straw had been perched precariously on the pile of my life. After all, if the pile toppled, it would be he who had to clean it up.

Plus, I had to tell him about Whitney.

"I already heard," he replied when I called and mentioned that I had news about Whitney.

"Really, from whom?"

"Syd told me. He thinks it's cool."

"He would. He'll be in California for all the drama to come. And did you know he left *her* dog with me?"

Jack chuckled.

"Yeah, you laugh now, but wait until the little thing poops on you."

"Do you mean the baby or the dog?"

"Either one. This is a nightmare." I took a deep breath and let it out slowly.

"Did you get Lucy settled?" he asked, trying, I knew, to change the subject.

"Yes, she's sleeping, I think."

"That's good."

"Yeah, that's good." But Lucy was the least of my worries at the moment. "We need to talk. I want to give Syd a going-away party, and we've got to start planning the wedding."

"You think you're up to a party? With Lucy there?" he asked.

"Yeah, I think so. Anyway, we have to do something for his send-off. Especially since he's going to miss the holidays." I paused for a second and then confided, "Besides, I think you should meet the Celtic music maiden before our son runs off with her, don't you?"

"I already did. Syd and I went to Burger Shack last week. She seemed very—uh, enthusiastic—about her music."

"You talked to her? What's she like?" When I had been to Burger Shack with the kids, Syd introduced me to her, but there had been no conversation. No interrogation.

"What you'd expect, I suppose. Weird, avant-garde. She bit the head off a snake while we were there."

"Fine, be a smartass. But when he comes home, *if* he comes home with a ring on his you-know-what, then be ready for me to say, 'I told you so.' "

More chuckling emanated from my ex, who was less than sympathetic to my worries. Since becoming fashionably gay, he had acquired some body art of his own. "Okay, we'll plan a party for our little rocker-wannabe so everyone can remember him in his current unadorned innocence. And we can get started on the plans for the wedding of our daughter to the father of her unborn child. Why don't I come over tonight?"

"Okay, great, I'll see you—"

"I'll bring my new partner. It'll be the perfect time for you to meet him."

I hesitated. I had wanted to meet Hunky Older Guy. I had wanted to somehow make him go away so Tad could have Jack, and I could feel things were right with the world. But now it just wasn't so important for me to become Tad's protector and defender, too, on top of all my other responsibilities. I had to draw the line somewhere.

"Great. I'd love to meet him," I said, sighing in defeat, feeling somehow that I was failing Tad. *Good grief!*

I took Lucy's dinner on a tray up to her room, and we ate together, chatting about nothing in particular. She picked at her food. It was the first time in two weeks I hadn't eaten a Weight Magic dinner. I poked my meatloaf and moved the mashed potatoes around on the plate. When I carried the tray back downstairs, I scraped the perfectly good food into the trash and grabbed a Pompeii Chicken dinner out of the freezer.

Guilt is a powerful motivator.

****

I had just cleared the dishes away when the doorbell rang, and I was taken aback when I opened it to find Jack standing there with Roger Austin from Coffee Heaven.

"H-h-hi," I stammered. I was so confused at seeing Roger out of context that I just stood there.

"Tess, can we come in?" Jack asked, a quizzical look on his face I'm sure matched my own.

Roger was the only one who seemed to understand what the hell was going on. "Hi, Tess. Nice to see you again. Small world, huh?"

"Yeah, small." Then the clouds parted, and I saw the truth. "Are you Hunk—I mean, are you Jack's business partner?"

"Yeah, and you, it seems, are the ex I've heard so much about."

I never missed an opportunity to shoot Jack a withering look, but the moment passed as I absorbed this news and the much bigger import of it.

Roger was Jack's partner, which meant Roger was *gay. Damn.*

"Well, well," I murmured, giving my voice time to recover from the high-pitched squeakiness that seemed to have overcome it. "Come in, please, both of you and sit down."

As Roger passed me, I caught a whiff of his cologne, my favorite, and looked down, catching a glimpse of his shiny loafers and pressed khakis, which appeared to have been sewn straight onto his perfectly proportioned body. I should have realized before that he was too good-looking to be straight.

I jerked my gaze back up to find him staring at me with an amused expression on his face.

He thinks I'm flustered. He thinks it's hilarious that he and Jack put one over on me. He thinks he has caught me off guard. Au contraire! My guard is on. It is so on!

I stepped back out of the tracking beam of Roger's gaze.

This is the man who stole Jack's affections from

Tad. Not to mention misleading me into thinking he was someone I could have a huge, donkey crush on. He and Jack must have had a big laugh at that.

"Let's sit in the den," I suggested. "Does anyone want coffee? You drink coffee, as I recall, Roger."

He chuckled, that soft rumbling sound I had fallen in love with on two sweet Saturday mornings.

"Yeah, do you have any half-caf venti mochas lying around?"

"Gee, fresh out," I said and took that opportunity to shoot *him* a withering look. "I do have a pot of regular full-caf made fresh this morning. I can warm it up."

Jack was quick. "We'll pass."

"Okey, dokey." I pivoted away from the kitchen and dropped into a chair across from them, wondering where my sixth sense had failed me. I could usually spot a gay man a mile away. But Roger had evaded all my defenses. *Damn!*

"Since I seem to be the last one to know you two were partners, maybe you could fill me in a little."

Jack looked amused. Clearly, he enjoyed my discomfort. "I met Roger a couple months ago at an entrepreneurial seminar. We hit it off and started talking."

Entrepreneurial seminar, my ass.

Roger leaned forward. "I had recently moved back to the States and was looking for a new challenge. Something I could sink my teeth into. Jack's business seemed just the thing."

Yeah, I'll bet it did.

Jack leaned forward. Excitement gleamed in his eyes. "Roger knows so much more about finances and expanding an operation than I do. I just know we're going to take it to the next level."

"Well, that's great, just great," I said with as much enthusiasm as I could muster, then I changed the subject. "Why don't we talk about the kids?"

Simultaneously, Roger and Jack leaned back against the sofa as if I had deflated them. For a moment, I felt guilty, then decided I just didn't care. "Okay, so about Syd's going-away dinner."

Jack said, "We can have it at Habanera. I'll close off the back room for the evening."

A party for Syd at Habanera would be festive, delicious, and a big send-off. It would also be a lot easier for me. But somehow, it didn't feel right. I wanted to give Syd's going away party at my house. I wasn't even sure that I wanted Jack to do the food. I wanted to do the food.

Peanut butter and jelly sandwiches with the crusts cut off. Pancakes that looked like teddy bears. Chocolate milk where the syrup was all lumped at the bottom of the glass.

Okay, it wasn't party food, but those were the things Syd loved growing up. Why couldn't I give him those things? Why couldn't he just stay home?

"That's sweet of you, Jack, but I don't think it needs to be a big deal. And I don't think Lucy's up to leaving the house yet, and I don't want to leave her alone at home."

Lame excuses, I knew. I didn't dare look at Jack. He'd see immediately what a cowering weakling I was about Syd leaving. So, I glanced at Roger.

He said, "Okay, how about doing it here. How about burgers on the grill? Something simple?"

How could it be this person I barely knew had read

me so spot on? I thought Jack was the one person in the world who understood me. But here was this new guy who seemed to have picked up on my need to mother my child.

Of course, he would be gay. I was cursed with attracting gay or dysfunctional men. I would shoot myself later.

For now, I needed to be constructive. "That sounds great. I'll get the word out. Now, about the wedding. I would like to do *it* at Habanera."

Jack smiled. "I thought so. I already booked it for the night you mentioned. I want you to work with Roger on all the details."

"What?" I asked, my head snapping toward Jack. "Why don't you do it? You said yourself Roger doesn't know anything about the restaurant business. Forgive me, Roger—but Jack, don't you want to be in charge of your own daughter's wedding? It has to be perfect. You can't put it in the hands of—of—an amateur." I nodded in Roger's direction, "No offense."

"None taken." He cut his glance to Jack. "I don't do party planning." He said it as if it were beneath him.

But Jack seemed unfazed. "I know, but I have several other events coming up, and you need to learn more about the business. You said so yourself."

"Yeah, about the business, the numbers, profits, loss. Not menus, and seating plans, and napkins made into ducks."

Jack chuckled. "We don't do ducks. They're more like fleur-de-lis, I think."

"See? I don't even know what they look like. I'm a businessman, Jack, not a party planner."

"It's a big part of the business, Roger. You can't

manage it if you don't know what goes into it." He stood, signaling the end of the meeting. "This will be a perfect event for you. Just big enough, nothing elaborate, pretty straightforward."

I was getting worried. This was my daughter's wedding, after all. "Wait a minute, Jack. I think you need to rethink this."

"Tess, I'll be involved. I'm going to leave the planning to Roger. It will be fine."

Fine didn't sound that great to me. I wanted fabulous, not fine. "You know, Jack, if Roger is unsure of himself about this, maybe you should—"

Roger stood to face me. "Whoa, I'm not unsure of myself. I've been a consultant in lots of different businesses. In my experience, they're all the same. You manage production, you manage customer service. You watch the bottom line."

"I'm sure you're very qualified to run a business, but this is an important event for me and my family. Maybe Jack should—"

Roger bristled, "Jack, hell! I'll plan your event. And it'll be the best damn wedding reception ever!" He stalked over to the door, then turned around. "What are you doing for lunch on Monday?"

"I beg your pardon?"

"Lunch, on Monday. So we can plan. I'll pick you up at eleven thirty."

Not quite sure what had just taken place, I stammered, "O-okay," to Roger's back as he stalked down the sidewalk.

As Jack slipped past me, following Roger to the car, I heard him chuckling.

****

My encounter with Roger the night before left me with two definite impressions. The first was Roger was infuriating and arrogant, but just as fascinating, intelligent, and handsome as I had previously thought. The second was Tad better be on high alert.

And I was just the one to sound the alarm.

"Tad," I panted as I did crunches on some contraption that forced me to curl into a ball, then spring backward into an arc. "I met Roger last night."

"Oh, him," he sneered.

"Yeah, he's holding Whitney's wedding hostage."

Tad rolled his eyes. "Yeah, he's trying to impress Jack with his business experience."

I sighed. "It seems Jack thinks he hung the moon."

Tad sniffed. "Jack is blinded by his resumé. South American embassies, European hotels, Asian corporations. It's pretty impressive."

"But he doesn't have direct restaurant experience. Jack's making him handle the wedding. I would have thought Jack would want to handle his own daughter's wedding. Instead, he just tossed it to Roger like a hand grenade."

Tad helped me off the last machine and walked me to the door of the locker room. "Well, I wouldn't worry about it. He hasn't left Jack's side once. It's like they're joined at the hip."

It dawned on me I might be able to help Tad hold onto Jack if I could keep Roger distracted for a while. I could put up with his handsome charm and unfailing wit as a sacrifice for Tad, if for no other reason.

****

Saturday night, the Thomasons gathered at my house for Syd's going away party. I sweated over a hot grill while everyone wandered in and out of the house, keeping me company. The combination of the white-hot coals, the thick, humid air, the exertion of party preparations, and my propensity for spontaneous self-combustion had me more lathered up than a prized racehorse.

I mopped my brow with a dishtowel, lifting the hair off my neck, wishing I were still in my short-hair phase. Paul came out onto the back porch, frothy beer in hand, and stared at me.

"God, Sis, you look like you're about to have a heart attack. Let me do that. Go inside and call the paramedics or something." He yanked the spatula from my hand and shoved me over.

I was about to gush my gratitude all over him when he said, "Looks like I took over in the nick of time. You're cooking these too fast. They're going to burn on the outside and be raw in the middle. Mom will love that."

That last sarcastic snipe was in reference to our sainted mother, who never met a cut of meat that couldn't be burned beyond recognition. In her opinion, eating raw meat was something heathens did. Civilized people enjoyed their meat charred and leathery. "They're perfectly fine," I countered. "But I will let you finish. Thanks."

I ducked inside the house, hoping to freshen up a bit before Sam arrived. I didn't want him to see me as flushed and damp as a lobster.

Head down, hurrying through the den, crowded with Syd's friends and family, into my bedroom, I didn't see the manly chest I ran right into. Hoping against hope it was Syd or my dad, anyone but Sam, I looked up sheepishly and was flustered to find that I had careened into Roger's well-honed torso.

I shouldn't have been surprised he was there. He had helped with the planning of the party, per Jack's request, through several phone calls and a food delivery the day before. But it caught me off-guard when I ran headlong into him. He smelled of aftershave and wore a navy blazer over khaki trousers, my personal favorite combination. Perfectly groomed, of course. Jack would have nothing less. Which made me even more aware of my own sartorial shortcomings.

Roger grabbed my upper arms to steady me and smiled. "Whoa, there." Then he must have gotten a better look, and his smile turned to a frown of alarm. I blushed even redder if that were possible. "Are you all right? Are you sick? You don't look well."

"No, no, I'm fine, really, just a little warm." I ducked out of his concerned embrace and raced for the bedroom, calling back over my shoulder. "I'll be right back. Help yourself to a beer."

Once in the sanctuary of the bathroom, I leaned against the doorjamb, panting. Then, I caught a glimpse of myself in the mirror. "Oh, my God! Paul's right. I look like I'm about to have a stroke." I splashed cool water on my face, touched up what little makeup I was wearing, and ran a brush through my hair, which was now plastered attractively to my head. I caught it up in a clip and pulled some strands out in what I hoped was a trendy touch.

"Are you all right? Roger said you looked like you were about to pass out." I turned to face Jack, who stood in the doorway of the bathroom we had once shared, staring at me with his brows stitched together, the way he used to when one of the kids fell down.

"I'm fine. Just a little warm, is all." I gave him my best, most dazzling smile by way of convincing him. "When did you all get here? Where's Tad?"

"Just a few minutes ago. Tad's putting the salad and beans in the kitchen and the dips and chips out for everyone to munch on. Of course, they're in a mixing bowl and two mismatched butter tubs. For Christmas I'm giving you some decent serving dishes. Yours are a disgrace."

I swept past him into the den, winking at him over my shoulder. "That's because you took all the good ones."

"What good ones?" Roger asked, walking toward me with a beer in one hand, a chip in the other.

"Men," I answered pointedly, hoping he'd get my meaning and leave Jack alone. But when his expression didn't change, guilt at my sudden dearth of hospitality overcame me, and I grabbed his arm, endangering the chip, and steered him across the room.

"Syd," I called to my son, who was busy introducing Slider to my mother.

I was surprised to see not only did she not recoil from the furry ball, but she reached out tentatively and then did something I had never, ever seen before. She held him.

Dogs were stinky, dogs were hairy, and dogs were dirty. She did not have dogs, and she certainly did not hold dogs.

Until Slider.

No wonder I hadn't been able to resist him. The furry beanbag must be enchanted.

Syd cocked his head at his grandmother, as stunned

as I was at her behavior, then laughing, turned toward me and Roger.

I introduced them, and they shook hands.

"Roger is your father's new business partner." I didn't intend it, but the words came out laced with sarcasm and with an emphasis on the word "business."

Syd didn't notice and nodded at Roger. "Cool."

"I hear you're going into the music business," Roger said, with the emphasis on the word "business." Okay, so he'd noticed.

My son, unschooled in the nuances of inflection as it related to sarcasm, launched into an explanation of his impending adventure. I waited for Roger to raise an eyebrow, smirk in ridicule, or say something patronizing. But instead, he offered to make a couple of calls on behalf of Bridget's band to old friends he still knew in the music industry, thereby endearing himself to my son for all time.

And damn it, to me, too.

"So, Roger, would you like another beer?" I asked, needing to make amends somehow for the roiling emotions this man engendered in me and the Jekyll and Hyde conversations they caused.

When I came back from the kitchen, beer in hand, I found Roger cornered by my mother. Before I could rescue him, Jack stopped me. "Paul says the burgers are ready. Is Lucy coming down?"

"Yes, she was going to rest until dinner, then I think she'll sit and visit afterward."

"Do you want me to go get her?" Jack asked, and I knew again why I loved him.

"No, that's okay. Rescue Roger from my mother and corral everyone for dinner. I'll bring Lucy down."

"Where's Sam?" he asked. And for the first time I wondered that myself.

"He should be here by now."

Chapter Eight

"I look like death on a stick," Lucy moaned and pulled the covers over her head. She lay in the bed, fully dressed and looking beautiful, if still a little pale.

She wore pants and a simple top, loose enough to hide the fact that the left side of her chest was bandaged and flat. Her eyes held the apprehension I knew she felt.

I reassured her as best I could. "You look ravishing. Now get up."

"Tess, I can't."

"Of course, you can. I'll help you."

"I thought I was up to it, but I'm not."

"Yes, you are. Look at you. You're dressed, you have on makeup, your hair is done. Let's go, you don't want to miss Paul's burgers. We'll probably hear Mom screaming from here."

"What?"

"Never mind. Let me help you out of bed."

She stood with little effort, the effects of the surgery having worn off, leaving only minimal pain and soreness and a good deal of trepidation at what the future held. I stood back and looked her up and down.

"Perfect."

"You can't tell?"

"Not a thing. You look great."

"Okay, okay. Let's get it over with."

"Geez, Luce, you're not going back to the hospital,

just downstairs for dinner. No big deal."

She tossed her hair and laughed a little, and I caught a glimpse of my friend bubbling to the surface. "Right. No big deal." She squeezed my hand. "Thanks, sweetie."

I kissed her on the cheek. "No problem."

We started down the stairs and when we got to the bottom, I said, "Oh, I forgot to tell you Jack's new business partner is here. His name is Roger. Close your mouth, Luce. It's no big deal."

She glared at me, "No big deal? There's a strange man downstairs, and I look like I'm coming off a four-day bender."

Before I could reassure her that it didn't matter how she looked because Roger was gay, we entered the den to the uproarious and heartfelt applause of my family. Lucy blushed, becomingly. Lucy did everything becomingly.

I spotted Roger across the room and strode toward him, Lucy in tow. "Lucy, this is Roger Austin, Jack's business partner."

"Roger, of course, I'm Lucy Trevain. Tess has told me *so* much about you." She flashed him her best and brightest smile.

I rolled my eyes and invited everyone into the dining room to go through the burger buffet. Jack got Lucy situated in a chair and offered to make her a plate of food. I went into the kitchen to fill glasses with ice.

Roger followed me and proceeded to pour himself a glass of wine. Apologizing for my erratic behavior seemed pointless, so I decided to shower him with hospitality instead. "Can I get you a plate? More wine?"

He gestured to the full glass.

"Oh, yes, well. Is there anything you need?"

"No, I'm waiting for the line to get a little shorter. This is a very hungry crowd."

"Yes, we're big on eating."

"You have a nice family."

I looked for the sarcasm in his face and, finding none, said, "Yes, it is. Thank you."

"And Syd seems excited about California."

The reason for the party suddenly hit me between the eyes. Syd was leaving. How could I have forgotten? I burst into tears and hid my face in a dishtowel.

Roger gathered me into his arms and patted my back. His jacket was stiff, and I dampened it with my tears. It was only seconds, but it seemed like long minutes that he held me until I regained my composure and stepped back, breaking the connection that had been so comforting.

"I'm sorry."

"Don't be," he said. "You've had an emotional week. First, your friend's surgery, then Syd, and then your daughter. It's a lot to take in."

I nodded my head in agreement.

"Not to mention the heinous birthday present." He looked at me sideways, a hint of amusement in his voice.

I busied myself chunking ice into glasses. "Yeah, remind me never to bare my soul to a stranger again. I'm guessing you knew who I was all along, some trick you and Jack cooked up. So funny."

He set the wine down and, with his hands on my shoulders, turned me to face him. "I had no idea who you were. How could we possibly have known you would be at Coffee Heaven on those days. And what possible purpose could it have served for me to keep my identity a secret from you?"

"I don't know. It's just a pretty big coincidence, don't you think?"

"Yes, I do." He picked up the wine again and sipped it slowly, then looked at me through slitted eyes. "Maybe *you* were following *me* all the time."

I laughed out loud then. "Yeah, right, I was spying on Jack's new partner." A twinge of guilt stabbed my chest, thinking about my plan to do just that by way of protecting Tad.

"So, we'll agree it was kismet, then."

"I suppose so. Sorry, I doubted you. I should have guessed that I'm not important enough for you and Jack to discuss—let alone plan covert operations around."

He smirked again. "Oh, you've been discussed. Plenty. Jack talks about you all the time."

I didn't know whether to be insulted or intrigued, so I went with the latter. "Oh yeah? What does he say?"

"He says you're an emotional rollercoaster."

That was certainly not what I was expecting. Too easy on the kids. A pushover for strays. A bad cook. But not an emotional rollercoaster. "Emotional?"

"Yeah, he says you cry at the drop of a hat, television commercials especially."

"Oh, for heaven's sake. I do not!" I threw the towel down on the counter and stalked back into the dining room, grabbed a plate, and began spooning food onto it with gusto.

Roger came up behind me, chuckling. "He also said you had a quick temper."

I glared at him and turned back to the table. *Quick temper, indeed.*

Just as I scooped up a burger and placed it on a bun, I heard my mother scream from the other room. "Don't anyone eat these. They're raw!"

****

Sam arrived about nine. He let himself in and sneaked up behind me, putting his arms around me in a gentle hug. I immediately recognized his subtle scent and the hands that held me, slender fingers, blunted on the ends, and the gold wedding band.

With a sigh of gratitude, I grabbed his hands in mine. "Hi, I'm glad you came."

He spun me around and bestowed a quick kiss on my cheek. "Wouldn't have missed it. It's not every day that we have a send-off for a roadie in a Celtic kitchen band."

"Tech crew," I corrected, smiling into his watery blue eyes.

As I prepared him a plate of lukewarm food, I noticed Jack introducing him to Roger. Unable to resist, I ticked off a mental list of pros and cons about both men: Roger, tall, handsome, worldly, sophisticated, funny, smart, and gay; Sam, tall, handsome, simple, warm, loyal, and unavailable.

I sure knew how to pick 'em.

After dinner, Whitney and Mark regaled us with their original send-off of Syd's Celtic kitchen band. There was raucous laughter as they banged away on the pots and pans with an assortment of spoons and spatulas. Syd didn't seem to mind and sat with Slider on his lap, stroking the little dog until he was limp as a rag doll.

I watched my sweet, not-so-innocent daughter, seemingly content in her situation, and wondered what the future held in store for her. For me? A grandmother. What a foreign notion it was and one I would have to work on comprehending over the next few months.

Sam sat next to me on the loveseat, his hands clasped in his lap, but our thighs touched from hip to knee. Such intimacy had never seemed unusual or wrong, except when I saw Roger watching me from his place on the sofa between Donna and my mother. He looked away, and I wondered if he wondered what the hell I was doing with a married man.

At that moment, so did I.

Irritated, I reminded myself what Roger thought or didn't think about me mattered not at all. But the truth was his opinion did matter. The opinions of everyone in that cramped room mattered. Those were the only opinions in the world that had the power to cause me pain.

And Roger, though a relative stranger and a newcomer to our family circle, had a relationship with Jack which gave him access other people didn't have, an information conduit even Tad didn't seem to share. I had never felt uncomfortable around Tad. Amused, maybe, but never uncomfortable.

Roger was different.

On the last roof-raising note of the kids' song, I jumped up and began clapping like a maniac. Anything to break the tension of the close proximity to Sam and the weirdness I felt around Roger.

"Dessert?" I questioned and before anyone could answer, I fled to the kitchen and began cutting pieces of cake. Sam followed.

"Are you okay? You seem a little jumpy."

"Oh, I'm worried, that's all," I said, and it was true. "About the kids and about Lucy. It's been a tough week." The echo of Roger's reassurance earlier filled my head.

"Well, that's understandable." He stepped forward

and hugged me to him. "It'll be all right. Syd is a bright boy. Whitney will be fine, and Lucy is a fighter. They'll all be okay."

His touch was warm and strong, and I relaxed in his embrace. The lingering tension I felt around Roger was lacking with Sam.

"Thanks," I repeated. "I'm glad you came."

"Me, too."

I wrapped my arms around him. Over his shoulder, in the other room, I could see Roger talking to Paul's boys, engaged in a conversation about the video game they were playing. I felt the tension rise in my body like a wall of heat.

I stepped back out of Sam's embrace and stood under the fan in the kitchen, letting the waves of cool air flow over me, fanning myself with the cake cutter. Sam chuckled quietly and picked up the ice cream scoop.

Donna came in to help, and I carried bowls out to the waiting throng. When I handed one to Jack, he said, "So, you and Sam seem as close as ever."

"Yes, we're close. We're very close," I said, with a conviction I didn't feel. "You should be happy. Now, you don't have to bring me any more strays."

"What does that mean? Are you serious about this guy? He's married, Tess. What if he's just using you? You know, to quell his...urges."

"Hold on there, Dad! I believe urge quelling is *my* concern. You should be happy to be off the hook." The mixture of embarrassment and frustration on Jack's face was too good to disturb, so I didn't dare tell him how far off the mark he actually was.

He stared after me as I went back to the kitchen for more bowls of dessert. I took a little bit of satisfaction in that.

****

An hour later, Lucy's head lolled against the back of the chair. She'd managed to stay vertical throughout the impromptu concert, the cake and ice cream, and the reminiscences of "little Sydney." But enough was enough.

"Come on, Sleeping Beauty, let's get you upstairs." I tugged her up with her good arm over my shoulder.

"Oh, no, Tess, I'm okay."

"You're catatonic, old girl. And you're going to bed. Say goodnight, Lucy."

As predicted, she said to the room at large, "Goodnight, Lucy."

Everyone offered cheerful farewells, and we trudged up the stairs, her leaning heavily on my arm. "I'm tired," she said when I got her into bed.

"No kidding! You've had a big evening. Real food, bad entertainment, and boring family memories."

"Your family is never boring," she said with a yawn. "I love them."

"And they love you, too."

"They're like my family."

My heart constricted. "They feel the same way about you, sweetie."

"Roger is cute," she offered out of the blue.

"You mean Sam," I corrected.

"No, Sam's married, but Roger is cute. You should date him."

"Boy, you are tired. You didn't even notice that Roger is Jack's boy toy du jour."

"Gay? Roger is gay?"

"Yeah, according to Tad, Jack can't stay away from

128

him."

"Really? How odd." Her words trailed into the abyss as she drifted off to sleep, and I was left to wonder what the hell she meant.

Downstairs, I ushered Syd's friends, my parents, my brother, his family, my daughter and her fiancé, my ex-husband, and his concubines to the door. Only Syd and Sam remained.

Syd was leaving that night to go to Bridget's. The band was driving to California early the next morning.

"Now, Mom, you must walk Slider in the morning and at night. Feed him once a day. This much dog food." He gestured to a cup in a bag he had stashed in the kitchen. "And here, use this." He handed me a rough-hewn pottery bowl. I turned its earthy beauty over in my hands. Celtic, no doubt.

Grasping for something to say to keep from crying, I blurted, "He's had his shots?"

Syd laughed. "Yeah, ages ago. He's good to go for another eight months or so."

"You'll be home by then."

"Mom, I told you I wasn't sure when we'd be home. It depends on if the band gets a recording contract in LA."

I shook my head, willing the tears to stay put. "You'll be back by then."

"Whatever." Syd shrugged, wise enough to let it go, given my fragile state. "I have to go. I'll call you in a couple of days."

"Okay," I mumbled.

I hugged my firstborn for dear life, wept into his ear, then let him go, as I'd done on all the milestone days of his life and hopefully would do on many more. But it wasn't easy.

"I love you, Mom," he whispered.

"—love—too," I sobbed.

Sam stepped up behind me and put his hands on my shoulders. I sank back into him, releasing Syd into the ether.

He opened the front door and walked down the sidewalk, into the embrace of his father who was waiting by his car. They talked for a moment, hugged again, then left.

I turned around and sobbed into Sam's chest. He held me close and patted my back until I caught my breath. When I was under control, he offered to help with the dishes.

"No, thanks, I think I'm going to leave them. We've both got work tomorrow, and it's late."

"Then I'll say goodnight." He ran his thumb down my cheek, wiping away the tears that lingered there. Then he kissed me, quickly, lightly, sweetly.

Before I could even open my eyes, he was moving down the sidewalk, hands in his pockets, whistling.

I closed the door and leaned against it. Slider ran up and plopped down at my feet, waiting to be picked up. I obliged him and slid to the floor, back against the door. Nuzzling the puppy to my cheek, I let him lick the salty tears that flowed down my face.

We sat there a long time, Slider and me. I tried not to think about the people I loved, and I wondered why I had never learned to whistle.

****

I crammed as much work into Monday morning as possible, having planned to take the afternoon off to drive Lucy to the oncologist. But before that, I had to endure a lunch meeting with Roger about Whitney's wedding reception.

I met Roger at Habanera at noon. He greeted me with a smile and offered to take me on a tour of the restaurant.

"That would be fun." I meant it. Jack had never taken me backstage before, but as a cooking show fanatic, I was fascinated with the idea of going behind the scenes in a trendy restaurant.

"Good, let's go." Roger led the way into the hustle and bustle of Habanera's kitchen.

Jack spotted us immediately, antennae tuned to Roger's vibration no doubt and waved hello. We waved back and kept a respectful distance by the double swinging doors while the chefs, sous-chefs, and waitstaff scurried about.

"It's a madhouse. How does anyone keep anything straight?" I asked, stepping gingerly aside to avoid getting run over.

"Well, it's strictly orchestrated. For instance," Roger said, gesturing to different parts of the room as he spoke. "They're making the salads; they're creating desserts; they're building entrees. Over there's where it all comes together, where Jack holds court. The runners gather the food and deliver it. It's a well-oiled machine."

Then, as if in slow motion, a runner with a tray full of entrees started past us through the right-hand swinging door into the dining room, just as a busboy with a tray full of dirty dishes came through the same door into the kitchen. The resulting collision was a sickening melee of china, food, and white-clad staffers hitting the floor.

And us.

Roger and I stood close enough to be christened with

a variety of delectable tidbits, some only slightly used, as they splashed off plates and bowls. The front of my dress was drenched in some red stuff; I got white stuff in my shoes and later found something green in my hair.

The runner stood transfixed, staring at the empty tray in her hands before she screamed at the busboy, "What the hell were you doing? You're supposed to go through the right-hand door! Not the left-hand door! Any moron knows you go through the right-hand door!"

Roger helped the poor busboy to his feet. "Why did you come through the wrong door, Jorge?"

"It was blocked by some people taking a picture. I didn't want to get in their way. I thought it would be okay just this once."

"That would be a *no*," the runner muttered.

"Okay, Leslie, that's enough," Roger soothed. "Go replace the order as fast as you can. I'll speak to the people at the table and comp their meal to make up for the wait." He turned to the trembling Jorge and put his hand on the young man's shoulder, then spoke to him, this time in Spanish, "You clean this up, Jorge. It's okay, but next time, just wait for them to get finished with the picture so you can come in the right door."

"You're not going to fire me?" Jorge said with eyes round as saucers.

"If we fired everyone who screwed up around here, Jack would be doing all the work himself," he answered, laughing.

Jorge hurried away to fetch a mop; Leslie rolled her eyes and headed back to the food prep area with her empty tray. From across the kitchen, Jack turned back to his cuisine crafting. He hadn't missed a beat.

Roger swiveled back to me, still standing there in

my ruined clothes, watching him turn a potential disaster into another moment in the day.

"Let's get you cleaned up, too. You've got the Brazilian Sampler all over you. Delicious, to be sure, but I had something else planned for lunch." After he smoothed things over with the table of diners, he led me to Jack's office and retrieved a chef's jacket and drawstring pants from the closet. "I'm sure Jack won't mind if you borrow these. He keeps them here to change into when he has to make an appearance in the dining room. Most of the time, when he cooks, he looks a little like you do now."

I took the clothes, ducked into the bathroom, and shrugged out of my soggy dress. The linen chef's jacket was starched and scratchy. I rolled up the sleeves. The soft striped pants fit loosely even on my thick middle, and I cinched them with the drawstring. My reflection in the mirror surprised me.

I was disheveled, hair tousled, but my cheeks were flushed, and my eyes shone. The odd clothing was comfortable and, I thought, rather becoming. I made a mental note to search for chef's clothing online.

I reentered the office, where Roger stood in his shirt sleeves, swiping bits of table forty-five's lunch from his pants. His jacket lay in a heap on the floor.

He looked up and smiled when I came in. I took note of his lightning-fast appraisal of my new attire. "Not bad. Toss your dress on the pile. I'll get it cleaned."

"That's okay."

"No, I insist."

I did as I was told and threw my dress on top of his jacket, which seemed somehow inappropriate—our clothing touching that way. But, oh well, things had changed; clothing wasn't as conservative as it used to be.

"Now, what?" I asked with a grin. "Are you going to throw things on me in the bar?"

"Well, it won't be a surprise now," he quipped. "I thought we might sit on the terrace and have lunch and talk about the reception. I promise everyone will keep their flying food to themselves."

"That sounds great. I am hungry. The stuff that landed on me smelled great."

We joked about the incident through lunch, which consisted of fried plantains, tamales rolled in banana leaves, black bean salsa, and a slaw that rivaled any I'd ever tasted. Eating outside was a rare treat in Texas, but the October air was cool, if not brisk, and thoroughly comfortable.

I told Roger we wanted the reception to be simple, traditional without being stodgy, and beautiful, romantic, and delicious. Even though Whitney's situation may be none of those things, it was important that we give her a wedding that could at least form a solid foundation on which to build a marriage…and a family.

"That's a pretty tall order," Roger said when I'd finished rambling about romance and flowers and cakes.

I blushed, feeling as if I'd revealed too much of myself in the process. "So, it's a lot to ask, huh?"

He smiled, and the little lines around his eyes crinkled with warmth. "No, not at all. I think we can do that. And more."

"More?"

"Sure, I have a couple of ideas."

Alarm bells went off in my head as I pictured donkey-shaped piñatas being smashed in the courtyard. "Like what?"

"No, let me surprise you. I'll get back to you in a week with the plan."

"Okay," I agreed, hesitant.

He must have read my expression because he took my elbow and steered me out of the restaurant into the bright sunshine. "It's going to be beautiful, romantic, delicious, and—what was the other thing?"

"Traditional without being stodgy," I murmured, feeling somehow déjà vu.

"Oh, yeah, that, too," he said. "Don't worry." Then, he looked at my chef's garb and grimaced, "I'm sorry about your dress."

I had already forgotten about our earlier mishap. I chuckled at my oversized clothes. "No big deal. I kind of like this look. They're going to love it at the doctor's office."

His grimace turned to concern in an instant. "What doctor? Are you going to the doctor?"

"No, no, I'm taking Lucy to the oncologist this afternoon. We're going to find out about her treatment."

"Oh." He relaxed a little. "Jack told me. I thought she was a real trooper last night."

"Yeah, I'm afraid we're in for a long haul."

"Well, she's lucky to have you."

"You know, everyone says that, but the truth is I'm lucky to have her. And I hope I can keep her a lot longer."

"I hope so, too. Let me know if there's anything I can do to help."

"Thanks, I will. And I'll be in touch about the reception."

"I'll call you later in the week."

I got into my car. "Thanks for lunch…both of them."

"My pleasure," he said, and I believed him.

****

The oncologist's office was in the same building as Jacob Volmer's, Lucy reminded me when we got out of the car. "You were supposed to be trying to seduce him, as I recall."

"Going out on a date is not seduction, well, not for anyone but you maybe. Anyway, I've been sidetracked. You, Mark, wedding receptions. I just don't have time to seduce Dr. Volmer. My dance card is full. Why don't *you* go out with him?"

Lucy gestured to her chest. "It seems obvious."

"Because he's seen you naked?"

She glared at me. "Oh yeah, that was an enticing sight, I'm sure."

"Might have been." I pushed on, not sure where I was going with it, but determined to convince Lucy she was still gorgeous and worthy of love. "You know, he's seen worse."

She rolled her eyes. "Trust me, he's not interested. I can tell."

"How would you know anything? The last time you saw him, you were three sheets to the wind. And quite alluring, I might add."

She laughed, and I felt a surge of triumph.

As I pushed open the door of the oncologist's office, Lucy turned to me. "Lucky for him, he'll never have to witness that sight again."

She stepped up to the sliding window and gave the receptionist her name before I could get in another decent repartee.

"Besides," she continued when she sat down next to me. "It's unethical for us to date because I'm a patient." She laid her hand on her chest, still lumpy with bandages.

"Anyway, he would never go out with me; he knows what's under here."

I smiled at her and handed her an old copy of some house magazine. "Yeah, a heart of gold."

Two hours later, we walked back into the hallway, bleary-eyed from an onslaught of medical jargon and armed with a rigorous schedule of radiation and chemotherapy. The oncologist had given Lucy a seventy-percent chance that she would be cancer-free at the end of it all.

Which meant there was a thirty-percent chance she wouldn't.

We walked without talking down the bleak corridor to the elevators, and I punched the button. The doors opened, and out stepped Jacob Volmer. We almost collided, which seemed to be my modus operandi around men: run into them first, get to know them later. It was a little more overt than shameless flirting, a little less obvious than full-frontal nudity.

"Well, hello there," he said with a quick smile, then his gaze shifted to Lucy. "How are you doing?"

"Good, quite good. We just came from the oncologist." She waved the sheaf of papers in her hand. "Ready to do step two."

"Great, you're right on track, then." He gestured to me, but his eyes never left Lucy's face. "And I see you have your faithful companion here with you."

I grimaced. Images sprang to mind of the frumpy housemaid in Victorian England pushing the aging dowager in her wheelchair.

Lucy put her arm around me and squeezed. "Tess is amazing. Beautiful, talented, smart, and caring. Quite a combination."

Oh my God. Now, I feel like a prized horse at auction. Next, she'll want him to see my teeth.

"I agree. You're lucky to have her," he said. This time, his eyes met mine.

Why do people keep saying that? I began to blush slowly, maddeningly.

I shifted the focus back to Lucy. "It's the least I can do for my best friend. Especially when she's so beautiful, gifted, funny, and wise."

Lucy cocked her head at me and mouthed the word "wise." I shrugged.

Jacob stared at me, then his gaze snapped back to Lucy. "Well, it seems as if the two of you have a mutual admiration society going there. Take care, and I'll see you next week." Then back to me. "And I hope to see you, too, Tess."

"I'm sure you will," Lucy said.

When the doors closed on the elevator, and we were swooshing down, I started to giggle. Then she started to giggle.

"That was awkward," she said.

"Yeah, he looked like he was watching a tennis match."

"The man is interested in you. It's obvious."

"You've got to be kidding. He was just being nice to your faithful companion. It's you he wants."

She insisted, "No, my money is on him asking you out when we go back next week."

"No way, it's you he's interested in. I could tell. Anyway, I don't think it's ethical to ask out the kindly caregiver."

She waved her good hand. "Screw ethical. All's fair in love and war."

"I don't think the AMA would agree with that."

"Screw the AMA."

I laughed as we walked out into the bright October sunshine.

Later that evening, Lucy and I sat in the den of my house, watching reality television and eating Weight Magic Parisian Chicken. Having exhausted Italy, we had begun to eat our way north through Europe.

Our evening had been a quiet one with Slider between us and Tuxedo pouting on the windowsill. We chatted about Syd's party, Whitney's wedding, and my encounter with Roger that morning. We didn't mention Jacob Volmer. It was the most normal time I had enjoyed with Lucy in over two weeks. Relaxation poured over me like a warm shower.

Then, during the tenth consecutive car commercial of the evening, she turned to me and said, "Tess, I'm afraid."

****

Sensible Shoes

By Tess Thomason

Fear is scary. Everyone thinks fear is that thing that grips your stomach and ties it in knots, makes your hands clammy, your heart race, and your voice squeak. Sure, fear does that.

When you see a rattlesnake, when you swerve to avoid a car accident, when your child runs into the street. Breath-stealing, adrenaline-pumping, in-your-face fear takes over.

We've all experienced that.

But what about more subtle terror? The mental kind that starts as a seed in your mind, then grows, planting roots, and sprouting leafless branches in every acre of your psyche.

Nameless, aching, pervasive, overpowering fear.

The fear of leaving home, the fear of giving birth, the fear of losing your parents. The fear of dying too soon.

You can rationalize it. You can intellectualize it. You can even trivialize it. But when all the "izes" are said and done, there it is, growing quietly in the back of your fertile mind.

It waits until harvest time when it's fully formed and dangerously strong and comes to you in the dead of night and wakes you up.

And you say into the darkness, "I'm afraid."

Chapter Nine

"Calm down, Ms. Thomason, I can only answer one question at a time," the nurse at Jacob Volmer's office insisted.

"I'm trying to get some information so I can help my friend," I answered.

After Lucy told me her fears, I spent a sleepless night Googling every question I could think of. The answers were contradictory, so I cataloged the questions on paper and decided to call the oncologist in the morning. But he had kept himself at arm's length from Lucy, never making eye contact, seemingly afraid to get emotionally attached to a real human being.

And so it was, in the dawn's early light, I realized it was Jacob Volmer who would give me the tools I needed to put Lucy's mind at ease.

The nurse said, "If you'll email me your questions, I'll get Dr. Volmer to answer them. Then I'll get back to you."

"All right, I'll send them now."

After I emailed the questions, I prepared to wait for the answers. My office phone rang about five minutes later. I picked it up, and was surprised to hear Jacob Volmer himself, his voice tinged with alarm.

"Tess, Miss Hanson told me you called. She gave me quite a list of questions. Is Lucy okay? Has there been a change in her condition?"

"No, no. She's fine, I suppose. There are a lot of unanswered questions. You said to call."

"Yes, I'm glad you did. No use speculating about things."

"Well, thank you. I appreciate that, but you didn't need to call me yourself. I'm sure you're busy."

"Not at all. I'm glad for the opportunity to help Lucy."

He proceeded to speak in detail about all the questions I had given the nurse. His answers were thorough, and I felt much better afterward. I told him so.

"Well, good. Then I've done my job. But..." He hesitated; the line went quiet.

I pictured his brilliant eyes and dazzling smile beneath the brushy, graying mustache. He reminded me of an Arabian sheik, fascinating and frightening at the same time.

"Dr. Volmer? Jacob?"

"Yes, sorry. I was just wondering if maybe I should come over and talk to her myself."

Stunned, I stammered, "W-w-well, s-s-sure. When do you want to come by?" Finding my voice, I rushed on, "How about tomorrow night? You can come to dinner."

He agreed, and we hung up. I stared at the receiver in my hand for a long moment after I heard the click of his, and then I smiled.

So, it *was* Lucy he wanted.

****

That night as I lay in bed, listening to the quiet of the house, hoping Lucy was asleep, I thought about my very odd day.

When I told Lucy about Jacob's offer to visit her,

she seemed somehow reluctant, considering he was about the most handsome man I'd ever seen in real life. But she finally shrugged and said okay, then spent the next hour trying to figure out what to wear that would be the perfect mix of convalescent mastectomée and sexy poodle.

Syd had called earlier, having reached California, and settled into a low-rent apartment. The band would be playing the next night at a club in LA called Celtic Cross. *Of course.*

He had asked about Slider, who now snuggled at my feet, not at the foot of the bed, but under the covers. At first, I feared he would smother down there, but he seemed to like the confined space. Maybe rebreathing carbon dioxide was okay for dogs. Anyway, there was some sweet comfort in having his furry softness next to my toes. And I had kicked off the covers in a hot sweat often enough to give him an occasional breeze.

As I drifted off, I thought I heard a light rapping noise, then a moment later, the doorbell rang. I glanced at the clock beside the bed. Midnight.

I got up, slipped into my comfy robe, and walked, heart thumping, to the door.

"Who is it?" I demanded.

"It's me, Donna."

"Donna? Donna Thomason?" I questioned, unsure I had heard the name correctly.

"Tess, please open the door."

"Donna, my God. What's going on?" I exclaimed as I unlocked and opened the door, ushering her in.

She dropped a suitcase at my feet and burst into tears. "I've left Paul," she said between sobs.

Maybe it was the hour or the half sleep I had been

in, but nothing made sense to me. "Where?" I pictured him getting coffee at the convenience store on the corner.

"At home. I packed my bag and left."

The sleepy fog in my brain cleared, "What in the world happened?"

"We had a terrible fight. He accused me of trying to wreck his career. He said I was useless as a wife and worse as a mother."

She broke down on the last word, and I folded her into my arms, afraid she would sink to the floor. We shuffled in tandem to the sofa in the living room.

"Sit down. I'll be right back. I'm going to get you some water."

When I returned, she was on the sofa, stiff and straight, with her hands folded in her lap. She had quit crying, but her eyes were dark with smeared mascara, and tearful streaks stained her perfectly blushed cheeks.

I handed her the water. "Okay, what the hell is going on?"

"We had a dinner party tonight for Paul's boss and an out-of-town client. It was a disaster. The caterers were late, and dinner was delayed. When they finally served, the food was only marginally acceptable to Paul. You know how he is about that sort of thing."

"Yes, he's a jerk about that sort of thing," I said, remembering the burgers. "Marginally acceptable? You mean burned? Raw? Cold? What?"

"Oh, no, nothing so dramatic. The sauce was too salty, the fish was slightly overcooked, the cake too dry. That sort of thing. He's very particular and has such exquisite taste. He notices everything."

I rolled my eyes. My brother's affected taste level was legendary in the family and a source of amusement to most of us. Apparently not so to Donna.

"As if that weren't bad enough, during dinner, the babysitter came downstairs to tell us one of the boys had pushed the other one into a table, and he had a bad cut on his forehead."

"Oh, my goodness, which one? Is he okay?" The boys were misbegotten little devils, but I didn't want anything to happen to them.

"It was Matt, and he was bleeding like crazy when I got upstairs. I was certain he needed stitches, so I excused myself from dinner and took him to the emergency room. I left Paul to serve coffee to his boss and the caterers to clean up."

"You mean the people stayed? They didn't have the decency to go home and let you and Paul handle an emergency?"

"They offered, but Paul insisted they stay. He said it was nothing and I could take care of it. Which I did."

I patted her trembling hand. "Of course you did. You're a very capable woman."

"Well, Paul doesn't think so. When I got home and put the boys to bed, he let me have it."

"Are you kidding? What did he say?"

"He said I was an idiot to hire incompetent caterers, that the food was disgusting, and he was embarrassed to serve it."

"Good grief! Did his boss complain? Did anyone say anything during dinner to make him think they were displeased?"

"Oh, no, they were lovely people and gushed all over the house and the food and how nice things were. Truly, Tess, only Paul, with his discriminating palate, would have noticed anything amiss."

"Oh, for God's sake!"

"Then he said if I hadn't hired a babysitter who was too young and inexperienced with growing boys, the accident with Matt wouldn't have happened. That it was all my fault."

"Now, wait a minute. The babysitter was how old?"

"Twenty-five. She's a graduate student in Child Psychology. Paul is so particular about who takes care of the boys. I always hire older women who have lots of babysitting experience, but this dinner was on the spur of the moment, and our usual sitters were busy, so I called the grad school to recommend someone."

Under my breath, I murmured, "My brother is an ass." Out loud, I asked, "What did you say to his accusations?"

"Well, what could I say? The food wasn't perfect, the sitter had let the boys get out of control, and I had hired them both. He was right. It was my fault."

She broke down sobbing. I grabbed tissues from the bathroom and handed them to her, snuggling her into the crook of my arm. I had to fight to keep from jumping in my car, driving to their house, and killing my brother.

I needed to be more constructive. I took a deep breath.

"So, Donna, sweetie, why are you here? If you agree that this is all your fault—which it isn't, but we'll get into that later—why did you leave?"

"Because Paul said we're partners in his career, and my job is to keep the house, take care of the boys, and entertain his business associates. He said I had failed in my part of the job tonight, and the results were disastrous." She looked at me with huge doe-brown eyes, and I noticed for the first time how sad they were, how sad she was. Broken and beaten and defeated down to her very soul.

"Oh, Donna, what a cruel thing for him to say."

"It's worse than that. He said I wasn't a fit wife or mother, and if he could, he would f-f—fire me!"

"Son of a bitch!" I screamed and jumped to my feet, more furious than I had ever felt toward another human being in my life. The fact it was my own brother made me even madder. The Thomasons were made of better stuff than that!

"What in the world is going on?" Lucy demanded from the stairway. She was clutching her robe around her, peeking over the banister the way a child does on Christmas morning.

"Geez, Lucy! I'm sorry. I didn't mean to wake you. Donna is here. She and Paul had a fight." I nodded toward the suitcase still in the entryway by the door. Lucy glanced at it and shook her head. She came down the stairs and arranged herself on the loveseat across from us.

I recapped the events of the evening for her, emphasizing my brother's insensitive behavior and the inanity of the charges against Donna, hoping my forlorn sister-in-law would see how ridiculous Paul was being.

It didn't work. When I was through, Donna looked at Lucy, whose mouth gaped open, and said, "He was upset. The dinner was a disaster, and it was all my fault."

My beloved Lucy was quick to respond. "What an idiot!"

"See?" I said to Donna, "Lucy agrees with me. Paul is way out of line here."

Donna shook her head. "No, he's right. He does everything for us, and I screwed up the two things I'm supposed to do for him—take care of the kids and be a good hostess. I failed him." The sobbing commenced again.

Lucy put one manicured fingertip to her chin. "Let me get this straight. He said he wanted to fire you. So, then, what happened?"

"I said if he were unhappy with me as a wife and mother, he didn't have to fire me, I would quit."

We clapped in unison. "Good girl! Way to go!"

"No," she cried, dismay etched on her face. "I said it in a moment of anger. It was wrong. I've left my home and my children. What was I thinking?"

Lucy smiled. "I think you were thinking pretty clearly. You're here. And he's home alone with the boys, right?"

"Yes."

"Why didn't you bring them?"

"He said he could do a better job of raising them. I guess he's right." She covered her face with her hands. Lucy and I looked at each other and winked.

I know what you're thinking.

"Donna, sweetie, everything is going to be fine. Trust us," Lucy said, patting her hand. "We have a little plan."

"W-w-what do you mean?" she hiccupped.

"Well, I think we should give Paul a chance to discover all the things you do for him. Things he never sees and knows nothing about. All the little things he'll have to do now that you've quit your 'job.' "

"I don't understand." Her bleary eyes glazed over in confusion.

"Let's have some coffee and lay out a little strategy," I said and ushered us all into the kitchen where we spent the next hour plotting my brother's demise over tiny squares of Weight Magic Italian Cream Cake.

****

The next morning dawned clear and crisp, with cloudless blue skies and the leaves from the sweet gum tree drifting down to carpet the front yard with crunchy color. I always loved fall in Texas, from the smell of wood burning in neighboring fireplaces to the pumpkins trimming front porches to the taste of crisp apples I bought at the farmer's market.

But this year, I hadn't put out pumpkins or gone to the farmer's market to pick up fresh produce. This fall was different. Forget seasonal niceties. Things at my house were crazy.

I realized this, standing on the back porch, warming my hands with a cup of coffee while I waited for Slider to christen some new place in my yard as his personal potty. He and I were slipping into a routine after several days of accidents in the house. But I couldn't figure out who was training whom. All I knew was I had gotten up early, so I would have plenty of time to make my coffee before I took him out back.

Having a dog had never been in my plan. But then neither had Lucy getting cancer or Donna showing up on my doorstep. Even as I accompanied Slider on his morning constitutional, Donna was inside talking to the boys on the phone, explaining to them that she was taking a little vacation with Aunt Tess and would see them in about a week. It was phase one of our plan.

We figured Paul would last about that long before he came crawling back to Donna on his hands and knees begging her to come home, a new leaf having turned over as he heaped appreciation and respect on her head.

Donna's self-esteem had hit such a low that she had no faith in our ability to predict Paul's behavior. But she promised to give it a few days, still unconvinced that the problems in her marriage were anyone's fault but her own.

Slider finished his business and yapped at my feet. We went into the house, where he promptly squatted down and pooped on the carpet by the coffee table.

"Slider, you little poohead—and I mean that literally—I can't believe you did that."

Donna hung up the phone and faced me, tears streaming down her face.

I said, "Well, that seems to have gone well. The boys will be okay. They'll be upset at first, but it's good for them to be with their dad. You can see them whenever you want, after all."

Her voice caught. "Oh, the boys are fine. Just fine. That's the problem. They're not upset at all. They think it will be fun to hang out with Paul. They're glad I'm gone." She broke down and sobbed, collapsing onto the sofa, head in her hands.

"Hey, they didn't mean it. They're probably trying to keep you from worrying about them. They're being thoughtful."

The arched eyebrow on my sister-in-law's face told me she knew I was lying. Her sons were a lot of things, but thoughtful wasn't one of them.

"Okay, never mind. But they *will* miss you. They're acting like school's out at the moment. You know, fun with dad, no rules, eat whatever they want, stay up late. They think it's going to be one big picnic. Then they'll realize there's no mom to help with homework, no mom to fix dinner for them at night, no mom to tuck them in.

They'll beg you to come home. And so will Paul."

She sniffed. "I don't know. I miss them already. And they hardly knew I was gone. Maybe I should just go home."

I took her hands in mine. "Donna, if you go home now, things will be as they were. Paul will think you're incompetent, the boys won't obey you, and you'll never get the respect you deserve. Please wait a few days. See what happens."

Before she could answer, Lucy floated into the kitchen in a confection of satin and lace that seemed to billow around her on an unseen current of air. "Hey, kids, what's up?" She poured a cup of coffee, then scoured the pantry. "What's for breakfast?"

I grinned at Donna, who smiled a little back at me. "Well," I said. "You must be feeling better. How about some eggs?"

"Eggs? Cholesterol? Oh well, who cares? You only live once, right?"

"Right!" I agreed and bustled around the kitchen, making breakfast for the three of us.

"So, Donna, did you hear from Paul?"

"No, I talked to the boys, though."

"Were they acting like they didn't miss you at all?"

Donna looked crestfallen. "Yes, as a matter of fact."

Lucy smiled and touched her arm. "That's exactly what I would do if I were them."

"What do you mean?"

"Well, if I were a twelve-year-old boy, the last thing I'd do is let on that I need my mommy to come home and take care of me, especially with dad standing there."

"I hadn't thought of that," Donna said, brightening.

"I think Lucy's right," I added, hoping to fortify the

little ray of sunshine that was somehow breaking through her gloom.

"Give them a couple of days, and they'll be begging you to come home, guaranteed."

Her phone rang, and Donna answered, "Hello, Paul." The ice in her voice almost cracked the sparkly case.

But we watched as the courage ebbed out of her and puddled on the kitchen floor. My brother must have been saying some harsh things. I mouthed to Donna to stay strong. Lucy went through a series of body-builder poses that made Donna stifle a giggle.

The firmness returned to her voice. "I'm sorry, Paul, but I won't be coming home in time to make dinner for your out-of-town client. And I won't be able to take care of the boys while you go out, either. I'll be staying here for a few days, and we have some plans of our own." She cut her eyes toward me and winked.

She paused while Paul apparently countered her refusal to be his slave, then answered in a calm voice, squaring her shoulders as her white knuckles gripped the phone. "I'm sorry you feel that way, Paul, but last night you told me in no uncertain terms what you thought of my wifely skills, my parenting skills, and my hostess skills. I'm sure you'll have no trouble finding someone who more closely meets your requirements. Have a nice day."

Then she hung up the phone, fell into the nearest chair, and cried her eyes out.

Lucy consoled her while I finished breakfast, mentally cataloging the damage I could do to my brother with various kitchen implements. We ate in silence, and then I said, "So, are you going to stay with us for a while until Paul offers you a proper apology and becomes a human being?"

Lucy rolled her eyes. "Gee, we'll all be dead by then."

Donna giggled, her eyes rimmed in red. "I guess so if you have room for one more."

"Sure, the more the merrier. It will be fun with just us girls." I glanced over at Slider, chewing on a corner of my sofa pillow. "And the little poopster here, of course."

****

While the idea of a constant coffee klatch with Lucy and Donna sounded oh, so fun, I began to feel the slightest bit panicky about the load on my plate.

So, I made a list, called my mother, and felt better.

Then, instead of feeding my apprehension with cheese and crackers, I called Roger to talk about the food for Whitney's reception. I liked living in a parallel universe.

"It's you!" he said, sounding almost excited, which gave me a little pang of sadness that I couldn't be excited, too.

"Hi, I wanted to check in. How are the plans coming?"

"I was going to call you today to see when you can come over to taste cake and some of the buffet items."

"Mmm, yum. How about tomorrow evening? I'll bring Whitney."

"She and Mark already came by. I have their votes. I just need yours."

"Democracy in action. Great. I'll see you at Habanera, about seven?"

"Bring a change of clothes." The laughter in his

voice was audible.

I chuckled. "Right. I'll just layer."

"Perfect." He clicked off the phone.

"Yeah, perfect," I whispered into the dead receiver.

****

That night Donna and I had the movie date Paul had thwarted a few weeks earlier. We left the house before Jacob arrived so he and Lucy could have time alone. Lucy had said we could stay, of course, but they didn't need a third *and* fourth wheel.

Whatever was going to happen between Lucy and Jacob was their business, and if I were being honest, I just couldn't worry about it. Jacob had already called her with the name of a surgeon she should schedule an appointment with, someone in another group practice, someone he trusted. The new doctor could handle the reconstruction when the time came.

Lucy's first chemo session was the next day, and Donna was going to drive her back and forth, a benefit I hadn't realized at first but was relieved to accept.

Plus, I was glad Donna had something to do. As the quintessential mother, she had hand-sewn her sons' Halloween costumes for ten years, and this was the first time they would be subjected to store-bought versions of whatever superhero the kids were wearing this year. That is if Paul knew how to order online. Donna was lifting nary a finger in her attempt to prove her worth to her ungrateful family.

Anyway, the movie was a disaster. We made the mistake of seeing a romantic comedy. I stupidly thought something light would cheer Donna up. Her perpetual malaise, coupled with Lucy's forced cheerfulness, had created a sort of stoic fatalism in me. The world was coming to an end. I couldn't do anything about it. Let's go to the show.

Bad idea. The first time the starstruck couple exchanged dewy-eyed glances onscreen, Donna burst into tears. We left the theatre and headed for Coffee Heaven, where, in my opinion, everyone felt better.

She cried into her latté, and after a while, I gathered her up, and we went home, parking in the garage. Since it was early, I expected to find Lucy and Jacob sitting on the couch watching TV but was surprised to discover the downstairs dark and quiet.

There was an empty pizza box on the counter but no other evidence of life. With a sinking feeling I went to the bottom of the stairs and said in a stage whisper, "Lucy? We're home."

There was no answer. Maybe Jacob had left early. Maybe she'd gone to bed. Hopefully alone. *God, help me, he wouldn't take advantage of her, would he? She can't have sex for who knows how long! She has cancer, for heaven's sake.*

Just as I was about to fly up the stairs and expose their exposure, Donna stopped me with a finger to her lips. She motioned to the front door. Without thinking, I opened it, and Lucy and Jacob nearly tumbled inside, still wrapped around each other, lips locked in a kiss.

Chapter Ten

Halloween slunk into town bringing with it a dank chill and howling wind Stephen King would have envied.

I had worried about Lucy all day, alternately scrubbing my brain of the image of my friend and her doctor exchanging bodily fluids on my stoop and fears about her first chemotherapy treatment. I tried not to dwell on any pain she might be having, the loss of hair, the nausea, all the horror stories I'd heard about chemo. Reality would be living in our house soon enough.

I was on my way to Habanera to eat cake with Roger. Lucy and Donna and their respective issues would have to wait until I was stoked on enough carbs to run the marathon that had become my life.

Besides I had left them with bowls of candy to hand out to the little ghouls and goblins who showed up on our doorstep. Paul had even called to ask if he could bring the boys by to trick-or-treat, and Donna's relief was palpable. Maybe my brother was coming around after all.

Roger met me at the door to Habanera and ushered me into a back room, avoiding any contact with waiters and trays of food. I appreciated the chivalry exhibited by my ex-husband's illicit paramour.

Lined up on a white-clothed table in the tiny room were five little cakes, each one a miniature work of art, resplendent with frosting roses, fondant geometrics, buttercream swirls, or sugary latticework. A stack of forks stood at the ready. It had been a month since I'd had anything more fattening than a Weight Magic Brownie Bite.

I began to salivate.

"So," Roger said, handing me a fork and gesturing to the first cake with a flourish. "We'll start simple. This is your basic white cake, with a raspberry jalapeno filling and traditional buttercream frosting. It's Jack's personal favorite," he added with a wink.

It was incredible, moist, and creamy, and with a kick of heat that would complement the rest of Habanera's buffet. But it wasn't Jack's wedding, and I didn't want to polish Roger's standing by picking Jack's favorite cake. So, I gave the others an undue amount of attention, oohing and ahhing over them.

Not that it was difficult to do. Never had I tasted such delicate pastry, such sweet nectar on a plate. It was a struggle to keep from gushing over each one, licking the fork clean, then setting it down, taking a subsequent plate from Roger, and sampling the next morsel from heaven.

It dawned on me that the last time I'd had a real cake was at my birthday party.

I set the fork down beside the remains of the last tiny cake.

"Which one do you like best?" Roger asked.

I couldn't lie. "The one with the raspberry jalapeno filling. But I like the latticework icing."

Roger smiled. "Interesting. Everyone agrees about the latticework. So, we'll do that, but it's a split decision on the cake."

"What did everyone choose?"

"You and Jack picked the jalapeno. Mark and Whitney chose the chocolate cake with the toffee ganache filling."

"Well, then, you get to be the tiebreaker, I suppose." I handed him a fork.

He took a bite of each one, keeping his expression blank, then set the fork down. "I have to go with the jalapeno as well. But I shouldn't be the one deciding."

"Well, Mark and Whitney should get the one they want. But I hate to lose the jalapeno." Gastronomic greed took over. "I know, let's do them both."

He grinned. "You mean have two cakes? We could, but Mark wants the groom's cake to be a giant chocolate chip cookie."

I grimaced. "Of course, he does. No, I mean alternate the layers. One chocolate, one jalapeno, and the top chocolate for their anniversary. Use the cream cheese frosting and put the latticework on the whole shebang."

"Done," he said, scribbling on a notepad. "Now, if you'll follow me, we'll sample the rest of the buffet items."

"But we've already had dessert. It's completely backward."

He took a step closer and let the notepad drop to his side. "Here at Habanera," he said in a voice as soft and low as distant thunder, with just a hint of a fake Latin accent. "We are risk takers. We live on the edge and pride ourselves on defying conventional ideas of order."

My breath came in shallow gusts. "Really?"

He laughed and stepped back. "No, the buffet stuff wasn't quite ready yet, and the cakes were drying out, so we did them first."

I steadied myself and laughed, a sort of nervous

twitter. "Oh, so here at Habanera, you don't take any risks?"

He took my elbow and steered me to a table. "Are you kidding? Raspberry and jalapeno!"

****

When I got home, a deafening racket from the living room assaulted me.

Donna and Paul were squared off against each other by the front door while the boys chased Slider around the coffee table with the pretend lightsabers that accompanied their intergalactic costumes. Lucy made weak attempts at grabbing the swords, but then one caught her on the shoulder and sent her flying backward onto the sofa.

"That's enough!" I screamed, rushing to my friend. "You two, give those to me and sit down in those chairs." When the boys hesitated, I glared at them and lunged a little forward. "Now!"

They threw the swords down and leaped into the chairs.

I turned back to Lucy. "Are you okay? Did they hurt you?"

"God, no, I'm fine. Just sorry I didn't catch the little hellions. Thanks for the rescue." She grinned a little at me and rubbed her shoulder.

I smiled at her, then reprised the angry mask I had used years earlier on the twins. Turning back to the boys, I bellowed, "What the hell is going on here? You could have broken something. You could have hurt the dog. You could have killed Lucy. What were you thinking?"

Jason opened his mouth to speak. I silenced him with a raised hand. "Do not speak. I am not interested in your excuses. You two just sit there while I deal with your parents."

Donna stared at me, mouth agape. "I'm so sorry, Tess, I—" I cut her off with a wave.

Paul glared at the boys, then at Donna, then at me. "You don't need to use that tone with the boys or me, Tess. They're just letting off some steam while I talk some sense into Donna."

"Frankly, Paul, I'm not interested in your excuses, either." I strode toward them. "Let me tell you a little something about your children. They are spoiled, disrespectful, unruly, and smart. They play both of you to get what they want because they see the weakness in your relationship."

Paul started to protest, but I waved him into silence. Surprisingly, he shut up. So, I continued, "These boys are going to end up in juvenile detention if you don't take them in hand. Give them some discipline, some instruction, some consistency."

He sputtered. "They go to school. Donna is responsible for discipline and education."

"Of course. And what are you responsible for?" I could see the laundry list forming in his head: I pay the bills, I put food in their mouths, I put a roof over their heads, blah, blah, blah. "Purely rhetorical question, I assure you. Let me ask you this. How do you suppose your children will respect their mother when you don't?"

"That's ridiculous."

"Is it? They never do a single thing she tells them because that's the behavior you model for them. They will never respect her until you do."

Donna had listened to this with her head bowed, beaten, and bloodied in the worst way, emotionally. She raised it then and whispered, "It's true, Paul. They think

I'm a servant because that's the way you treat me. They're rude bullies to everyone but you."

Then I watched the most remarkable thing. Donna straightened her shoulders and swept the tears from beneath her soft, wounded eyes with the back of her hand. "Now, Paul, if you don't mind, I'd like you to take the boys home. We've disrupted Tess's house enough, and I need to see to Lucy."

She turned to the boys, who started fidgeting. "Jason, Matt, go with your father." They didn't move. The face of anger she presented as she stomped toward them made them jump a foot and run for the door.

I handed the swords to Paul, who looked as if his world had been rocked to its core. He followed the boys out the door. Donna slammed it behind him, swayed backward on her heels, then ran sobbing up the stairs to her room.

I helped Lucy off the couch and up the stairs to her own room. "How'd the chemo go?" I asked as I got her into bed.

"Piece of cake," she replied without smiling.

****

The next day at work, I forced myself to focus on the blank screen in front of me. I sat that way for some time, fingers poised above the keys, waiting for the muse to invade my psyche.

Ruth had been understanding about my personal issues so far, but I figured at some point she'd put a hit out on me. I needed to up my writing game and quick.

So, I studied my fingernails and chastised myself for never getting a manicure. I looked at the pictures on my desk, I double-checked my email, then I surfed for dresses to wear to the wedding. Maybe I'd get a manicure for that.

My muse was obviously at the mall because I couldn't think of a single funny, wise, relevant, or poignant thing to say to the women of Dallas.

The morning flew by in a flurry of wasted minutes and lost hours. Then, it was time for lunch.

Sam had asked me to meet him at a nearby deli, which was not a part of our usual work week routine. When I pulled up, I saw him standing in the doorway, punctual as always. After ordering the low-fat, taste-free special, we gathered our food and settled ourselves at a table near the window. Outside, the bustling strip center teemed with lunchtime errand-runners and eatery-goers.

Inside wasn't much different. We tried to talk over the clang of silverware and conversation, but it wasn't easy.

"So, how's the wedding coming?" he asked.

"The food and cake are ordered, flowers, dress, church, just about everything's done. We need to get the invitations out. Whitney's coming over this weekend to do that. We're on track. A fast track, but a track nonetheless."

"That's good." He stared at his salad plate, distracted.

I waited for him to tell me the reason for our lunchtime rendezvous.

"I heard from my daughter last night."

"Susan? How is she?"

"Well, she's coming for Thanksgiving."

His only child lived with her husband, David, and son, Steven, in Arkansas. Sam had told me Susan worshipped her mother and was so devastated by her illness she rarely visited, unable to bear Julia's lack of recognition. Because of her infrequent visits, I had never met her.

Sam looked at me as if my response to his news were critical.

So, I lied. "That's wonderful. I'm so glad. Is she bringing David and Steven?"

"Yes, I think so." He moved the lettuce around his plate. "I just don't know if it's such a good thing. She gets so upset when she sees Julia at the nursing home."

"Maybe she's ready to deal with the way Julia is now. She must know you would love to see her."

"I think that's why she's coming…to be with me for Thanksgiving. And to meet you, of course."

I looked up to see him smiling at me. My heart softened at his need for my help in dealing with this. "That will be fun. You'll have to join us for Thanksgiving."

Sam relaxed, letting out the breath he'd apparently been holding in anticipation of my response. "Thanks, that's great. I couldn't figure out what to do with them. Our house would be so bleak without Julia. And restaurants are all closed. Unless you want Chinese."

"We can't have you eating Chinese on the most American of all holidays. It's all settled. You'll come to our house." I beamed, hoping to hide any trepidation I felt.

After all, who wouldn't want to meet the daughter of the married man she's dating whose sainted mother is institutionalized?

****

Preparations for Thanksgiving in Thomason world began around November tenth. We would be descending on my mom and dad's house for the celebration, but while Mom had her hands full with the turkey, Donna and I did most of the other cooking, which was to say I did most of the cooking, and Donna appeared with platters and trays prepared by a trendy caterer.

This year was different.

This year Donna was out from under the condescending disapproval of my brother, and she was going to rock the kitchen.

At least that's what she said.

She began rifling through my cookbooks and sat for hours with a pad and pen, going through recipes, and making a menu any TV chef would envy.

There were beans and yams and stuffing and salads, none of which were recognizable as standard Thanksgiving fare. All had a little something unexpected: raisins and pecans in the yams, oysters in the stuffing, crunchy peanuts in an Asian salad. Desserts laced with liqueurs. Curried fruit. It sounded delicious and exotic. And hard to make.

But she was so enthusiastic and eager to show her own prowess in the kitchen that I couldn't argue. Besides, it took her mind off Paul and the boys. Even Lucy got excited about helping, offering to sit on a stool at the counter and chop.

I watched them chatting about ingredients and techniques, surrounded on the sofa by my cookbooks, which weren't nearly as worn as the ones Jack had taken with him. I loved them both and had to fight down the wave of motherly protectiveness that washed over me.

"So, Lucy, is Jacob coming to Thanksgiving?" I asked, curious to get the latest on the smooching couple.

She blushed and nodded. "I invited him. I hope you don't mind. He said he'd come, but you know, we don't know each other very well. Thanksgiving's still a few weeks away. Anything can happen."

I giggled. "Yeah, it looked like anything was about to happen the other night."

She screeched and threw a sofa pillow at me. "Yeah, you two. Thanks for the *bad* timing!"

Donna looked up from her scribbling and laughed. "I'm sorry we interrupted you from discovering his true 'bedside manner.' "

Lucy blushed again, a deeper shade this time. "Nothing was going to happen. Geez, it was our first date. Besides, he's the one who told me to go easy on extracurricular activities for a while."

That made me think of my lack of extracurricular activities with Sam. "The way things are going, you'll probably beat me to the bedroom."

Donna added. "That makes two of us."

****

Lucy struggled through the next three weeks of chemo, sick and lethargic, with moments of dark despair coupled with rock-solid resolve. And then her hair began falling out.

I heard her screaming from the upstairs bathroom and took the stairs two at a time. "What's wrong? Are you all right?"

She stood in her bathrobe, pale and thin, holding two handfuls of her glorious blonde hair. "Look! Look! It's happening!"

I took the clumpy hair and tossed it in the trashcan, then bundled her into my arms. She sobbed a little. I tried consoling her. "Sweetie, we knew this was coming. It's right on schedule. In fact, I think this whole thing is very punctual."

I felt her giggle against my shoulder.

I pushed on. "So, what was our strategy for dealing with this? Remember the scarves? Where are they?"

She pointed to her bedroom but didn't move away from me. So, we walked like conjoined twins into her room and rifled through the dresser until we found the scarves we had bought online a few weeks earlier.

There were six in all, silk and shimmering, with a Hermes among them, along with other prominent designers. Nothing in my wardrobe cost as much as one of those scarves, but at that moment, none of them were worth a handful of my friend's hair.

I picked one, all pastel and sherbet colors, and tied it around her head, hoping for the right effect. She glanced into the mirror, patting it into place, then suddenly tore it off, retied it, kissed me on the cheek, and said, "Perfect. Let's get ice cream."

Denial and ice cream always went together in my house.

****

Things were falling into place for the wedding. The invitations had gone out for the celebration which would be the first Saturday of December. Dresses, tuxes, attendants, cakes, food, flowers, favors, a limo, and a honeymoon, albeit brief, were all accounted for.

And by some miracle, Syd had called and said he would be in for the wedding, arriving in time for Thanksgiving. Bridget would be spending time with her parents in Cincinnati. I was thrilled.

Roger and I had communicated by email since the day of the cake tasting, but I had one more meeting with him before the wedding. We needed to finalize seating and centerpieces. Whitney was supposed to come with me but had a conflicting doctor's appointment.

"It's okay, Mom, I trust you and Roger. And, the truth is, I don't really care who sits with who."

"Whom," I corrected without thinking.

Whitney shot me a withering glance. "Whom. Anyway, just make sure the attendants and their dates have a table and put everyone else where you want them."

So, while it was tempting to put Jack with my Aunt Lula, the icon of the conservative right, I would behave and keep appropriate species together.

After all, why make things more complicated than they already were?

"Hi." Roger welcomed me with an outstretched hand, which I took, trying to ignore the welcoming warmth of his touch. "How are things? Lucy and Donna, for instance."

I gave him the latest info, careful to speak in pride-protecting generalities, but appreciated that he asked. Then, we got down to business.

After an hour of table settings, place cards, floating candles and miniature white lights, Roger set his pencil down. "I'm starving, let me buy you dinner."

I cocked my head. "Buy me dinner? At your own restaurant?"

"Ah, no, I was thinking of somewhere else. I'm tired of Mexican food." Then he rushed to add, "Although it's the best Mexican food this side of Acapulco."

I laughed. *"The Dallas Tribune* isn't the only newspaper I read. So, you can relax. You're allowed to eat somewhere else. Call it research."

"Good idea." He leaned in closer. "So, will you come and do some research with me?"

I dragged my gaze away from his eyes, which were hypnotic, brown and warm and chocolaty. Delicious eyes.

"Sure," I said, with feigned casualness, gathering up papers and pens and shoving them in my purse. "Where shall we go?"

He suggested we research Greek food, so I told him about a place called Capri. It had kitschy fake windows looking out on sparkling Mediterranean villages, whitewashed in sunlight. If I squinted, I could pretend I was there on a cruise.

"Don't tell Jack, but Greek is my favorite food," I confided to Roger, who swore he'd keep my secret. I ordered a platter filled with lamb and moussaka and dolmas, with creamy cucumber yogurt sauce for dipping. Roger knew his way around Greek cuisine and ordered saganaki for an appetizer—Romano cheese, deep fried, then set ablaze at our table to cries of "Opa! Opa!"

My taste buds (which had atrophied on weeks of Weight Magic dinners) had a blast. So, did I. We talked nonstop about everything from the weather in Texas to our philosophy of education. In between we laughed like crazy at the same things.

I was sated by the conversation, the food, and the easy companionship Roger and I seemed to share. I was reminded of dinners in the early years with Jack, the man I thought was my soulmate, who turned out to be a great example of why gay men made good friends. When the baklava came, with its flaky pastry and layers of sticky, honeyed goodness, I asked for a to-go box.

I would enjoy the tasty tidbit at home with a glass of milk and a painful longing for the man who seemed impossibly perfect for me.

****

Sam and I always went to dinner on Wednesday. It was Mexican dinner discount night at our favorite restaurant, La Fiesta. We always got there in time to avoid the lines; we always ordered the special; we always got a sopapilla to share. This was ritual. This was comfortable. This was us.

But the Wednesday before Thanksgiving, his daughter Susan and her family were coming in from Arkansas, so we shifted our date night to Tuesday, so he could take the family out to La Fiesta on Wednesday. I would be busy chopping, stirring, and serving as Donna's sous chef for Thanksgiving. It would work out—for everyone.

We went to Angelo's, a sappy Italian restaurant in an older, urban neighborhood called Lakewood. Drippy candles, Dean Martin music, painted murals on stone walls, plastic grape vines twining around the ceiling, and twinkling lights peeking out of the leaves set a more romantic tone than La Fiesta ever could have.

We must have looked like an uncomfortable first date because the hostess seated us at a quiet, cozy corner table.

Sam ordered red wine and after our first glass was poured, he held his up to me. "What shall we toast?"

"How about friendships and family?" That felt safe.

"Friendships and family it is." We clinked glasses.

We ate in the silence reserved for elderly couples, commenting on the décor and the food every once in a while. We finished the bottle of wine. "So, are you looking forward to Susan's visit?" I asked while we waited for spumoni at the end of the delicious meal.

He looked away, staring at the mural on the wall.

"Of course, but it's always difficult when she comes. Susan is devoted to her mother but refuses to accept her condition, so rather than come down and confront it, she continues to call the house and send letters and pictures as if nothing were wrong. She can't bring herself to see her mother that way."

He paused, looking distant, unhappy, lonely. I felt sorry that I'd mentioned something that could make him so sad.

He swirled the last of the wine in his glass and stared into its depths. "You know, I miss Susan so much. And Steven. What she doesn't realize is she's cutting herself off from me, too. And when Julia dies, she won't have closure. I'm afraid she'll never get over the guilt of not saying goodbye."

I was saved from giving some lame piece of advice by the arrival of the spumoni and our subsequent oohs and ahhs regarding its cool creaminess.

While we waited for the bill, I said, "Maybe this time Susan will see that she needs some connection with family. If you take her to see Julia, she'll realize at last that she has to move on." I leaned over the table and touched his hand. "You all have to move on."

Sam stared at our hands, then up at me, his eyes more watery blue than usual, heavy with emotion. "Tess, you are a wonderful person, so generous and kind. You're the one thing that keeps me going."

My heart swelled with affection for this dear, sweet man. I squeezed his hand and smiled.

****

An hour later, we were making out on his sofa.

Don't ask me how it happened. I'm not sure. But he asked me back to his house for a nightcap—something we had never done.

He lived in a comfortable, predictable Dallas ranch on a quiet suburban street lined with pecan trees. Inside, it was as if time stood still the day he took Julia to the nursing home. Pictures were everywhere. Sam and Julia getting married, Susan as a baby, Susan growing up, Susan in her cap and gown, Susan and David getting married, Steven as a baby, Steven growing up—the circle of life on the mantel, the piano, the coffee table.

They were a family, at least they had been, until they were ravaged by illness, the way my family had been ravaged by unexpected revelation, and Lucy's had been ravaged by suicide, and Donna's was now being ravaged by arrogance and the need for power.

I thought of my parents' house, with its mantel of pictures, and smiled at the thought of a family intact and healthy, at least from the neck up.

Sam didn't notice any of it. Sam was like a man on a mission. The floodgates of his libido had opened, and there was no dam in sight. He closed the front door behind us and gestured to the sofa. "Sit down. Do you want anything to drink?"

"No, thanks, I think I had enough at Angelo's."

He sat next to me. "Tess, you know how I feel about you."

"Not exactly, no." And that was true. We hadn't talked about our feelings for each other. Up to then, there had been an unspoken pact between us to keep things simple, uncomplicated, un-physical.

"Well, then, this is how I feel about you."

He slammed into me, knocking me backward against the sofa pillows, kissing me hard somewhere between my lips and my chin. That shocked us both, and he lifted his face from mine. "I like being with you. You make me laugh. You're smart. We have great conversation."

He started kissing me again, this time more softly. Hands began to roam—his, not mine. My mind raced back through his catalog of assets. Laughing, smart, good conversation. I had that same relationship with National Public Radio. But I didn't want to make love to it.

He came up for air again. "I need you, Tess. I need for us to be more than friends. I need to touch you, to kiss you. I need to feel you close to me."

This was wrong, and I knew it. Red flags waved in every part of my wine-soaked brain. He needed me. I needed him, too, But I wasn't hearing the word I longed to hear from Sam. And I wasn't feeling it myself.

Love.

Where was the love?

This was Italian decor, rich food, and red wine. But it definitely wasn't love.

If I didn't stop him now, there would be regret. His for cheating on his beloved, unknowing wife; me for allowing myself to be used by someone in need. I'd had enough of that already.

And there was the small but important matter of letting another human being view my nakedness before I was ready. No matter I had been losing weight—yes, I knew it—Tad's cruel scale didn't lie. No matter the lights were dim. The lights would never be dim enough.

I had to somehow extricate myself from this situation without further demeaning either one of us.

I grabbed Sam's hands just shy of dipping into my blouse and held them tight between us, then I kissed him one last time. "Sam," I whispered against his lips. "We can't do this."

"Tess, I need you."

"Yes, you said that, you crazy, romantic fool. And as tempting an invitation as that may be, we can't do this. You will hate yourself and me, too. And you know it."

He sighed, and his weight sagged against me on the couch. "Dammit, I know. It's just been so long, and I thought maybe it was time we had sex."

Just as he said the word "sex," the door flew open, and Susan, David, and Steven bounded in.

Chapter Eleven

"Daddy!"

"Susan!"

"Sam!"

"David!"

"Grandpa!"

"Steven!"

"Oh, Lord in Heaven!"

That last was me as I scrambled upright on the couch and rearranged my disheveled clothes, mussed hair, and destroyed self-respect.

Being caught *in flagrante delicto* when you're seventeen is one thing; when you're fifty, it's entirely different, let me tell you.

"Daddy! What in the world is going on? Who is this woman?" Susan sputtered while holding her hand over Steven's four-year-old eyes. David looked amused. I liked him immediately, despite my blushing embarrassment.

"Susan, this is Tess Thomason. I've spoken to you about her, I believe."

"You told me you had a lady friend, Daddy. And that she was *elderly*."

My head snapped around to see Sam do some sputtering himself. "Well, what I meant was she wasn't *your* age, Susan. I didn't want you thinking I was dating some cute young thing."

I stood up then. "So, Sam, what *did* you tell Susan about me? That I was wrinkled, toothless, and wore corrective shoes?"

Sam hurried to mitigate the damage. "No, Tess, I never said *elderly*. I may have said older." He turned to face Susan. "I didn't want you to be upset that I had a friend."

"A friend? Daddy, you were nearly ripping off her clothes."

"Whoa, there, just a minute," I said, feeling the need to defend myself since Sam wasn't inclined to do so. "Number one, your father and I are consenting adults. And number two, no clothes were ripped here this evening. As near as I can figure, no clothes have been harmed in any way."

Before she could return volley, I turned to Sam. "You need to take me home now." I picked up my purse and moved to the door, where Susan, David, and Steven were still standing. They moved away.

I smiled as sweetly as possible at them and said, "I hope to see you all on Thanksgiving." I glanced down at Steven who looked a little confused at all the ruckus. "There'll be pie."

He grinned.

****

Sensible Shoes
By Tess Thomason
"Your Thighs—Your Enemy"
"Face-Plucking: The New Addiction"
"What's So Bad About Belly Fat?"
"How Wrinkles Affect Body Art"
I have taken to reading popular (and not so popular) magazines to get ideas of what is on the minds of women

of a certain age. There are stories on decorating my "cool, curtained outdoor living room" or finding the right handbag at a price "you can afford." There are features focusing on a couple who have come to blows over the thermostat setting or one about a woman who has hitch-hiked her way around the world.

I don't even want to drive downtown.

But the ones I can't tear my eyes from, the ones that beckon me over my full shopping cart at the checkout line, the ones that hold me riveted while I sip my Weight Magic bouillon at lunch are the ones that scream at me, "You're fat, hairy, and old."

I know about my problem thighs. I'm aware that belly fat is the new clarion call of healthcare. I have wondered how many other women spend a full hour plucking every hair from their chin, upper lip, and lower eyebrows. Okay, the wrinkled tattoo thing hadn't crossed my mind, but I bet it has a lot of other aging gen-Xers worried to death that their upper arm twaddle will render their old boyfriend's name unreadable.

I don't want to be reminded of my shortcomings at the checkout counter.

I go to the grocery store for respite, as odd as that sounds. It's quiet there, cool, calm, except on Saturday morning or just before a football game. I go off-hours when I can spend leisure time wiggling eggs, tapping melons, and reading labels on the backs of noodle boxes. I poke the roasts, squeeze avocados, and thank God for such luxuries as feta cheese and Kalamata olives.

I am forced to shop for Thanksgiving groceries, because I doubt my all-American family will give up a single calorie of their traditional turkey and dressing dinner. And even though my house is stocked with enough Weight Magic meals to last through the winter, I still have two other women living with me who need nourishment. Plus, and I don't discount this—I have certain needs, too.

Sugar-free ice cream, fat-free hazelnut creamer, and lo-cal whipped cream in a can. Dieting is all about cream.

No one who cares about the needs of another human being could ask me to give those up.

Sexual, spiritual, emotional…yes, the grocery store is all those things. But there's more to it than that.

I'm serene at the grocery store. And alone.

Like you, I'm not alone that much. My sweet family, friends, and co-workers are around—a lot. So, an hour of heavenly solitude is welcomed. And protected.

When I come to the checkout line, I'm aglow with health and love and goodwill for the whole human race. I've thoughtfully chosen small luxuries for myself, healthy fare for my friends, and disinfectant bathroom wipes. I'm feeling good about myself and my life.

And then the screaming starts.

I'm bombarded by mean, hurtful barbs. "Cankles are the New Love-Handles." I'm not even sure what cankles are. But I know they're bad, and I've probably got them.

My self-esteem deflates, my newfound glow dims, my shopping cart is now the symbol of all that is bad in me and the world. I hand over my two hundred ten dollars, after the reward card, and skulk out to my car, magazines tucked under my arm, thankful that I escaped the curse of wrinkled body art.

****

I unloaded the groceries from the car, stopping long

enough in the kitchen to switch on the ceiling fan and swig a bottle of water. Late November and I was moist and steaming as a bread pudding, not from the exertion of Thanksgiving shopping, but from a hormonal imbalance that seemed to rollercoaster along no matter the season.

I had just stuffed the last can of yams into the groaning pantry when I heard Whitney yelling through the house, "Mom! Mom, are you here?"

"In here, honey."

She came into the kitchen, headed straight for the fridge, and poured herself a glass of milk. When she turned around to face me, it was evident she'd been crying.

"What's wrong?" I demanded.

"Nothing." She turned away to stare out the window and for an instant, I felt like we were living a soap opera moment.

"Okay, then, how's Mark?"

"Oh, Mom!" She wheeled around and buried her head in my shoulder, her body wracked with sobs. After a minute or so, the sobs became muffled gasps, so familiar to a mother's ear. The sound of a child regaining control in the safety and security of a mother's arms.

So, I ventured again, "What's wrong, Whitney? Is the baby okay?"

"The baby's fine." She sniffed.

"And Mark?"

"Mark's fine, too."

"Okay, so what's up, then?"

"It's me, Mom. I'm a mess. I'm so worried this is a mistake. This wedding."

Although I envisioned dollar bills taking flight

through open windows, I shoved the image aside and concentrated on being compassionate and wise with my daughter, who was so clearly in distress. "What happened? Did you have a fight?"

"No, we never fight."

"A disagreement? A misunderstanding?"

"No, he's wonderful. Sweet and sympathetic when I'm tired or cranky."

"Money, politics, religion?"

"No, we're really in tune with one another, which is unusual in Texas."

I nodded, then waited, but she just sat at the kitchen counter, silent, sipping her milk. "So, what's got you so upset?" I ventured, at last.

"I think it's just what we've been talking about."

"That you and Mark seem perfect for each other?"

"Seem perfect. But no one's perfect, are they? What if we're just on our best behavior? What if after the wedding, we find out we have these huge chasms of difference between us?"

"That seems unlikely, honey. You've been living together for months. Any glaring issues would have come up by now."

Whitney stared into her now-empty glass. Then she said, without looking up, "It happened with you and Daddy."

I was by her side in an instant, clasping her head to my bosom, guilty for being blind and naive and marrying someone trapped by culture and fear of a family steeped in narrow-minded, religious dicta.

I lifted Whitney's sweet face in my hands to gaze into her eyes, so like Jack's. "Whitney, sweetie, it was another time. A gay man was stigmatized and marginalized. Gays and lesbians fought their own biology, desperate not to lose family, friends, and careers, everything.

"Society was cruel to them, and it still can be today, and your dad was a victim of that. So was I.

"He never intended to lie to me or hurt me or you and Sydney. He loved us then like he does now. It just became too hard to deny who he was to himself and everyone else."

"But, Mom," she protested. "Look at you. He left you all alone. He has Tad, but you don't have anyone."

Surprised by the turn the conversation had taken, I answered, "I have Sam."

"Yeah, but you and Sam are just friends. You don't love him, and he doesn't love you."

Surprised she had noticed, I replied, "We care about each other, we do. It's complicated."

"What I see are two lonely people who eat Mexican food once a week."

A need to defend my relationship rose, but I thought it better to focus once again on Whitney. "Enough about my love life or lack thereof. We're talking about you."

"Well, I don't want to make a mistake and end up alone."

The unspoken "like you" lingered in the air.

"Do you love Mark? Or is all this about making a home for the baby?"

"Maybe at first, but now, I'm not sure."

"Then here's a question that may help clarify things."

"Okay."

"If you weren't pregnant, would you still marry Mark?"

Whitney got up, poured another glass of milk, and grabbed two cookies from a package that had escaped the pantry.

Sensing the need for more ammo, I added, "In other words, if you lost the baby tomorrow, God forbid, would you go through with the wedding?"

Her mouth dropped open as she stared at me, and then she grinned. "Yes, absolutely, yes. I mean, it's been fast and crazy because of the baby, but the wedding is just as I always dreamed it would be, and I wouldn't change anything. And I guess the more we've planned for the baby and the wedding, the more we've gotten to know each other. I suppose it's no different than people who have been together for a long time. We've just compressed our learning curve into a shorter span of time." She paused. "So yes, even though we've done it all sort of backward, I'd do it all over again."

"So, do you think this is cold feet—normal pre-wedding jitters?"

"I guess. It's such a big step, and I look at you and Dad and Aunt Donna and Uncle Paul, and I don't want it all to go south."

Chagrined at being a bad example of marital bliss, I scoured my mind for a happily married couple to display in front of my daughter. "Look at Mamaw and Papaw. They've been married for over fifty years. And happily, I think they'd say." I sat down at the counter next to Whitney. "Honey, there are no guarantees with marriage—ever. But we take a leap of faith. We believe in love and a life shared, in family and continuity, in legacy and in the right to have a partner advocate for us."

"That's what Sam does for his wife, isn't it, Mom?"

"Yes, that's what Sam does. He still loves her very

much."

"And Daddy still loves you, doesn't he?"

"Yes, I think so, but in a different way. It turns out you can love someone very much and not want to sleep with them."

Whitney smiled. "I guess so, but that's a little bit weird, you know, Mom, to have two guys love you that much, but to never have sex with either of them."

"Thanks so much, sweetie, I hadn't thought about it that way."

"Sorry, Mom, I didn't mean to make it seem so pathetic."

"Good grief!" I slapped her bottom with a dish towel as she stood to leave. "I feel so much better now."

"Me, too," she said and hugged me hard. "I'll see you tomorrow."

"Come early. I need help getting things over to Mamaw's house."

An hour later, as I was heating up a weight Magic Acapulco Chicken Wrap for lunch, I struggled to read the directions through the tears falling on the box.

I am pathetic. And alone.

****

Despite my personal pity party, I reveled in the unmistakable fall-ness that had come to Dallas. I shuffled through waves of leaves on the way to the car and lugged armloads of logs in from the pile outside to restack by the fireplace. We didn't often build a fire in Dallas, but I wanted to be ready at a moment's notice anyway, should a blizzard rain down upon us.

Sensible Shoes
By Tess Thomason
We don't want a white Thanksgiving in Texas. That

would be wrong on several levels. What we're after on this fall-ish of all holidays is crisp. Like the bite of a big red delicious apple, the crunch of vivid leaves underfoot, and the crackle of flames in the fireplace.

We want it cold enough that you need a bathrobe to fetch the newspaper, that you pull a thick sweater on over the turtleneck your mother hates.

"It makes your head sit right on top of your shoulders, like a linebacker."

Oh yeah, crisp like the crack of helmets and shoulder pads in the November air on a Sunday afternoon.

The snap of fresh beans in a bowl on my grandmother's lap, the sizzle of roasting pumpkin seeds, and God knows about a dozen other sights, sounds, scents, and tastes all signal fall.

At least here in Texas.

But Autumn is more a state of mind than a state of place. And no matter where you are, whether deep in snow or basking on a beach, I hope your season and its attendant celebration is warm and cozy.

As it should be.

****

Thanksgiving seemed unusually chaotic, even for the Thomason household.

Syd had arrived that morning, and Whitney and Mark picked him up from the airport. They all descended on my house in a flurry of hugs and kisses.

Upon seeing Syd, Slider danced a jig, then promptly pooped on Syd's shoe.

I burst out laughing. "Well, that's an appropriate welcome-home gesture, I think."

Donna and I had been up since dawn continuing the

preparations begun the night before. But things hadn't gone well. We were frantically juggling pots and pans in the oven and on the stove, trying to fulfill Donna's vision of Thanksgiving with a twist.

It was twisted all right.

"Taste this," Donna had asked me that morning. "Does this taste right to you?"

I sampled the spoonful of yams she offered me. "I don't think they're done."

I picked up the recipe card from the flour-dusted counter. "The recipe said to cook it at four hundred fifty for thirty minutes."

Donna's mouth dropped open. "Four hundred fifty? I didn't read it right. It's only on three hundred fifty."

"We'll just turn it up and put them back in."

"No, we can't. The curried fruit is in there, too. It has to be on three-hundred-fifty."

The lower oven was full of spiral-sliced ham roasting away at an even lower temperature. Donna had opted for a ham instead of a turkey, opining about taking risks and stirring things up a little. I had acquiesced because she seemed so excited about the prospect of change and because it seemed to be the theme of the fall that year, and why the hell not?

"Okay, we'll just send the kids to Mom's early with the yams, and she can cook them, plus the rolls. They cook at four hundred, too."

Donna went to get the rolls, some new kind she had chosen instead of the brown and serve brickbats we were used to. We had put them in the fridge to thaw. She squealed.

"What's wrong?"

"They're just little balls of dough. I thought they

were supposed to rise."

I checked the wrapper, still on the counter. "Uh oh. We were supposed to put these in a warm place for a few hours to let them rise. They'll never be ready in time."

Donna's lower lip quivered.

I picked up a dish towel, blotted the sweat from my upper lip, and turned on the ceiling fan. I could have single-handedly warmed those dough balls into giant puff pastries in my armpits; I was so hot. Which gave me an idea.

"Okay, don't panic." I turned to Whitney, still standing in the doorway awaiting instructions. "Take these to Mom's also. Tell her to put them in a warm oven—like one hundred fifty to let them rise for an hour or so. I'm sure they'll be fine." I wasn't sure about anything at that point, but why panic?

The kids left, and I went upstairs to check on Lucy while Donna made the Asian salad with peanut sauce and noodles.

Things upstairs were not much better than below.

Lucy sat on the edge of the bed, half dressed, head bowed, a gorgeous autumn-hued scarf in her hand, tears dropping on her bare knees. I sat down next to her.

"What's wrong, sweetie?" I ventured.

She sniffed and looked at me with sunken eyes, red-rimmed from a combination of chemo sickness and crying. "I don't have the energy to get dressed, and I want to go to your folks so much, but I don't think I can make it."

"I'll help you. We can do it together. You'll be beautiful."

"I don't even care about being beautiful. I just want to wear some pants." She giggled a little. And so did I.

"Okay, then, let's start with pants."

Fifteen minutes later, leaning on my arm, with a swipe of blush on both cheeks and the lovely scarf tied around her bald head, she went downstairs.

We got to the kitchen in time to see Donna take a big swig of rum before pouring the rest of the bottle into the batter for her cake.

****

By noon, with pots and jars tucked into the trunk of the car, a tipsy Donna, shaky Lucy, and I headed over to the elder Thomason home for what would prove to be the least traditional Thanksgiving dinner in the history of the world.

Yes, the entire world.

It started out steeped in tradition. The parades were over, and the pregame festivities blared from the television with an array of ex-football players predicting one outcome or another.

Jack helped in the kitchen, but we shooed him out as he kept looking longingly into the den, some remnant of testosterone calling out to his vestigial maleness to join the game-day fun. He snuggled onto the couch next to Tad. It occurred to me I had yet to see the change in their relationship Tad had worried about weeks earlier when Roger came onto the scene. Unbidden, the image of Roger, tall, elegant, and more fun than a theme park came into my head. I sighed.

So, Mom, Whitney, Donna, and I finished lunch while Lucy sat at the kitchen table, slowly polishing a silver serving platter. She had insisted on helping, and this was a chore I felt wouldn't be too taxing for her or important to the meal if it didn't get done.

Donna was a wreck. Contrary to my hot flash-induced inspiration, the rolls didn't rise quite as much as needed. And while the yams were done, the curried fruit seemed runny. But the salad, laced with crunchy Asian noodles and a decadent peanut dressing was beautiful, and a rich chocolate cherry rum cake baked in the oven while we set the table.

Donna, rather rum-soaked herself, wrapped napkins in strips of raffia to coordinate with her Pilgrim-themed Thanksgiving tablescape.

The doorbell rang, and before anyone could get to it, Jason and Matt raced in and straight for their mother. She beamed at first, but her smile quickly dissipated when the boys were eager not to shower her with affection but with tales of all the perks Paul had given them and how great their life was without her. At last, they plopped down right in front of the TV so several of the guys had to adjust their vantage point. Paul said hello to everyone, and took a seat, with a nod to Donna.

He looked like someone who had gotten the wind knocked out of him.

The bell rang again, but this time, I opened the door to Sam, Susan, David, and Steven, who smiled at me and asked, "Is there gonna be pie?"

"You bet." I smiled back at Steven and then at Sam, who had the good graces to kiss me on the cheek despite Susan's glaring. I said to him, "Why don't you take David and Steven into the den and introduce them to the guys. Football pregame is already on."

"Great!" he said, with over-the-top enthusiasm, probably relieved I was still speaking to him.

I took a foil-covered pan from Susan. I peeked inside to see a green-bean casserole. At least there would be one traditional dish on the table. I said, "Mmm, this looks delicious. Thank you so much. Why don't you come with me? The women are huddled in the kitchen as usual."

She looked a little unsure, glanced after Sam and her husband as if she might make a break for it, but then said okay, and followed me into the kitchen where I introduced her all around.

Her gaze landed on Whitney's well-rounded belly. "Oh! When are you due?"

Whitney patted the mound affectionately. "In February."

"Boy or girl?"

"We don't know yet. We want it to be a surprise." She laughed a little. "Not that it hasn't been up to now."

"I'm sorry?" Susan asked, confused.

"Oh, never mind," Whitney answered, recognizing my headshake as a warning. "Being pregnant is such an adventure for a woman."

"That is so true, although I think the fathers have a crazy time, too. Everything changes for them. I'm sure your husband would agree."

"Well—" Whitney stammered, looking for the right way to tell this perfect stranger about her husbandless condition.

And before I could say anything to help, Mom chimed in. "Oh, dear, no, she's not married. Well, not yet. The wedding is in two weeks. You'll have to come!"

As I expected, the look on Susan's face was like someone who'd smelled a decaying body. "Thank you so much for the invitation, Mrs. Thomason, but I'm afraid we'll be back in Arkansas by then."

And not a moment too soon, I'm guessing.

She had the courtesy to ask if she could help with

lunch, so I put her to work chopping pecans to sprinkle on the ambrosia.

About that time, Jack breezed into the kitchen. "The game starts in forty-five minutes. We better get this show on the road, or we'll never get the boys to the table. Tad threatened to make me sleep on the couch if he missed halftime. It's Cher."

Susan looked up from her chopping. "My mother never allows the football game to interfere with Thanksgiving dinner. It's a sacred time at our house, and no one would dare question that."

"Susan, this is Jack, Whitney and Sydney's father. Jack, this is Susan, Sam's daughter," I said by way of deflection.

She cocked her head to one side. "Whitney and Sydney's father? Oh, of course. Hmm. Who's Tad?"

"My partner."

This time the look was more as if she were watching someone burn the flag. "Oh, how nice. My mother used to work with someone whose brother was a homosexual."

Oh God.

Jack smiled at the hapless woman. "Do tell."

"Yes, she said they did everything to try to make him change his mind, but he decided to stay that way. My mother always says we have to love the sinner, not the sin." She smiled with ignorant innocence.

Oh God.

"Sinner?" Jack repeated as if he were too stunned to utter anything else.

I was formulating my own response when Lucy chirped, "Oh, Susan, around here, we practice 'Judge not, lest ye be judged.' How does your mother feel about that one?"

Score one for our side.

Unfazed, Susan said, "Oh, yes, that's one of my mother's favorites. She tolerates all minorities."

Oh, my dear God in heaven.

Jack stiffened. I put my hand on his arm.

"Susan," I said with as much calm as I could muster. "We don't consider homosexuality a sin or a minority. And furthermore…"

The doorbell interrupted the rest of my rebuke. "I'll get it," Jack offered and hurried from the kitchen, relieved no doubt to be away from the weirdness of being denigrated while in the safety of the family home.

I heard the voices at the front door but was still surprised to see Roger come into the kitchen carrying an enormous bouquet of fresh fall flowers arranged in a tall vase amidst a cadre of tiny pumpkins. He handed it to me with a kiss on the cheek.

"I hope I'm not putting you out too much. Jack invited me weeks ago, but we weren't sure my flight would get in on time."

"Flight? Where have you been?"

"Scouting locations in the state for other restaurant sites. Austin, Houston, San Antonio, Waco."

I studied the flowers, all vibrant oranges, golds, yellows, and greens while I willed my pulse to slow. "They're beautiful. You didn't have to, but I'm so glad you did."

"Well, you and your mother can share them. I appreciate all the work that goes into Thanksgiving dinner. Then, we consume it in an instant. Crazy, when you think about it."

"Well, then we should give these to Donna. She's

done most of the work for this particular feast."

I presented the flowers to Donna with a flourish. She took them, burst into tears, thrust them back at me, and raced from the room. I turned around to see Paul standing in the doorway.

"I'll take care of her," he said.

"Be gentle. She's had a tough morning," I called after him.

Paul took a few steps, then turned back around to face me. "Maybe I haven't done a great job of showing it, but I love my wife." He turned on his heel and followed Donna up the stairs.

Lucy gave me the thumbs up.

Roger escaped, too, to join the other men in the den.

Susan stirred the ambrosia. "So, are you dating Roger, too?"

"Me? Heavens, no! He's Jack's partner."

"Jack has two partners? You know, my mother told me that homosexuals are promiscuous. No wonder Tad wants him to sleep on the couch."

"Oh, for God's sake," I muttered under my breath. "Let's just get dinner on the table. Susan, can you carry these yams into the dining room?"

Blissfully unaware that she and her mother were woefully behind the cultural eight-ball, Susan carried food to the table as did the rest of the women, and Jack, who had recovered from the earlier exchange, cast me sidelong looks that had me rolling my eyes and mouthing "I'm sorry."

I had never seen a hint of bigotry or narrow-mindedness in Sam, and I found myself wondering where he had been during the rearing of his child. It seemed where he was reserved and quiet, Susan was opinionated and vocal.

What I didn't realize until the ham was served was she was channeling her mother, and the worst was yet to come.

Chapter Twelve

Dad carried the huge ham into the dining room and set it on the table.

We clasped hands and bowed our heads for the traditional blessing but were interrupted by Susan, who said in a stage whisper to David, "Ham? For Thanksgiving? Where's the turkey?"

Donna answered with a slurry chirp, "I thought we'd do things a little differently this year. You'll find surprises throughout the meal. I hope you'll enjoy the change."

Paul smiled at Donna. "I bet it will be delicious." We all stared at him.

Who is this guy, and what happened to my brother?

Stricken, Susan said, "But Thanksgiving is all about tradition. We do things the same every year. My mother makes the same foods. We watch the parades and then put puzzles together afterward. And turkey, well, turkey is just *required* for Thanksgiving."

I expected Sam to shush his child at least, if not scold her for her rudeness, but instead, he busied himself with his napkin. When I elbowed him in the ribs, he ventured, "I think everything looks very good, Susan. Why don't you try it? If you don't like it, we'll find some turkey later."

I thought he had perhaps grown a second head or morphed into an alien blob. Turkey later? Was he kidding? Everyone knew you could get Chinese food on Thanksgiving and not much else.

The blessing forgotten, we passed bowls around the table. Susan took them as they came to her, sniffing each one and looking at it as if it were a petri dish of fungi. She put a few spoonfuls of various foods on her plate, including the heinous ham.

And then, she was given the bowl of Asian salad.

"Peanuts? Are there peanuts in here?" she cried, horrified, and thrust the bowl back into her father's hand. "I'm allergic to peanuts. I'll *die* if I eat peanuts, you know that, Daddy!"

Sam set the bowl away from him. "I'm sorry, Pumpkin. I didn't notice the peanuts. I haven't had to worry about that in a long time, and I just forgot. Look, they're way over there. They won't hurt you, honey. It's okay."

Susan sniffed and mumbled, head down, but loud enough for everyone to hear, "Peanuts for Thanksgiving? Who in the world serves peanuts at Thanksgiving dinner? What kind of Thanksgiving is this, anyway?"

Donna, exhausted, stressed and still feeling the effects of various cooking liquids, stood up, knocking her chair backward so it crashed onto the hardwood floor. "I just wanted to make a nice Thanksgiving dinner and show everyone I can cook, too, even though Paul won't let me, and I can be creative and useful, like Tess, and I can contribute to the family, too."

And then she fled the room.

Paul was on his feet in an instant, rage coloring his face a deep red. He glared at Susan. "Who the hell do you think you are saying those things about Donna after she worked so hard?" He tossed his napkin on the table and followed his wife down the hall.

And at that moment, Paul became human in my eyes again, and I thought there might be some hope for their marriage after all. But first, I needed to deal with Susan, and Sam.

I was furious at Susan for insulting Jack and hurting Donna, but even more furious with Sam for allowing his daughter to run roughshod over my family without a word. If she'd been my daughter, I'd have taken her to the woodshed.

Oh, to hell with it. I don't care if she's my daughter or not.

"Look, I don't know what your mother taught you, and frankly, I don't care. But clearly, she didn't teach you any manners." I ignored Sam's sputtered protests and wagged my finger in Susan's face. "When someone invites you to their home, you should graciously accept anything that's offered. And if you cannot for some reason eat something, such as peanuts, then you should pass it along without a word."

Susan's mouth dropped open. "Daddy, are you going to let her say those things to me?"

Sam turned to me. "Tess, may I speak to you?"

"Of course," I said, and we both left the table, where everyone sat staring into their empty plates, terrified to make eye contact.

We barely reached the den before I turned on Sam. "Why didn't you say anything to her? She's been acting like that all morning."

"Tess, you need to understand what she's been through. Losing her mother, but not losing her mother at the same time. It's terribly hard on her."

"I see that, but it's no excuse for her rudeness. She

can't take her unhappiness out on other people that way."

"Well, I think your family needs to be more patient and understanding. You're not perfect either."

"Perhaps not, but at least we don't intentionally hurt one another at family events."

"She didn't intentionally hurt anyone."

"She insulted Jack for being gay, Donna's menu choice, and our family celebration in general. If it's not intentional, then it's something else."

"What do you mean?"

"I mean, she's spouting insensitive ignorance she learned from somewhere. Perhaps she needs someone to tell her some truths and give her some guidance."

"Don't tell me how to parent my child, Tess. Not when one of yours runs off with a musician and the other is pregnant out of wedlock."

I couldn't believe what I was hearing. Was he passing judgment on Whitney and Syd? "What?"

"Well, let's just say that it's understandable they would be immoral, given their father is gay."

The blinding light of fury behind my eyes nearly knocked me backward, but in an instant, it was gone, and, with red-hot clarity, between teeth so clenched they threatened to break off, I snarled. "Get your family, and leave my house. Now. I never want to see you again."

An immediate change came over Sam, and he slumped. "Tess, I'm sorry. I didn't mean it. I'm just upset about Susan. Please forgive me."

"It seems you've given me a glimpse into your true self, Sam. And I want no part of it. You and Susan have some issues to deal with, and I think you need to do it without me."

"You're going to let this destroy what we have?"

"What we have? Sam, what we have is a dry, lifeless, loveless union of two lonely people. There's nothing to destroy, especially after today. Now, go home."

He stood, shoulders down, and went back into the dining room, where he announced, "Susan, David, Steven, we're leaving. Come on."

Steven argued, "But we haven't eaten. I'm hungry."

His dad bent down and whispered something to him, and without another word, he followed his father out of the room and to the front door.

Susan stared at her father and around the table. "Where are we going? Nothing's open today. Where will we eat?"

Sam, in a rare show of parenthood, snapped, "You should have thought of that an hour ago."

Susan turned from the table, then stopped and turned back to us, tears streaming down her face. "My mother always has turkey for Thanksgiving."

I closed the door behind them just as Paul and Donna came back into the room. We took our places at the table, clasped hands and listened as my dad said, "Father, we thank you for this food we are about to eat and all the other blessings you have given us." But instead of saying Amen as he had for the last fifty years, he added, "And Lord, please help those poor folks find some turkey."

Amen.

****

Sensible Shoes
By Tess Thomason
Family traditions can be complicated. One clan's passion is another's poison.

Witness Thanksgiving.

There are those who say that the holiday is not complete without turkey, dressing, parades, and football. My family, rooted in Texas tradition, would agree. We are big on candied yams with marshmallows on top, homemade pecan pie, and green bean casserole made with canned soup.

Other families may embrace creamy ambrosia salad, with or without coconut, or mac and cheese. And it may not be "right" without them.

This year, we stepped away from tradition and welcomed a new Thanksgiving paradigm. We did it because one of our family members needed the change. And so, because we love her, we moved past our "needs of the many" to embrace the "needs of the one."

That's what you do for family.

And after all, we still had the fundamentals in place.

We had the gathering around the table. We had the sharing of the meal. And we had the watching of the football.

We had moments of stress and moments of relaxation. We had tears and laughter. There were children and elders. There were dear, old friends and new, tentative ones.

And yes, there was a kid's table, and the kids actually ate there this year.

We, like other families, are going through changes, and our Thanksgiving celebration was a microcosm of that change. We have someone getting married, someone going through illness, a baby on the way, and someone leaving home for the first time.

It was hard for some of us to accept things were different this year. But everyone was okay once we got over the shock and awe of it. We ate ham instead of turkey, for heaven's sake!

And we survived.

****

No sooner were the dishes done than Roger appeared at my elbow. Whitney and Mom had gone off for a nap. Donna found a puzzle, and she and Lucy were hunched over the coffee table working on it. The rest of the men were either intent on the television or snoozing in front of it. Perhaps, unlike Jack, Roger had never spent time in the locker room of male bonding that was football.

"Can I help?" he offered.

I folded the dish towel and laid it on the counter. "All done."

"I should have come in sooner."

"What about the game?"

"Halftime. I'm not a big Cher fan."

So, stereotypes are not always accurate.

"And we're losing. So, I thought I'd see if you needed help. But bad timing."

"Perfect timing. How about another piece of pie, and we can sneak off to the living room."

"Sounds good."

We took the pie and cups of fresh coffee into my mother's gold-brocaded living room. The sixties still lived there and would never be allowed to grow up. We sank into the narrow-armed sofa.

Roger voiced what we had all been thinking but no one had dared utter throughout the strange meal. "That was a rather bizarre Thanksgiving dinner."

"Oh, you think?"

"Is that typical of Thomason Thanksgivings?" he

asked, with a twinkle in his eye.

"No, no, usually we sacrifice a virgin. Sadly, we didn't have any of those handy."

We both laughed. It felt good, like cleansing the palate between courses.

Roger said, "It's none of my business, but things between you and Sam seemed a bit strained."

I chuckled. "You could say that." I didn't want to share the horrible things Sam said with anyone, especially someone who could carry it back to Jack, so I left it at that.

"Well, I hope you're able to work it out."

"Oh, I think maybe Sam and I have reached a parting of the ways."

"Wow, that bad, huh?"

"Yeah, pretty bad."

"Are you okay?"

I searched my heart for a moment, delved into the recesses, and pulled back the dusty curtains that were my feelings. What I discovered there was not the heartache or panic or chasm of loneliness I felt when I lost Jack. No, what I felt was, yes, relief. Surprising, unexpected relief. It was over. *Thank God.*

"I'm better than okay. I'm fine. I'm great." Roger's quizzical expression made me smile. "I know, it's weird, but it's all good."

He smiled, then, too, and I noticed the crinkling around his eyes and the silver glinting in random strands of his hair. "Good. I'm glad for you, then."

We sat for a moment in comfortable silence, then I asked, "Did you find any good locations for Habanera?"

"Yes, several. Texas can never get enough Mexican food, even more so if it has a twist, a hook to bring people in."

"And Habanera has the hook?"

"Yeah, it does. Jack, for one. Handsome and personable, he's great with people and food. And he has a unique culinary point of view."

"I love it when you speak 'Chef.' Tell me more." I was flirting. I knew it, but I couldn't help myself, and what harm could it do, anyway?

"Well, we have a blog and are trying to get other social media exposure for Jack as an Influencer. One day, I'd like to get Habanera and Jack featured on a cooking show."

"That would be amazing!" It had never occurred to me that Jack could be a television chef. But I had to admit he'd be perfect. It was brilliant of Roger to think of it.

"We need to start locally. I've arranged for him to appear on *Good Day, Dallas,* here in town after the first of the year."

"Oh, my gosh! Wow, that would put him on the map!"

"Well, it would get us on the road. The actual map might be a long way off." He chuckled.

"He's lucky to have you," I said, masking the jealousy I felt.

Another long silence passed before Roger asked, "So, how are the gift cards coming?"

I laughed, remembering our "chance" meeting at Coffee Heaven so many weeks earlier. "Not bad. I've put two of the four to good use so far. I'll use one before the wedding, and the remaining one will be my reward."

"Reward?"

"Yes, I'm going to be a little selfish come Christmas."

He raised his coffee cup in a salute. "Good for you. I think you need to be a little selfish. You spend a lot of time taking care of everyone else."

I blushed. "I didn't think it showed that much."

"Trust me, Tess, everyone notices."

While it was nice to have someone say such complimentary things to me, I was unused to flattery, and I blushed even deeper.

Roger continued, "In fact, I think you deserve a reward, too, and the events of today have given me an idea."

"An idea? What kind of an idea?"

"Well, I was wondering if—"

"Tess," Donna stuck her head into the living room. "Something's wrong with Lucy. You better come."

****

Lucy was burning up, flushed, and lethargic. Mom's ancient thermometer read Lucy's temperature as somewhere between eighty-five and one-hundred-twenty-seven. Unsure what to do, I called Jacob.

"Get her to the hospital; I'll have her doctor meet us there."

The "us" in his voice was a relief.

Roger, Jack, and I bundled Lucy into my car, and I drove her to the hospital with Roger cradling her in the back seat. The rest of the family followed in a caravan of cars.

The staff hustled her into an exam room immediately. It paid to be dating a rock-star surgeon, I surmised. Roger parked my car, then came in to sit with me.

Looking for something to take my mind off Lucy, I said, "You were about to ask me something at the house."

"Oh, yeah, it can wait."

"That's okay. I need to think about something else. What is it?"

"Okay," he said, smiling. "I was wondering if—"

"How is she?" Whitney demanded as she came in, leading the others through the double doors and into the emergency waiting room.

"She's in with the doctors now," I answered.

"How long before we know anything?" Donna asked, brow furrowed with worry. Paul hovered next to her.

"I don't know. We haven't been told anything yet."

"Well, then, we just need to wait," Jack said. He and Tad sat in the chairs across from me and Roger. Everyone else draped themselves around the room in small clusters. After a moment of silence, the low hum of chatter began.

Jack asked Roger, "Did you find any good locations for Habanera's expansion?"

They began to talk about possible cities for the restaurant. Tad looked bored. I dozed. Thanksgiving had been stressful on a few levels.

A scrubs-clad nurse showed up in the waiting room doorway.

"Is there anyone here for Lucy Trevain?"

We all stood up. "We're her family," I said, and it was the truth. "How is she?"

"Dr. Volmer will be in to speak to you in a moment."

We all sat down.

Jacob came in a moment later, and we all stood again. He saw me and walked over. I braced myself for whatever—I didn't know.

"She has an infection," he said.

"An infection? Of what?"

"The oncologist, Dr. Hightower, isn't sure. We've called in the surgeon I referred Lucy to. He's on the way."

"So, what are you doing in the meantime. Is she still running a fever?"

"Yes, but Dr. Hightower put her on antibiotics, and the fever should come down soon. We just need to figure out where it's coming from."

"So, you're keeping her here overnight?"

"Absolutely. We need to watch her. We'll see where we are tomorrow."

"Can she have visitors?" I asked.

Jacob looked around the room, taking stock of the concerned faces. "Well, I suppose, but not all at once. Can some of you wait until tomorrow?"

The combined Thomason clan, extended friends, and family giggled. I had to laugh. We did make quite the picture.

"No, I'll go in alone. Everyone's here for moral support. Lucy's part of the family, you know."

He nodded. "Yes, I do know. She's talked about you all and she's so grateful, especially to you, Tess, for all you've done. You *are* her family."

Whitney spoke up, voice quivering. "We love her. And we don't want anything to happen to her."

Jack added, "Please take good care of her."

Jacob smiled. "We will. She's in good hands. I don't want to make any promises, but she doesn't seem to be in any immediate danger."

Donna sat down with a heavy sigh. "That's good news. She looked so weak and flushed at the house. I thought she was going to pass out."

Jacob said, "You did the right thing to bring her in. She'll be much better tomorrow." Then he turned back to me. "So, do you want to see her now? She'll be sleeping soon."

We went back to the room where Lucy was hooked up to machines that blinked and whirred and blipped and dripped. Her eyelids drooped, but she smiled when she saw me.

I crossed the tiny room in a single stride and grasped her hand. "What in the world got into you?"

"I couldn't let a whole holiday go by without some drama."

I laughed. "I thought we'd had quite a bit already."

"Yeah"—she smiled—"but it wasn't all about *me*!"

I squeezed her hand, birdlike in mine. "This was your way of getting attention, huh?"

"Yep, it worked, too, didn't it?"

"Sure did." I watched as she struggled to stay awake. "Look, sweetie, I'm leaving. The whole gang is out there, and I need to get them home. You can only have so much fun in one day."

She smiled. "See you tomorrow."

"See you tomorrow." I turned to leave.

"Tess."

"Yes?" I turned back, my hand on the curtain.

"I love you." She snuggled into the pillow; her head lolled to one side.

"I love you, too."

That night when I got home and Donna and Sydney had gone to their rooms, I sat with Slider on my lap at the kitchen counter and ate a Weight Magic Americana Turkey Pot Pie and a beautiful golden brown, warm-from-the-oven dinner roll. It had somehow escaped the tray that carried the others to my mom's house and had risen to its full glorious roundness in the warmth of my quiet kitchen. It was delicious.

And I was thankful.

****

"Tess?"

I heard Sam's voice when I picked up the ringing phone the next morning at work, and I slumped in my chair. I was furiously trying to finish a column about the evil hemline conspiracy, and I didn't have time for handholding or arguing, either one.

"Tess, we had a terrible misunderstanding yesterday. I said some things, and you said some things. And now, well, there's an elephant in the room."

"You think?"

"Yes, I think we need to clear the air."

"Sam, I think we said all there was to say yesterday."

"I'm sorry I said those things about your kids and Jack. You know I didn't mean them."

"I accept your apology."

There was a long silence, then he said, "Well, aren't you going to apologize to me?"

I took a deep breath to steady the growing anger I felt. "No, Sam, I'm not. I think Susan was the one who needed to apologize to Donna and the rest of my family."

"She couldn't do that."

I let the breath out in a whoosh. "I know. I know. That's why we need to let it go now."

He sighed. "I don't want to let it go, Tess. Let you go. I need you. I don't know what to do."

"I think you're going to have to spend some time,

some uncomfortable time, helping Susan confront the truth. And I think you need to do that without me in the way."

"What do you mean? Are you breaking up with me?"

I smiled. "Oh, Sam, we aren't even together enough to break up. Your wife and Susan are always between us. The elephant in the room is them."

"But Julia could go on for a long time the way she is."

"And you and Susan have to come to terms with that and figure out how to move on with your lives. Sam, you're *both* unwilling to let her go. You just handle it in different ways. You're guilty, and she's frightened. Maybe you can help each other."

He was quiet for a minute, then said, "There's a support group at the Alzheimer's Center."

"Well, that would be a great first step."

"You could come with me," he said.

I hardened my resolve.

"No, you have to do this alone. The truth is I've been using our relationship as a crutch to keep from moving forward with my life, too."

"What do you mean?"

"Well, I spend all my time taking care of other people—Lucy, Donna, Whitney, Syd's dog, even you. I can't remember the last time I did what I wanted to do."

"I thought you liked taking care of everyone. Being the mother to everyone."

"It's not that I don't like it. But there's got to be something out there that's, well, more about *me*."

"So, like you want to play an instrument, learn a language? We could do that together."

"No, it's not like that." I sighed and rubbed my hand across my eyes. "I think this is something I need to do on my own. I think maybe that's what self-discovery is all about."

"Self-discovery?"

It had been a long time since I'd thought about anything but the moment. What had to happen right then. What other people needed from me right that second. I no longer knew myself very well, what I thought, what I wanted. "Yeah, I need to discover myself, I guess. Explore new places. Have new experiences. Meet new people."

"Like Roger?"

That had come out of left field. I laughed. "For heaven's sake, where did that come from?"

"I saw how close you two are."

"Don't be silly. He's gay. And apparently a rival for Tad."

"Could've fooled me. You just never know anymore."

Yeah, you just never know.

Chapter Thirteen

Sensible Shoes
By Tess Thomason
The Christmas season, Yuletide, Advent, whatever you call it—the four-week period between Thanksgiving and Christmas is without a doubt my favorite time of year.

Sure, I know it's commercialized and crazy busy and materialistic, and the true meaning of the season has been lost in the tawdriness of tinsel and twinkling lights.

Frankly, I don't care.

I still love it. I am mesmerized by the riotous light display my neighbor stages every year, beginning the weekend after Thanksgiving.

I'm a sucker for the store windows, the sales, the extended hours, and the special holiday shopping bags.

I decorate every inch of my house with the same tired decorations each year, including the crèche scene Sydney made in elementary school before Christ was banned from Christmas.

I hang candy canes on the tree and all the handmade ornaments, including the one Whitney made from Popsicle sticks. We think it's a snowflake, but who knows. She can't remember.

I drink homemade spiced cider from an old snowman mug. We eat from special Santa plates. And I wash them by hand.

No amount of trouble is too much at Christmas. I shop, wrap, cook, go, come, clean, plan, listen to the same Christmas albums, and watch It's a Wonderful Life *for the hundredth time. It always makes me cry with such joy at the resiliency of the human spirit.*

So, while this year may be more hectic than most, pockets are more empty than usual, and spirits may be sagging lower than in years past...Christmas is here.

****

Bah, humbug! The thought of dragging the Christmas tree box out from the closet under the stairs was more than I could face.

Lucy was home from the hospital, staying in bed or on the couch and taking an armada of infection-fighting drugs. The fever was just a low-grade annoyance now but was not gone, so they had suspended her chemotherapy until she recovered. Because of that, she felt a little better but was still weak. I was just worried.

In my usual fashion, I burdened Mom with the news of Lucy and then busied myself with preparations for Christmas and the wedding, which was now a mere ten days away.

Someday, I would tell my grandchild that a superhuman effort had been made to keep him (or her, we still didn't know) from being a cute, little bastard child because no one in their right mind would plan a wedding between Thanksgiving and Christmas, especially if family dramas like cancer recovery and marriage separation were playing out in their house.

I didn't mean to sound so harsh, but I was unraveling just the tiniest bit as I dragged the tree box, duct-taped within an inch of its life, into the living room.

We would have a Christmas tree, by golly, despite

my bad mood. It would be heresy not to. I couldn't do that to the menagerie of weirdness living in my house. Something would be normal, and that something was the tree.

Lucy sat grinning at me from the couch, Tuxedo on her lap, as I ripped open the box and dumped it on the floor.

"What?!" I demanded, glaring at her.

"Nothing. You're just so cute when you're in the Christmas spirit." She giggled.

"Shut up." I stomped to the bottom of the stairs and hollered, "Sydney!"

"He's walking Slider," Lucy offered.

"Well, that's something, isn't it?" I came back into the living room and stood across from Lucy, hands on my hips. "How about Donna, oh, Font of All Knowledge. Is she here?"

"No, Paul and the boys picked her up a while ago to go to their holiday pageant at school."

"Well, two Christmas miracles in one night. I may faint with joy."

"Yeah, you're stuck here with me, and as we both know, I'm not to leave this couch. Although I can hand you ornaments." She gestured to the tree, lying in three pre-lit pieces on the living room floor. "As soon as you get this thing put together."

I plopped down on the couch next to her. "Lord, will this year never end?" I put my head in my hands, more as a dramatic gesture than anything else.

Lucy was unaffected. "Oh, cut it out. You know you love Christmas. Now, get your ass up and show this tree who's boss."

I did as I was told, and about twenty minutes later,

we were sipping spiced tea from Santa mugs and staring at the nude, twinkling tree.

"Perhaps I could leave it this way," I ventured. "We could have a natural Christmas, no tacky tinsel, no boring balls, no handmade angels."

"Hmm, not even this?" She held up Whitney's snowflake.

"Okay, maybe this one. Snowflakes are natural, after all." I took it and hung it on the tree, right in the middle of the front. It had never had such a place of honor before.

"And this?" She held a tiny baby carriage, the ornament I bought after the twins were born.

"Okay, that one, too. What's more natural than a baby?"

"Right, and this?"

An hour later, long after Sydney had come in and started helping, the array of ornaments was hung. We sat in the dark and marveled at the glory of it all, shimmering and glistening and twinkling just as in years past.

I pitied the people who had a tree with elegant silver balls and dignified white lights.

As we were about to turn off the glittering array and head up to bed, the door flew open, and Donna came in, crying.

Since Thanksgiving, she and Paul had been talking on the phone almost daily, alternately flirting in whispered tones and screaming their lungs out at each other. I knew the day was coming when she would return to her family and her home. I just hoped the changes she needed would have occurred by then.

"What's wrong? Is everyone all right?"

"Yes," she blubbered. "Everyone's fine. The play

was cute. All about Santa's toy shop. Jason was an elf, and Matt was a-a—a reindeer."

"So, what's wrong?"

"Well, the boys wanted ice cream after the play, and even though it's a school night, I thought it would be okay since it was a special occasion, and other families were going. But Paul said no he thought they should go straight home and to bed. And we argued about it."

"I'm sorry you argued, but at least lately you're sharing your opinions. I mean, you used to do everything Paul said without question, right?"

"Yes, that's true."

Lucy said, "So an argument is a good sign, then."

"I suppose so, but the argument really wasn't the problem."

"What do you mean?" I asked.

"Paul got so angry I was arguing with him. He said he'd given me all this time to come to my senses, and he couldn't believe I was still being so stubborn."

I shook my head. "Oh, dear. It doesn't seem he's come very far, does it."

"That's what I thought. But then he apologized and said it was okay, that we could get ice cream, but that when the kids flunked school, it would be my fault."

"Oh, passive-aggressive. Now, we're getting somewhere," Lucy said, rubbing her hands together.

"That's good?"

"Yes, it means he feels trapped, frustrated, like he's not in control. It's a way of getting to you through guilt, but his hands are clean because he said it was okay with him."

She didn't answer for a moment, contemplating. "Oh, I think I get it."

I asked, "So what did you say?"

"Well, I ended up deferring to him, of course. I didn't want the kids to flunk school. So, then the kids were mad at me because we didn't get ice cream. I ended up being the bad guy."

"Funny how that works, isn't it?" Lucy shook her head. "My mother plays that game all the time."

Donna asked, "How do you stop it?"

"With my mother, I don't because I don't care."

I offered, "But you can shut Paul down by saying, 'That's right, but I think we'll go ahead.' Then he's lost his ammunition. And you still get ice cream. Unless, of course, you believe the kids will flunk because of it."

"Don't be silly," Donna said. "They're way too smart to flunk because of one late night."

"Well, in that case, you're gold," Lucy said.

Donna sniffed once and then brightened. "Okay, so you think I've made progress?"

"Of course," Lucy said with confidence.

"I agree. He's on the ropes." I hugged Donna.

"I hope you're right. I'd like to be home by Christmas."

After she had bounded up the stairs, cheered by our conversation, I looked at Lucy, who shook her head. "Maybe by next Christmas."

"If she's lucky."

****

If Donna were going to be at my house until Christmas or beyond, then I would get the good out of her. I had no compunction about asking her to do any and everything to help me with the wedding. It kept her busy and moved things along much faster than anything Whitney and I could have done alone, given that we were still working during the day.

So, Donna and Lucy, when she felt up to it, wrapped votive candles in tulle and ribbon for the place settings, tore petals from silk flowers for the centerpieces, shopped for snacks to take to the church, and tied bows on the ecru ceremony programs.

It turned out Donna was a gifted party planner, as I should have suspected from all her practice hostessing for Paul. Wedding gifts poured in, and she set the most beautiful table in the dining room to display them after Whitney and Mark unwrapped them. Then she catalogued each one in a lace-covered scrapbook she made for the bride and groom.

I must admit I was grateful she and Paul had not quite made up. I needed the help.

Lambkin Lennie would arrive any day. I sighed with relief when she emailed to say she'd be staying at Mom and Dad's. Our only remaining bed was the foldout in the den, and while I had enjoyed having Lucy and Donna stay with me, now that Syd was home, too, I wasn't looking forward to tripping over yet another person in the kitchen or bath.

Plus, it kept me from having to tamp down my inevitable jealousy at Lennie's carefree, high-rolling, jet-setting, wine-drinking, cruise-taking, elbow-rubbing life.

Don't get me wrong, I loved my sister. I did. But no two people were ever less alike than she and I. My domestic yin was her global yang. My familial black was her unfettered white. My path of least resistance was her road less traveled.

She was the me I was too afraid to ever be.

I sighed and folded a pile of towels to take upstairs.

****

Sensible Shoes
By Tess Thomason
Expectations unmet are a recurring theme when you hit fifty. Entering the second half of one's life (okay, I'm optimistic, there are new medical advances every day) gives one pause for thought about things left undone in the first half.

Dreams discarded, begun, perhaps abandoned, or set aside amidst fear of failure, or worse, fear of success. Dreams with too high a cost: relinquishing of family or friends, home, familiarity, security, prestige and power, or money. Dreams that crashed against the rocks of physical, emotional, or mental shortcomings.

At fifty it's easy to rationalize the loss of dreams, to categorize them and file them and closet them away in shoe boxes, neatly labeled and stacked in the dark.

We don't dare blow the dust off and open them up because, at fifty, it's hard to become a rock star, an airline pilot, a neurosurgeon, or the President of the United States when all you've been is an insurance salesman, a teacher, or a truck driver. Or a writer and a mother.

At fifty we come to terms with who and what we have become. It's okay I'm not a rock star. I didn't even know that's what I wanted to be until I was thirty-five. And by then, I had outgrown spandex and spiked hair. So, at fifty maybe I'll sing in a choir or in the shower or to my grandchild.

And that's okay by me.
****

"You look amazing!" Lennie squealed when she saw me. "My God, you've lost like a hundred pounds!"

"About twenty, actually, but thanks, I think," I said, hoisting her suitcase into the back of my car at the airport. "You look wonderful as always. Is that new hair?"

She fluffed her cute red pixie cut with one hand. "You like it? I'm not sure. Antoine said it suited me, but what does he know? I've only been going to him for six months. I'd been with Serge for five years. He knew every strand of my hair. It was devastating to lose him."

"Did he die?"

"God, no! He went back to Belgrade. An immigration thing."

I touched a hand to my hair, still straight and brown, still grazing my shoulders, thanks to whoever was working at The Clipper Shop on Saturday.

Geez, I need to get a life.

"So, what's been going on with you?" she asked, checking her lipstick in an enameled compact. "I hear you have Lucy with you and Donna and Sydney. It must be a madhouse."

"Well, it's pretty crazy, like a giant slumber party. Only there's more crying."

"Yeah, I can imagine. How is Lucy?"

"Not sure. She's had to suspend chemo because of this infection, and she just seems weaker all the time. Donna and Paul are sort of inching their way back together, but I never realized how big a jerk our brother is."

"Oh, I had an inkling. What I don't understand is how he got that way. Mom and Dad didn't do that to him, did they?"

"I don't think so. I think maybe it was college and some fraternity he was in: Macho Woman-Haters Phi Psi

Chi. Anyway, it's high time Donna got some of her own back."

Lennie giggled. "I hope things work out for them, maybe before Christmas, for the boys' sake, at least."

We pulled into the driveway at Mom and Dad's just in time to see Donna stomp out of the house with Paul in hot pursuit. She wheeled around and threw something at him that looked like a card of some sort. He ducked and swore and loped back into the house.

I looked at Lennie. "I wouldn't hold my breath."

****

The dust-up between Paul and Donna seemed to be about the wedding. Not Whitney's, although that was the catalyst. Matt and Jason had spent the night with my folks. My match-making mother had invited Donna over for lunch, knowing Paul would be coming to pick the boys up during that time.

As I heard from a tearful Donna later, they were all having a lovely time, eating chicken salad sandwiches, and discussing the upcoming nuptials. Donna was studying the invitation and reliving her own wedding.

"It was beautiful," Donna told the boys, who were leaning in, elbows on the table. "We were married at a park, on a bridge covered in flowers, overlooking a gurgling brook."

Appearing in the doorway, Paul chuckled. "Yeah, which the minister fell into right before the ceremony."

"Sweet!" Jason said, high-fiving his brother.

Donna glared at Paul. "It was unfortunate. It seems he had tippled a bit beforehand, but the wedding was still beautiful."

Mom patted her hand. "It was, dear. Never mind the gnats."

"Gnats?" Matt asked.

"The gnats were thick as thieves because of the stifling humidity, I guess. We could barely cut the cake."

"Gross!" Matt exclaimed.

"It's okay," Paul continued, laughing out loud by now. "We were saved by the rain."

"Geez, what a disaster." Jason breathed.

Indignant, Donna argued, "It was not a disaster. We got through the whole ceremony and the cake-cutting before the rain started. The food was in the pavilion, anyway. We didn't even get wet. I thought the whole thing was rather romantic."

"Maybe for you," Paul said, and according to Donna, this is where he went astray. "I would have preferred something a little less...outdoors."

"So, you hated our wedding?" Donna questioned, admitting to me later that she maybe overreacted a little. "I guess you wish now we'd never gotten married! Why don't you divorce me, then, and marry someone else! *Indoors!*"

That was the point at which she stormed out of the house, with Paul in pursuit. The card she threw back at him? The invitation to Whitney's wedding.

****

Lennie settled into Mom's guest room in about a minute and called me right away, whining she was bored and had a surprise for me if I would please, in the name of all that was holy, come get her.

Ever the sucker for a surprise, I rushed right over. I quickly found out Lennie had heard about the gift cards from my mother and had made an appointment at Patchouli for both of us to have our hair and nails done as a sort of pre-wedding girls' ritual.

"I know you'll never use the card on your own," Lennie said when I began to sputter my usual protests. She picked up my unadorned hand and tossed it down like a rotten tomato. "These nails do not belong on a grown woman. It is high time you came to the party, missy, especially the wedding party."

I sighed. That was all I ever did around Lennie. Sigh and follow along behind, terrified of being left out of the fun, scared to death the fun would kill me somehow. It had always been that way. Why should anything change now?

We opened the door to Patchouli and immediately wafted into the reception area on a cloud of herbal deliciousness. The place was infused with an array of scents, one comingling with the next in the most erotic of ways. It was intoxicating, and I immediately understood why women got their nails done once every two weeks. They had to. They were addicted to the opiates in Patchouli's air and must return for a fix. The nails were just an excuse.

"Mmm," I murmured to Lennie.

"Mmm, is right," she whispered. "This place is aromatherapy heaven. I have to buy some of that."

I chuckled. Of course, she did.

We were robed in clouds of soft baby blue and led, swaying slightly, to recliners where our hair was washed, including a scalp massage that brought tears to my eyes. I asked to have my hair washed again, you know—rinse and repeat—but was turned down by a smiling, beatific angel in a rubber smock. "I get that all the time," she said.

Then we were led to chairs at side-by-side stations, and I knew I wasn't at The Clipper Shop anymore. We were given glasses of white wine, chilled to perfection, and an array of magazines from which to choose. Because my brain was fogged by the mixed scents in the room and the tingling of my scalp, I chose *Teen Weekly* and found myself scanning an article on the pros and cons of the latest social media challenge.

A moment later, I knew why going down the Lennie path had always scared me. A young, robust woman named Miagi (pronounced Mee-ah-gee with a hard gee) approached me, full of life and multi-hued hair.

"Hi. Mom of the Bride, huh? Well, you need something special for the big day, don't you?"

Before I could say a word, Lennie grabbed her by the elbow, and the two put their heads together for a few moments. Forcing myself to engage my relaxed brain, I interrupted. "Hey, my hair and I are over here. What are you two planning?"

"Oh, I was just telling Miagi what I think we should do with your hair."

"Well, shouldn't *you* tell *me* what you have in mind?"

They looked at each other and shook their collective heads. "No," Miagi said. "I think you should trust me to make you look fabulous."

"Don't take this the wrong way, but I don't even know you. You could be the worst hairdresser in the world. I could end up looking like I did in sixth grade after my mom gave me a home perm."

Miagi was unfazed, but Lennie stepped in anyway. "Tess, for God's sake, no one says 'hairdresser' anymore. She's a 'stylist.' And you should know I have Miagi do my hair every time I come to Dallas because she's so good. So calm down." She put her hands on her hips and stared at me. Then she threw in another "for

God's sake" for good measure.

"Okay, then." I raised my hands in surrender. "Do with me as you will. I'm sorry if I insulted you, Miagi. But this may be about the third time I've ever had my hair done."

Lennie rolled her eyes. "Good grief."

Miagi said, her mouth quirked up in the slightest of smiles, "I better do a good job, then. It has to last a really long time."

Three hours later we emerged into the dusky Dallas twilight, Lennie looking as she had gone in, perfect. I, however, had experienced a transformation of epic proportions. My long, stick-straight brown hair was now a short bob streaked with blonde highlights. And my misshapen, clear nails now boasted an elegant gel manicure.

And, as usual, the gift card provided by my overly generous family covered a fraction of the cost.

****

Sensible Shoes
By Tess Thomason
What price beauty?
I'll tell you…an exorbitant one.

I admit I'm not a girly girl. And I'm not sure if that's genetics or logistics. About the time other girls were practicing their goth eyeliner, I was trying to put on makeup without poking myself in the contact lens.

While my sorority sisters buffed, polished, and painted their nails as shown in Glamour magazine, I chipped the you-know-what out of mine, typing articles for the school paper.

After a while, I gave up.

So now, it's not that I don't have time or money, I

simply don't think of it. I've grown used to my unadorned fingernails, my embryo eyes, and my Plain Jane hair.

But today things changed.

In preparation for my daughter's wedding, I have been girlified. My nails are manicured in shimmering turquoise, my makeup is glowing and radiant, and my hair is newly cut in a sleek, blonde bob.

I look gorgeous.

What price beauty? One gift card, an additional two-hundred-dollars-plus-tip, and a relaxing day with my sister. Priceless.

Chapter Fourteen

That night, I turned heads at the rehearsal. My mother wept. My kids crowed with pride. Jack wolf-whistled, which was weird, but my dad was the sweetest.

"You look just like your mom at that age." Then he kissed me on the cheek.

I had met Mark's parents once before, months earlier at his birthday party, before the gift cards, before Lucy, before the baby, before Donna, before the wedding. Before my life turned upside down. Before Lennie cut my hair.

"Goodness, Tess," Kathy Horton gushed when she saw me. "You look fabulous. I nearly didn't recognize you."

I'm sure she didn't mean that the way it sounded.
"Thank you! I feel ten years younger."

"Well, you look it!"

Or that.

Her husband Ben chimed in, pumping my hand, his jovial laugh filling the room. "Just make sure you don't upstage the bride!"

I laughed, too, enjoying this rare moment. "No chance of that, I'm sure."

We had included Roger in the guest list for the rehearsal because of all his help with the reception. He was practically a member of the family now anyway, although Sam's cryptic remark about him did rocket through my consciousness when he walked over and took my hand.

"Wow, this is a great new look for you. Gift card?" he asked, continuing to hold my hand, which I didn't mind.

"As a matter of fact, yes, that and a particularly sneaky sister." I pulled him over to where Lennie regaled several men with her latest exploits in the Amazon.

Roger didn't react to Lennie the way other men did, which surprised me. Other men swept their appreciative gaze down the length of her well-honed body or struggled to keep from stammering some inanity. I had seen it happen many times before, and tonight was no exception. But Roger shook hands, then apologized for interrupting her story, and steered me out of the circle of panting men.

He didn't pant, he didn't stare, he didn't stammer. It was then I was reminded that, yes, he was indeed gay. Sam was nuts.

"So, can I get you a drink?" he asked, smiling.

"Sure, something light, please. I've heard too much about tipsy mothers-of-the-bride. I'm determined to be dignified, stodgy even."

Roger winked at me. "Not looking like you do tonight. You couldn't be stodgy if you tried."

My cheeks burned. I didn't care if he was off-limits. A compliment was a compliment. And it counted twice coming from him.

The rehearsal went off without a hitch. The wedding party consisted of Mark and Whitney and two attendants each, including siblings, plus an usher or two. The minister, a longtime friend who had baptized my kids and counseled me when Jack and I broke apart, was a pro at wedding etiquette, and since we had not hired a bridal consultant, that was a blessing.

Another blessing came in the form of the calmness that had settled over Paul and Donna, who had overcome their earlier blowup. They spent most of their time talking about Christmas plans and staying out of earshot of the boys, who had their heads buried in video games, as usual.

The dinner, hosted by Mark's parents and held at a hotel near the church, was uneventful and gracious, featuring a delicious plateful of something I couldn't remember, much like the rest of the evening, which sped by at a breakneck pace.

There was a slideshow set to current music, which Syd had put together, complete with colorful transitions and titles. The whole thing was quite charming, showcasing Whitney and Mark from birth to college and through their short, if intense, courtship. At the end we all cheered and cried and stood and saluted the engaged couple with half-empty glasses of whatever was handy.

Roger stayed by my side the entire evening, acting, as it were, as an attentive escort, for which I was grateful. There were couples all over the room, and it was nice to be at the elbow of a handsome, intelligent, interesting man. If only for one night.

When I got home, I tiptoed in, trying not to disturb Lucy. She had been so under the weather due to the infection and the drugs she hadn't left the house since she'd come home from the hospital.

Sitting on a stool in the kitchen, I drank a glass of ice-cold milk and prayed the wedding would be as smooth as the rehearsal, but I was aware of the old wives' tale that says the opposite. So, like any old wife would do, I opened the freezer and pulled out a slice of Weight Magic Fudgy Brownie Delight and lifted a little prayer to the wedding gods.

****

Overnight, the gods and the old wives turned against us, and the day dawned stormy and menacing.

I was sure there was an adage out there about a wedding day that starts rainy, but I hadn't heard it. And neither had Whitney when she called in tears the morning of the big day.

So, I made one up.

"Sweetie, haven't you heard the old saying about rainy fall weddings bringing a harvest of blessings?"

"Really?" she blubbered.

"Of course, I think it was Benjamin Franklin or…or…Susan B. Anthony, who said it."

"Who's Susan B. Anthony?"

I rolled my eyes. "Never mind. Hang up, get a cup of coffee, put on your sweats, pack up your stuff, and get yourself over here."

"Okay."

Twenty minutes later, the doorbell rang. I hollered for whoever to come in, assuming it was Whitney.

Jacob Vollmer strolled into the den, shaking raindrops off an umbrella. He looked dashing in a fisherman's sweater and cords. "Hi, is Lucy home?"

I struggled to keep from laughing. First, because he sounded so much like a kid asking a child to come out and play, and second, because he thought Lucy would be somewhere else.

She hadn't been downstairs all morning. I figured she was sleeping late, recovering, and storing up her strength for the evening's festivities.

I composed myself. "Sure, I'll get her."

I flew up the stairs and into Lucy's room, where I found her stuffing two feet into one pants leg. She must have heard Jacob's entrance from upstairs. "Why is he here?"

"I have no idea. Haven't you talked to him?"

"Not in several days. It was his idea for me to recover in peace and quiet."

I lifted one eyebrow.

"I know, I know." She chuckled. "Not a lot of that around here."

"Well, let me help you before you throw yourself on the floor."

A minute later she was heading down the stairs with me hovering for support. I left them in the living room and went into the kitchen under the auspices of making coffee, knowing full well I would be able to hear most of what they said.

Lucy spoke first. "Jacob, I wasn't expecting you. Was I?"

"No, I should have called, but I had to see you. I've let you recover enough, I think."

The next few sentences were muffled, probably by indiscriminate hugging and kissing.

That must be nice.

Jacob ventured, "So, I was thinking that I would take you to the wedding this evening if you like."

"That would be terrific! I've been wondering how I could get out of Tess' hair today. She's got so much to do, and she doesn't need to worry about me. And with you, I wouldn't have to go so early. It's a win-win for everyone but you."

"How do you figure that?"

"Well, you have to deal with the slow, sickly girl who gets tired so fast. No late night for you. Oh, and no dancing. And not much drinking, either. I'm afraid it's a lose-lose for you all around."

"No, that's the evening I was looking for."

"And that's why I lo—like you so much."

Jacob replied in a husky voice, "I lo—like you, too, Lucy."

More muffled discussion followed, intermingled with loud smacking noises. I decided they could get their own coffee.

****

Sensible Shoes

By Tess Thomason

There are so few things that have survived from ancient times. In fact, the only thing I can think of is religion and specifically its rituals and trappings.

I'm not sure if it's fear or fondness that keeps us hanging on to the time-honored traditions, but it's always evident in the wedding ceremony and reception. The ritual of the wedding has amazing staying power.

It seems from generation to generation, the only things that change are the fashions, the food, and the music.

When my ex-husband and I got married, I wore a lace gown with huge, puffed sleeves and the biggest bouffant veil ever crafted. We danced to Rod Stewart and took one step beyond cake and punch with trays of hors d'oeuvres.

At my daughter's wedding, she wore strapless satin, and the groom was in starched white with a bronze cummerbund. The reception was at Habanera, her father's restaurant, with a full dinner and music by a local DJ.

But some things never change and were identical to weddings the world over for millennia past: the processional, the exchange of rings, the vows, the prayer, the pronouncement, the kiss, the recessional.

Even the unity candle is still a part of many American ceremonies, although some brides now choose to mix layers of colored sand in a vase. No matter, mantels still boast the resulting candle or vase until it is crowded out by baby pictures.

Families gather, toasts are made, first dances are watched, cakes are cut, garters and bouquets are tossed.

Rituals familiar and beloved are continued. And the circle of life goes on and on.

I think there's something comforting in that.

****

I was probably not the first Mother-of-the-Bride (MOB for short) who nearly missed the processional. After settling Whitney in the bride's room, getting the videographer acclimated, side-stepping the photographer, showing the men where to get dressed, and setting up the snacks in a third room, I could start getting dressed.

My newly short hair had plastered itself to my head in damp layers, a result of my exertion coupled with a hot flash of mammoth proportions that swept over me the minute I sat down. I fanned myself with a snack-sized bag of cheese crackers from the hospitality basket.

The cooling-off period took longer than usual, but I didn't want to put my beautiful bronze-colored dress on damp skin, so I sat there in a tee shirt, watching as Whitney posed for pictures with first this friend and then another. She was glowing and very pregnant.

I let Lennie do my makeup, too tired for once to insist on doing everything myself. She painstakingly applied eye shadow in two shades, expertly swiped blush across the apples of my cheeks, defined my lashes with layers of mascara, and painted a luscious mouth with the precise shade of scarlet to complement my eyes.

"What do you think?" Lennie asked when she spun me around. I looked in the mirror and gasped a little at the transformation. There was color, but not too much; drama, but not too much; and enough subtle sex appeal to make me blush for real.

"My goodness." I breathed, afraid to speak lest the spell be broken.

"Mom, you look amazing." Whitney squeezed my shoulder.

I hugged Lennie. "Thank you."

"You're welcome," she whispered.

She and Whitney slipped my dress over my head just as the photographer and videographer insisted they get pictures of me with the bride. But first, I had them take a picture of me with my sister.

For the first time I could ever remember, I felt as pretty as Lennie.

Then, we staged a few pictures with Whitney. I loved having the opportunity to straighten her veil and clasp her necklace as they snapped away.

I whispered a few motherly tidbits in her ear. "I know it's too late to give you the sex talk," I said, patting her rounded belly. "But I will tell you, in spite of your very pronounced indiscretion, I am immensely proud of you. I think Mark is a great guy. I want only wonderful things for you. And I love you desperately."

She hugged me close and whispered back, "I love

you, too, Mom, thank you so much for everything."

Donna stuck her head in the dressing room door then and said, "It's time. They've started the next to last prelude song."

Lennie and the camera people hurried out. Whitney went to meet her father, and I was following them when I realized I didn't see my parents in the throng gathered by the doors to the sanctuary. *Where are they?*

After a moment of searching, I found Mom by the snacks. I asked her where Daddy was.

"In the men's room, dear," she said. "It's his enlarged prostate."

"I appreciate knowing that, Mom. And I know Dad would be so glad you shared, but we need to get you in line. I'll find him."

I handed her off to Sydney who would escort her and my dad to their seats and went in search of Daddy. I found him in the men's room down the hall, scrubbing at a spot on his tuxedo shirt.

"Daddy, what's wrong? We need to line up."

He looked up at me. "I dripped coffee on my shirt. See?"

There was a faint wet spot on the shirt, and I suddenly had the most powerful protective feeling toward my father, the man who had held me in his hands at the beginning of it all. I was overcome with love for him and my mother.

It's so strange how these things hit you.

"No, Daddy," I answered him, regaining my composure, "I think you got it all. I'm sure no one will notice. It's time to start. Let's go."

I looped my hand through the crook of his arm and hurried us out and down the hall to where the line had formed, and the strains of Pachelbel's Canon in D began. Sydney grabbed Mom, and I shoved Dad down the aisle after them.

I hugged Whitney one last time and winked at Jack, who had tucked her hand into his arm. They made a striking couple, and my breath caught in my throat.

What the hell is wrong with me? Pull yourself together, girl.

Sydney materialized next to me and led me down the aisle to my seat.

I think I was smiling.

****

The actual ceremony was somewhat of a blur, seen through tears and unutterable fatigue. At one point, I almost dozed off.

But it was beautiful, and Whitney and Mark stared lovingly at each other, and Whitney's dress draped elegantly over her bulging belly, and I didn't even care.

I glanced down the row at my family and stole a peek behind me. The church was not full, but almost so, with friends and family from both sides of the aisle, people who wished the new couple well. People who would form a foundation of love for Whitney and Mark to build their newly joined life upon. People who would be gossiping like crazy later.

When the ceremony was over, the bride and groom and their attendants danced down the aisle and out of the chapel to a current popular tune I sort of recognized. Non-dancers, Jack, and I followed, laughing. And when we got to the narthex, we hugged and kissed and congratulated each other as if it were all our doing.

Which, in a way, it was.

****

The reception, too, was a blur of activity, congratulations, food, dancing, and fun. I wandered from table to table, thanking friends for coming, introducing myself to strangers, stopping to nibble on the various concoctions Jack and Roger had come up with to make the buffet more memorable than any I had witnessed.

The DJ's playlist was mostly unfamiliar to me, but I found I didn't care what he played. I had a wonderful time, and everything went beautifully. I danced with Mark and Syd and Jack and even had one musical moment with Whitney, but I couldn't take my eyes off Lennie.

She was breathtaking in a silvery gray sheath that skimmed her slender body. On her feet glinted rhinestone-studded sandals with six-inch heels. And although she'd been dancing with every man in the room, eligible and otherwise, she was still powdery cool. I tamped down my lifelong envy and made my way over to her, grabbing a couple of champagne flutes on the way. I handed her one, and we sank into two chairs at the edge of the dance floor.

"The whole thing is fabulous, Tessy," she said, saluting me with her flute and taking a long draught.

I sighed. "It has turned out well, hasn't it?"

"It's perfect."

"Well, not perfect. I'm sure Whitney could tell you all the imperfections. But I doubt anyone else would ever notice."

"I certainly can't find anything wrong. It's just as I knew it would be."

"What do you mean?"

"It's warm, beautiful, welcoming, elegant, but comfortable somehow. Just like you."

I searched her face for sarcasm or teasing but found none. "You're serious."

"Of course. You always know how to make everyone feel special. You have a knack for entertaining effortlessly. Look around you. Everyone's having a great time without any embarrassing, tacky party antics."

I was about to thank her for the compliment when the DJ started playing the "Chicken Dance," and dozens of people flocked to the dance floor with their hands cupped incongruously at their bottoms.

I laughed. "Spoken too soon, I think."

"Don't worry about it. I once went to a wedding where the culmination of the evening was chugging a whiskey shot every time the couple kissed. I've never seen more drunk people trying to find their cars in my life. It was carnage."

I feigned leaving. "I'll be right back. I have to tell Jack to cancel the whiskey shots."

We both laughed. Then I said, in a more serious tone, "You know, one of the best things about this whole wedding has been getting to visit with you. You're so busy being a jet-setting celebrity journalist that we never get to see you."

Lennie demurred. "Not a celebrity, I assure you."

"You're a celebrity to us. I can't imagine having your life. Wearing gorgeous clothes, traveling to exotic places, hobnobbing with imams and emirs and shamans and whatnot. Do you have to pinch yourself sometimes?"

She slumped a bit in her chair. "The truth is, Tess, I'm a little tired of it all. I miss all the holidays. Mom and Dad are getting older, and I feel like I've abandoned them. I barely even know Matt and Jason, not that I want to, but still." She grinned.

"Yeah, but you have such freedom, no responsibilities except to yourself, no one's schedule but your own. You've seen the world. I've seen North Texas."

"Oh, Tess, you can't imagine how lucky you are. Surrounded by people you love and sharing your life with them. You're doing things that matter. Things that will last. You're building the future. I see things that have already been."

I'd never seen this side of Lennie, and I was stunned. I had always thought she was perfect and perfectly happy. "Lennie, I've always wanted to be you."

She put her flawless, manicured hand on my arm. Tears shimmered in her eyes. "And I've always wanted to be you."

I hugged her close, and we both murmured, "I love you" into each other's ear. Then she tugged me to my feet. "Enough of that crap. Let's dance."

The DJ had taken a break after the humiliation of having to play the "Chicken Dance" and Sydney's phone provided the music. The singer's voice urged someone to "Put a Ring on It." Dozens of women flocked to the dance floor, including Lucy, who had stayed at her table the entire night. It was great to see her get a little of her groove back. But Donna was the big surprise, shimmying like a diva. Paul almost licked his lips, watching her.

When the song was over, Lennie and I grabbed Daddy and led him onto the floor where we danced to Bruno Mars. Donna and Lucy and Whitney joined us to create a moment suspended in time. Every camera in the room flashed at the picture we made, and I knew it would be one I would treasure. We led Dad back to his table. Mother took his hand, tears shimmering in her eyes.

"See, Mom, we brought him back in one piece," I assured her with a kiss on her damp cheek.

Lennie glanced my way and winked. Before I could speak to her, an elderly neighbor whisked her back out onto the dance floor, and our moment was gone.

I wandered over to the cake and was considering whether I wanted a second piece of the delicious jalapeno version when someone tapped on my shoulder. I turned to find Roger there, looking dashing in his black suit.

"Hey, there," he said, "care to dance?"

Jack and Roger had danced with nearly everyone in the room all evening. I'm sure they felt it was their duty. I didn't think anyone would have cared if they had danced with each other. Tad and Jack certainly had done so, and no one had raised an eyebrow. Roger seemed to enjoy dancing first with one smitten female guest and then another, beguiling them all with his charms. *Why shouldn't I dance with him, too? I'll probably never get the chance again.*

I took his outstretched hand, buoyed by several glasses of wine. "I'd love to."

He led me onto the dance floor, snugged his hand into the small of my back, and pulled me to him. I went willingly.

He held me close, and in a move I didn't think twice about until later, I rested my head against his shoulder and let my fingers weave their way through the hair at the nape of his neck. Nothing had ever felt more natural.

I found myself swaying to Tony Bennett singing "The Best is Yet to Come."

I thought he might be right.

And then it happened.

Two burly policemen strolled into Habanera, meaty fists clutching the collars of two boys who squirmed ineffectually against their iron grasps.

"Matt! Jason!" Donna screamed and ran toward them, with Paul close behind. "Are you all right? What happened?"

"What the hell is going on, officer?" Paul demanded.

"Sir, are you the father of these young men?"

"Yes, I most certainly am. And this is their mother. I'm Paul Thomason."

"Well, Mr. Thomason, it appears your sons here got into a little mischief out in the parking lot."

Matt disagreed. "We didn't do anything wrong."

Jason added. "Yeah, it's what you're supposed to do at weddings."

The second policeman, still holding Jason, said, "They were writing on the cars with these." He held out two bottles of shoe polish.

Donna covered her face with her hands. "Oh, God."

Paul said, "Well, officer, it's customary to write on the bride and groom's car."

"Yes, sir, that's true. But I'm afraid your sons took it a bit farther."

"So, they wrote on other people's windows?"

The first policeman shook his head. "Not just on the windows. I'm afraid they've also taken out a few fenders and hoods."

"Oh, God," Donna repeated, her hands muffling the sound.

"Oh," Paul said, "Well, I guess they didn't understand the concept that it's only the bride and groom's car that gets the well wishes. I'm sure everyone will understand, and we'll take care of any expenses."

The second policeman said, "There's a little more to it, Mr. Thomason. Maybe you should come see for yourself."

An entourage proceeded to the parking lot consisting of the two policemen, still in possession of the heinous felons, Paul and a reluctant Donna, plus one hundred of our closest friends and family, and a few curious waiters.

None of us were prepared for the scene that greeted us.

The parking lot of Habanera was full to overflowing with every kind of car imaginable, and, since this was Texas, a preponderance of SUVs and trucks. And each and every one of them boasted some lewd, disgusting, or nasty word written in huge white letters, mostly misspelled.

There was a collective gasp, followed by more than one person choking back laughter. That was probably the waitstaff whose cars were safely parked out back. Several poor souls went running for their cars.

"Oh, my God, oh, my God," Donna said over and over.

"Officer," Paul said with steely calm. "Go ahead and do what you like to my sons. My wife and I will meet you at the police station."

The policeman gave Paul a look of respectful understanding and whipped out a pair of handcuffs. The other officer followed suit.

"Dad! Mom!" Matt screamed as the cuffs snapped shut. "What are you doing? We were just having some fun!"

Jason yelled, "Dad, tell them to let us go! Get us out

of this! Mom! Do something!"

Donna buried her head in Paul's shoulder, hands over her ears. Paul turned to Jack, who was standing next to me, and said, "Tell everyone I'll take care of any damage to their cars. They just need to call me." He watched as the boys were led to the patrol car. "And tell them we're sorry. Especially Whitney and Mark."

He led Donna to their car, which had been spared from shoe polish epithets. They followed the patrol car, with Matt and Jason crying in the back seat, out of the parking lot, and away from the scene of the crime.

People straggled back inside. Jack sent the busboys to the lot with wet cloths, hoping to reduce some of the damage and keep people from having to drive home with misspelled obscenities on their cars. Many of the men joined in to help.

A few people left, heading no doubt to the car wash.

But the rest stayed, enjoying more cake and wine, until the bouquet was thrown, and the garter was tossed.

When the traditional rituals were complete and the DJ finished his last set, people said their goodbyes, offering condolences about the boys, getting Paul's number, and grabbing the personalized Christmas ornaments Whitney and Mark had created as favors for their guests.

In the confusion over Jason and Matt, we had forgotten to put out the second box of ornaments, and the first one emptied quickly. While everyone lined the entrance of the restaurant to send off the bride and groom, I ran to get the other box.

When I got back to the entrance, the lines were breaking up and the limo hired to whisk away the happy couple was gone. And so was the happy couple.

Wait a minute! What happened here? Are they gone? And I didn't get to say goodbye?

I waited for someone to tell me that wasn't the case, but the longer I stood there, more people grabbed an ornament from the box I still held and headed to the parking lot, telling me what a wonderful time they had.

"Jack!" I hollered and headed toward him, standing at the end of the sidewalk, talking to the photographer. "What the hell?"

"Oh, there you are! We looked for you. Where did you go?"

"I went to get the other box of favors. Why didn't you wait for me?"

"The kids knew everyone was in a hurry to get their cars taken care of. They didn't think you'd mind."

"Didn't think I'd mind? Are you kidding? I just wanted to say goodbye and tell Whitney how much I love her." Unexpected tears ran down my cheeks.

Jack grabbed my shoulders and looked straight into my eyes. "Don't you think she knows that? For heaven's sake, Tess. Look around you. There's nothing but a big mountain of love here, and you built it."

"I didn't do all this. You and Roger did most of it."

He shook his head. "I'm not talking about the reception. I'm talking about the family. You're the hub, the fulcrum, the glue—whatever you want to call it. No one would be here if not for you."

The tears kept falling. "I don't think so. I feel like everything is slipping away from me. It all seems like chaos. I can't fix anything."

"Think what things would be like if you weren't here. Lucy, Donna, Whitney. We'd all be in a world of hurt, my girl, if you weren't holding things together.

We're lucky to have you."

"That's what people keep saying, but—"

"Yeah, well, they're right."

He kissed me on the cheek, squeezed my shoulders, and said, "Now, turn around and wait for it." He spun me around.

"Wait for what?"

As I stared down the street, I saw a long, white limo round the turn, come toward us, and stop at the curb. The door opened and Whitney jumped out and ran toward me, veil flying behind her.

"I couldn't leave without saying goodbye to you, but I couldn't find you, and we wanted everyone to be able to take care of their cars, so I made them turn around and come back." She flew at me, all tummy and arms and tulle, and hugged me hard.

I sobbed into her hair. "Oh, sweetie, I went back for the stupid ornaments. I'm so glad you came back. I love you so much."

"I love you, too and thank you, thank you for such a beautiful wedding. It was amazing."

"You're amazing."

"No, you're amazing."

Jack stepped in. "You're both amazing, but Whit, you and Mark need to get some sleep. You have an early flight tomorrow."

Mark had gotten out of the limo by this time, and he came around the car, shook Jack's hand, and hugged me. "Thanks so much, both of you, for everything."

Whitney slipped into his embrace. "And let us know how it turns out with the boys, okay?" She giggled a little. "They really are little monsters, aren't they?"

"Yeah, maybe this will teach them a lesson."

Whitney and Mark got back into the limo and rolled down the window to wave. I walked over to the car. "Wait, don't forget this. It'll help you remember this night." I handed them one of the ornaments that had been my downfall.

Whitney smiled, eyes glistening. "Don't worry, Mom, we're never going to forget it. Thanks to you."

They drove off down the street, and on the back window of the limo, in white shoe polish, was written "2 BUTTHEDS."

****

Sensible Shoes
By Tess Thomason
A wise woman once wrote that it takes a village to raise children, and I think that's true. When children go wrong, who's to blame? Poor parenting? Youthful exuberance? Or society for glorifying inappropriate behavior through movies, TV, and music? Or celebrities who prove to be less than favorable role models through their indiscretions? Or the schools for failing to teach right from wrong?

I tend to think it's all the above. Of course, parents are to blame for raising hellions who grow up learning to flaunt authority, hate ethnicity, and fear diversity. What about parents who bail their kids out of every scrape, so they never learn responsibility or self-control. And then there are the powerless parents whose children seem predisposed to bad behavior and poor choices. What can they do?

Sure, kids want to have fun, take risks, and sometimes even rebel a little. Those are stepping stones on the path to adulthood, and they help us learn what works and what doesn't. But there need to be boundaries, schedules, rules, structure, and procedures. Kids need to know parents, teachers, police officers, doctors, and yes, even lawmakers, are figures of authority and deserve respect. That there are people who know more than they do.

Yes, I do think society has a role in raising responsible children, and showing them right from wrong, good from bad, and wholesome from nasty. We need to clean up our airwaves, our music, our magazines, our online discourse, wherever children are or have access to. Parents need to use oversight and program blockers, whatever tools live in their arsenal, to let kids be kids, but protect them from inappropriate material. Do I want censorship? Heck, no. I want parenting.

And last, I wish we could idolize a better class of people than overpaid athletes, actors, and that strange group of characters known as "celebrities" who haven't done anything but end up as paparazzi fodder. In fact, let's not idolize anyone. Idols tend to tarnish. Let's all work to be everyday role models.

After all, it takes a village.

Chapter Fifteen

After Mark and Whitney left, I hurried back into Habanera to find Lennie, Roger, and the restaurant staff packing up presents, pictures, guestbooks, bouquets, and a variety of odds and ends, without which it seemed impossible to stage a wedding.

Jack and I joined them, and in a few minutes, we loaded things into my car. What I hadn't realized was it had taken several trips, plus Whitney's car, to get it all to Habanera, and the load seemed to have grown exponentially. It wasn't going to fit in a single vehicle.

Roger said, "Put some in my car, and I'll follow you home."

"That's out of your way, isn't it?"

"Not as much as it is for Lennie. And Jack has to stay to lock up. It makes sense, and I don't mind at all."

A little thrill went up my spine. An extension of the evening spent with Roger was always welcome. "Okay, then, thank you. You know how to get there if we get separated."

Fifteen minutes later we were unloading things from my driveway into the house.

When we were through, I offered him a drink. He accepted, and I felt that little thrill again.

I poured two glasses of wine and handed one to him. "Thanks so much for everything. All your work on the reception, your patience with me and Whitney, this—" I gestured to the pile of wedding paraphernalia on the sofa and coffee table. "Everything."

He took a step forward. "It was nothing. I was glad to help."

"It's like you've become a member of the family."

He smiled, and a warmth spread through me.

He said, "I was so lucky to meet Jack. My relationship with him has changed everything for me."

Whoa. Of course. His relationship with Jack.

I took a step back and murmured, "I'm glad." An awkward silence filled the room. I schooled my expression into a smile. "Let me walk you out. You're probably exhausted."

A flash of something—disappointment? Surprise? crossed his face. "Uh, sure. It's been a long day."

When the door closed after him, I locked it. Then I turned out the lights in the den. And with more reckless disregard for my own health than I had exhibited in four months, I walked deliberately into the kitchen, poured myself a glass of whole milk, and ate the three donuts left on the counter from breakfast.

It didn't help.

****

The next day I had lunch with Lennie. She would leave for Kenya in a few days, and I wanted to spend a little more time with her. Ours had been a surprising reunion for me, one I wanted to prolong. It was as if I'd made a wonderful, new friend.

We met for a salad at La Toscana, a quiet little bistro in a trendy uptown shopping center.

As we were perusing the menu, beads of perspiration popped out on my upper lip. I fished in my purse for something to fan myself with and found a receipt from the drugstore.

"Good grief," I exclaimed.

Lennie looked up from her menu and cocked her head. "Are you all right? You're sweating."

"Yeah, hot flashes. They're the worst. I guess you haven't gotten them yet."

"Oh, yeah, I got them for about a minute, then I went to my doctor and said, 'I cannot do this; give me something.' So, I'm on hormones."

"Aren't you worried about side effects?"

"I guess I'm more worried about my silk blouses."

I laughed. I didn't own a silk blouse, so the problem hadn't come up. "But what about breast cancer? After what happened to Lucy, I'm not taking any chances."

"Yeah, it's a risk, I know, but I'm all about risks, right? Anyway, Mom hasn't had any trouble with that."

"A lot of things can happen at her age. She's always been the Rock of Gibraltar, but you never know," I mused.

"Well, she's getting older. They both are."

"I don't know what I'd do without Mom to burden with all my problems."

Lennie laughed. "You, you've got to be kidding. You don't have any problems." She seemed genuinely surprised.

"You must have missed the news about my divorce, Lucy's cancer, our brother's separation, and my pregnant daughter." I smiled, thinking of the fall I'd been through. "And don't forget the inevitable cleanup from Jason and Matt's little escapade last night. Who's gonna blame who for that mess?"

"You mean you talk to Mom about all that stuff?"

"Yeah, what do you talk to her about?"

"The scenery, the weather, the food, wherever I am, I guess."

I laughed then. "We're the yin and yang of phone calls, too. And I bet she likes yours more. No worries."

"Yeah, but not much of anything. It might be nice to think about something other than what I'm having for dinner."

"Well, I do need to reduce my dependence on Mom. Give her a little less stress."

"Well, then," Lennie said, patting my knee with a manicured hand. "You can tell me all your woes. I'd love for us to talk more."

I picked up my phone and punched some buttons.

"What are you doing?" she asked.

"I'm putting you in my favorites."

****

The newspaper column had become something of a catharsis for me. I was able to funnel day-to-day frustrations and observations into the somewhat anonymous vehicle. Of course, I wasn't writing an op-ed piece about health care or military spending. There wasn't much threat in writing about holiday decorating or cutting coupons.

The truth was I enjoyed writing the column. I also enjoyed the low-level attention it afforded me. Readers emailed with comments and questions and ideas for columns. I occasionally found flowers or cookie bouquets on my desk with cards reading "You helped me" or "Thanks for making me smile today."

Who would have ever guessed anyone out there read *Sensible Shoes*, much less that it meant something?

So, I was not surprised when Ruth called me into her office the Friday before Christmas. I was expecting a pat on the back and the customary year-end bonus. I could use it when the wedding expenses showed up on my credit card bill.

"Sit down, Tess," she said.

I did so without trepidation.

"You've done an amazing job on the column this fall."

"Thank you. I'm surprised to admit I enjoyed it a great deal."

"Yes, I can tell, which is why this is especially hard for me."

So, I'm not getting a bonus?

She continued, leaning back with her fingers tented in front of her, partially obscuring her craggy face, "Sylvia is coming back. *Fashionista* returns on New Year's Day. So, we won't need *Sensible Shoes* anymore. We can't afford to have two columnists."

I felt as if her manly fist had punched me in the stomach. "So, I'm going back to Lawn & Garden, then." It would be hard to go back. But I had only missed one season. I could pick up the column with "Keeping Poinsettias Alive," always a seasonal favorite. I shoved aside the weight of disappointment.

"Well, the truth is Stan has done a good job with Lawn & Garden, and of course, we don't pay him as much as we pay you. He doesn't have the years of experience. And I'm sure you realize with newspapers struggling as they are, we have to cut corners everywhere we can. I'm sorry, Tess. We'll be letting you go. Your last column will be on New Year's Eve."

I struggled for breath, and my hands shook so violently I had to clasp them tightly in my lap. "You're firing me?"

"We're asking you to retire. We can offer you a package and bridge you to early retirement age, which is fifty-two." Her voice was quiet and more motherly than I had ever heard it.

I wanted to vomit.

"Isn't there something I could do instead? An online column? I'd take a cut in pay." Panic rose like the tide in my throat.

"I'm sorry, Tess. There's nothing I can do. The newspaper is in trouble. *Fashionista* sold a lot of advertising."

"I don't understand. Have those advertisers left?"

"No, but we're sure they were just waiting for *Fashionista* to return."

"Oh, I see." I reached deep down and dragged up some self-respect from the soles of my feet. "Okay, then, well, thank you."

I stood and left the room. And my life for the last twenty years. I felt as alone as I did the night Jack walked out on me.

****

"Bastards!" Lucy cursed.

She watched from the sofa as I wrapped Christmas presents, but it wasn't the season that had her so upset. It was merely the last in a string of epithets she had hurled at the management of the newspaper. She voiced my feelings, so I let her rant until she fell back on the sofa pillows, exhausted from the effort.

In the weeks since the infection at Thanksgiving, she had not made much progress toward recovery and, indeed, seemed weaker to me. She had restarted chemotherapy, and, of course, that didn't improve either her mood or her energy level.

Slider jumped on her lap, and she snuggled him close. Syd had confirmed his plans to stay through Christmas, then journey with Bridget and the band to Ireland, where she hoped to connect with her roots and acquire some authentic Celtic instruments. An image of Bridget playing a fiddle and Syd on a tin whistle in a low-ceilinged Irish pub sprang to mind.

"What are you going to do?" Lucy asked, shaking me from my jiggy reverie.

"I don't know. Look for another job, I guess. God knows where."

"You keep your benefits, though? Medical?"

"Oh, for a while, I'm on COBRA. But it's expensive and runs out after eighteen months."

"I'll give you the name of my people. I've been doing my own for years."

"Okay, thanks."

I wrapped in silence for a while, then instructed my phone to play holiday music. After a moment, Enya sang something festively Celtic, and I smiled to myself, wondering if Bridget and Syd would run into her somewhere wildly, remotely Irish.

"You know..." Lucy broke the ethereal quiet. "Maybe now is the time to do some soul-searching. Discover what you want to do with the rest of your life."

I remembered my last conversation with Sam about my journey of self-discovery. I had never taken the first step but had run headlong into Whitney's wedding plans and now Christmas.

"What is it you'd like to do?" Lucy pressed.

"I don't know. The only thing I've ever done is write. And some gardening. And raising children. And wrapping presents." I gestured to the one in front of me, the fourteenth for the baby. When I looked under the tree, it seemed the preponderance of gifts was for Little Baby, who still had no sex or name. But I didn't care. It was something I could do in the midst of my middle-aged meltdown—I could outfit a baby.

"Let's make a list of all the things you can do," Lucy suggested. "It will help hone your job search. And maybe give you new possibilities to explore."

"Okay," I said, setting a rare gift for Sydney aside to wrap later. "Although I can't imagine what good this will do."

"Come on," Lucy encouraged, "where are those rose-colored glasses you're so fond of?"

"Smashed to pieces on the rocks of despair," I quipped, half joking.

But an hour later, amidst much raucous laughter, we had a list of about fifty things I could do or enjoyed, ranging from organizing shelves to teaching grammar.

I looked it over and smiled. "I am an amazing girl."

Lucy tilted her head back and laughed. "Yes, you are. Glad you finally noticed."

"Which of these should I pursue? The ability to sew on a button or my knack for planting tulip bulbs? So many choices, no chance in hell."

"Let's group them into general categories and attach some kind of job to them." She studied the list, pen poised to write down the supposed pursuits that would solve the problem of creating my future income and keeping me off the streets or from moving in with my parents.

After another hour, we had come up with a dozen or so jobs I might realistically pursue, including training to become a master gardener, writing a book, teaching school, or working as a personal assistant.

"I figure I have about six months of savings before I go belly up, so no hurry," I said, setting the lists aside and heading to the kitchen. Slider bounded after me. "How about dinner?"

Lucy answered, "Okay, but where's Donna?"

****

We didn't have a clue where Donna was. It seemed the third member of our slumber party triumvirate was MIA. We had seen her seldom since the day after the wedding when she had come back to the house, looking like the cat that ate the canary—a big hairy canary named Paul.

She and Paul seemed closer to reconciling than ever and had begun what she called "dating" nearly every night. She would come in at all hours or not at all. I was simultaneously elated they seemed to be working things out, concerned they would relapse if Paul got complacent, and ticked off that she was behaving like a smitten teenager while living in my house. It wouldn't have surprised me to find she was sneaking out through an upstairs window when my back was turned.

Was I an annoyed housemother, a supportive friend, or a worried sister-in-law?

Mostly, I was tired of thinking about it.

So, when Lucy asked, "Where's Donna?" My response was a terse, "I don't know, and I don't care."

But I was a little curious when Donna came breezing in as Lucy and I were eating Weight Magic Texas Beef Barbecue dinners from the Americana collection.

"Hi, girls." She waved. "I've come to get my stuff. I'm moving back home."

Lucy exclaimed. "That's wonderful."

I wasn't as excited. "What happened? Are you sure?"

"Oh, yes, it's been great. We've been spending time together, reconnecting, you know. Paul is a very passionate person. And he loves me. He bought me this as an early Christmas present." She held out her arm for us to admire a diamond tennis bracelet.

"It's beautiful, Donna. But what about you, besides jewelry, what's changed in your relationship?" I was skeptical and ignored Lucy's raised eyebrow.

"Well, he's much more of a gentleman. He asks my opinion in a restaurant, about what I want to order. He compliments what I'm wearing and comments on my hair."

Lucy smiled. "That's all good. That's progress, right? He used to dictate those things and insult you."

Donna nodded vigorously. "Yes, true. He doesn't do that anymore."

I said, "That's wonderful. He's sharing control of the boys and the house, giving you freedom?"

Donna hesitated. "I won't really know all that until I move back in, will I? You said he was on the ropes. He's begging me to come home. Telling me how much he needs me."

Red flags popped up in my head. "Oh, Donna, until you hash out those things and come to some understanding, they aren't resolved, and everything can go back to how it was."

"It won't!" she disagreed. "I won't let him do that to me again, and he knows it. Things are different now. It won't be the way it was."

"But you don't have any guarantees."

"Geez, Tess, there aren't any guarantees about

anything. You lost your job. Lucy has cancer. Whitney got pregnant. Where are the guarantees with all that? You don't have control over your life or anyone else's. It's all just a big game of chance."

"But you can make choices, Donna."

"So can you, Tess, but look at you. Your children are gone, and now you don't have your work. I don't want to be like you. All alone. I want my husband and my children and my life back. I love you, and I'm so grateful for what you did for me this fall. And because of it I'm stronger, and I'm ready to go home and be a partner to my husband instead of his maid, his hostess, and his concubine. I'm sorry if you don't think so."

I stood there as if I'd been slapped and watched her go up the stairs to her room. When she came down ten minutes later, I was still there, numbed by the barrage of truths she had thrown at me like grenades. Lucy sat on the sofa, stunned into silence.

Donna thumped down the stairs, her big suitcase barely zipped. She hugged us both. "I love you, I do. This has been so fun, and I'll be forever grateful. But it's time for me to go home to my family."

She stepped through the front door and was gone.

Chapter Sixteen

I worked a half-day on Christmas Eve, sending out a round of goodbye emails and packing the remaining personal items on my desk into a plastic tub. I realized I had amassed weeks of vacation, so I decided to take the rest of the year off. I would finish my last column at home, and that would be that.

Neat and tidy. Just as I liked it.

Besides, I couldn't take the well-wishers and their sad faces and solicitous hugs. My email overflowed with outraged rants and tearful tributes. My emotions were like exposed wires. One more touch and I would ignite in a conflagration of tears and screams.

Okay, it wasn't that bad, but I was sort of on edge.

I thought Lucy and I could enjoy a quiet evening at home, wrap a few straggling presents, concoct a few tidbits for the midday feast tomorrow, and argue about whether to watch *It's a Wonderful Life* or *Miracle on Thirty-Fourth Street*.

Perhaps we would watch them both, and I would use the beloved Yuletide traditions as an excuse to release the floodgates of emotion that threatened to overwhelm me.

Or I could just drink enough eggnog to float a cruise ship, pass out, and wake up in the New Year, past all the pitying looks and self-doubts.

No, everyone's coming to my house tomorrow. I

have to, at least, be vertical.

So, Lucy and I ordered pizza, drank wine, and ended up watching *Sleepless in Seattle*, and I cried like crazy anyway.

She dabbed her eyes as we watched the credits. "You know, Jacob and I are talking about moving to Seattle when I'm finished with chemo."

"Oh my gosh! I love that idea!"

"Yeah, he loves it there and has some family in the city and could start a practice there."

"And what about you? What would you do besides drink coffee and look fabulous?"

"That sounds pretty darn good, but I would work with him as the office manager."

"Wow! This sounds serious. What's the deal with you two, then?"

She got quiet and looked at her lap, then up at me, eyes glistening. "I love him, Tess. And I know he loves me. He tells me all the time."

"Well, then, I think it's wonderful. And this calls for a celebration. Wait right here." I jumped up and ran into the kitchen, where I scrounged in the freezer for something festive but found only ice cream.

Then, in mid-scoop, I stopped cold, convulsed in racking sobs I fought to keep quiet so Lucy wouldn't hear me. I knew why I was crying. And I hated that I was so weak and vulnerable.

I had lost my job. Lennie would head to Kenya before New Year's. Syd was going to Ireland in a few weeks. Whitney was settling into her new home and her new life with Mark, anticipating the birth of their baby. Sam was out of my life. Donna and Paul had reconciled. And now Lucy was leaving.

I'm alone.

Slider danced around my feet, sensing food was in the offing. I picked him up and snuggled him close. Tuxedo rounded the corner, saw my infidelity, and pranced off in search of Lucy. "It's just you and me, bud," I whispered in Slider's floppy ear. He licked the tears from my face in what I took as a sign of unity.

I set him down, grabbed the bowls of ice cream, doused them in chocolate syrup and whipped cream, and went back into the den.

Lucy was lying on the couch, her arm slung over her face. When I shook her, her skin felt hot beneath my fingers.

"Hey, are you okay?" I asked, setting the bowls on the coffee table.

She swung her feet around and sat up. "Sure, just tired. Is it warm in here, or just me?"

"Damn, Luce, you know I can't tell the difference anymore." I shoved one of the bowls at her. "Here, this will help."

We downed the ice cream and walked up the stairs arm in arm.

****

Christmas Day dawned clear and cold, at least cold for Texas, enough that I pulled my robe on to take Slider outside. The air was crisp, and I could already smell the smoke from someone's fire. So, I grabbed a couple of logs from the stack and took them in with me.

Minutes later I had a fire crackling in the grate and that same smell wafted through my house, the scent of warmth and season and family. I wished I felt the way my house smelled.

I tossed cinnamon sticks and cloves into a pot of

water and set it on the stove to simmer. Why not pull out all my seasonal stops in an effort to get into the spirit? It was Christmas after all, my favorite day of the year.

Sydney came downstairs in time to help me get the turkey in the oven. Mom and I had decided to do the traditional turkey-stuffing-cranberry dinner after the Thanksgiving fiasco. Donna didn't care; she was ensconced back home, enjoying her family. We had not even heard from her in a few days.

But we had changed one thing from the Thomason tradition. This year, Christmas would be at my house, not just to take some of the strain off Mom but also to keep Lucy from having to do too much traveling.

It seemed everything was changing.

Most of the food would be coming in with the family, but the turkey and dressing were my area of expertise, and I dispatched them in short order. Then I busied myself setting up tables with Sydney's help.

"How many are we now?" he asked, unfolding card tables and chairs.

"I counted sixteen, including Jacob and Roger."

"How about if we mix it up and don't have a kiddie table? Jason and Matt are the only real kids, anyway. At least until the baby comes."

I agreed, and Syd started working on place cards.

I hadn't bothered Lucy that morning, thinking she'd need to rest up for a long day of fun and festivity. But when I went upstairs at ten o'clock to check on her, I was surprised to see her still in her jammies, sitting on the side of the bed.

"What's up?" I asked.

"Don't know," she said, shaking her bald head. "I just don't feel well. I'm really warm."

I felt her forehead. She was still running a fever, maybe a higher one than the night before, and worse, she felt clammy, too. "Can you get dressed?" I asked.

"Oh, sure, I'll be down in a while."

The doorbell rang.

"Go on," she urged. "I'm fine. You've got company coming."

"I hate leaving you."

"It's not your fault I'm sick during the busy holiday season."

"Yeah, you have such bad timing. Why couldn't you have cancer during Lent? It's so depressing, then, anyway. It would have been so much more appropriate."

I left her laughing and ran down the stairs in time to see Syd usher Paul and Donna into the house, with Matt and Jason right behind. They were all laden with food trays, gaily-wrapped presents, and huge smiles.

"Boys, please set the presents under the tree and put the food in the kitchen for me," Donna spoke with a motherly authority I had not heard before and the boys obeyed without a word. Since the wedding, they had been under "house arrest," grounded from everything fun, including video games. The punishment seemed to have worked.

"Wow," I mouthed at her behind Paul's back.

She grinned and winked.

Paul turned around and said, "Donna, honey, tell Tess your big news."

She beamed at him. "I've decided to start an event-planning business. Handling intimate, fancy dinner parties in people's homes for business or special occasions."

I was stunned at the notion that quiet, submissive

Donna had blossomed into an entrepreneur. "My goodness! That's wonderful! I'm so excited for you. When do you start?"

"I already have a New Year's Eve party lined up for some business associates of Paul's. It seems they appreciated my entertaining skills. And now that I've discovered I love to cook, it seems like a perfect idea."

I glanced at Paul, who glowed with husbandly pride. It was a look I hadn't seen before, and it suited him better than the jackass face he'd been wearing.

"Well, I couldn't be more surprised or thrilled for you!" I said, and I meant it.

At least someone was moving forward with their life.

The doorbell rang again, and I moved to answer it. Mom and Dad came in with a pile of presents and covered casseroles, followed by Lennie, who carried several grocery sacks, which, according to tradition, were filled with a pumpkin pie, cherry pie, and cheesecake.

They all trouped into the kitchen, while I welcomed Tad and Jack, overburdened with delicious goodies, who headed straight for the kitchen as well. They were followed by Jacob, who carried an armful of presents, one perched precariously on top, like a deliciously mysterious cherry, in a very tiny light blue box.

"So, Lucy tells me you all are thinking about moving to Seattle," I ventured, after we had tucked the gifts under the tree.

"That's right. As soon as she's well enough, of course. I'm going to start a practice there."

"I think it's a great idea. And I'm so happy for the two of you."

"Thanks." He smiled his handsome sheik-ish smile and disappeared up the stairs.

Before I could join the others, the bell rang again and I opened it to see Roger standing there, wearing a red sweater and Santa hat, holding an enormous poinsettia.

What a charming dork. He's so like me.

I glanced down at my own outrageous holiday sweater, populated by lamb's wool snowmen, a present from Sydney years earlier.

"Love the hat," I said, grinning.

"Love the sweater," he answered with a kiss on my cheek. I blushed. I couldn't help it.

"Merry Christmas," I said.

"Thanks very much for having me. And my sister in California says thank you, too. She doesn't have to feel guilty for going skiing in Tahoe this year." He handed me the plant.

"It's my pleasure to help assuage your sister's guilt," I said, and I meant it. "This is lovely." I placed the gorgeous flowering specimen on the coffee table.

"Roger, can you open the front door?" Jacob called down the stairs. He came down with his arm around Lucy, who was still in her jammies but now sported one of her silk scarves and cashmere coat.

I rushed to meet them. "What's wrong?"

"She's running a fever, and I want to be sure it's not anything. We're going to the hospital."

She must have sensed my worry because Lucy said with a wan smile, "Don't worry, Tess. We'll be back in time for pie."

"I'll come with you."

"No, absolutely not. You've got a house full of

people. Enjoy your family and your day, sweetie. I'm fine."

"Lucy, I can't let you go alone."

She patted my hand in the way grownups reassured small children and pets. "I'm not alone. I have Jacob."

I looked into the stoic face of the doctor who loved my friend. "Yes, you do, thank God." I stepped off the stairs, opened the front door, and forced a smile onto my face. "Okay, then, I'll see you back here later."

"I'll call you," Jacob said with a reassuring nod.

Lucy yelled over her shoulder, "Merry Christmas, Tess. Save me some cheesecake."

I watched until their car disappeared down the street. When I came back into the house and closed the door, Roger was standing there with his arms open, waiting for me to step into them and begin sobbing.

****

It was only moments before I regained my composure, dried my tears with the backs of my hands, smiled up at Roger, and, taking him by the hand, went into the den where everyone was gathered, oblivious to the drama heading to the hospital.

It was easy to camouflage my feelings and lose myself in yet another of the Thomason celebrations, especially when Whitney and Mark breezed in, smiling and happy in their newly minted wedded bliss.

Lucy is fine. It's just a small infection like before. Nothing to worry about. She'll be home soon, and if not, I'll go see her tonight. She'll hate missing Christmas, but we'll celebrate then. We'll eat cheesecake.

The rest of the day was charmed. We toasted Donna's new venture, wished Sydney well in his travels to Ireland, oohed and ahhed over the adorable layette gifts Whitney opened. If Mark had wished there had been something more manly among the gifts, he didn't let on, which I loved.

Mom was flush with joy when Daddy presented her with two tickets for a cruise to the Mediterranean, leaving in early March.

Lennie was preparing to leave in a few days for Kenya and a photo safari at a game preserve. Her gifts, I noted, were mostly canvas and khaki, an odd combo of rugged and chic which suited only her.

After the last present was unwrapped and the dishes cleared away, Tad passed around a tray of champagne. When he handed me one, he said in a conspiratorial tone, "I've been meaning to tell you, you look fabulous. You've really made a lot of progress this fall."

I smiled. "My clothes fit better, but I didn't think I'd lost a lot of weight."

"Oh, yes, quite a bit." He turned away, handing a flute to Lennie.

The combination of working out, eating Weight Magic food, and walking Slider had made a difference, I knew, but I didn't think it was enough to notice. I appreciated that Tad did.

"So, why the champagne, Dad?" Whitney asked, handing hers to Mark and picking up an iced tea instead.

Jack pulled Roger over to stand beside him. "We have an announcement to make."

My God, they're getting married.

My heart leaped to my throat. I looked at Tad, but he hadn't changed his expression.

"We're ready to launch a new catering venture. It'll be a spin-off of Habanera called Hot Tamales. It's set to debut around wedding season in the spring."

Roger continued, "We'll have a huge, restaurant-quality catering truck, which can set up indoors or out for up to a hundred people and offer food cooked onsite while guests watch."

Jack added, "Thanks to Roger's amazing marketing skills, one of the cooking networks has already expressed interest in doing a feature on us as part of a series on high-end food trucks."

I began fanning myself with a bow I'd picked up off the floor. It was at that moment, as I shed the snowman sweater and tossed it on the hearth, that I realized Donna was right.

I am a pathetic loser.

****

Around dinner time, with my house deserted, I tucked Jacob's blue box in my bag, wrapped a piece of cheesecake in foil, and headed for the hospital. Jacob had not called and didn't answer his cell phone. I tamped down my rising worry and found Lucy's room on the third floor in the same oncology wing she had frequented for her surgery and chemotherapy.

She was sleeping fitfully, the machines humming, beeping, and dripping as usual.

"Lucy," I whispered. "It's me, Tess."

She roused, opening one lazy eye. "Hi, how are you?"

"I'm fine. How are you?"

"I'm mad at my mom."

"Was she here?" I couldn't imagine that Edith Trevain had come to the hospital. Maybe she had called her daughter. It was Christmas, after all.

"She's gone to play bridge. She won't let me go out with Bobby Johnson. She says he's not good enough for me. His dad's a plumber. I like Bobby. He makes me laugh. And he's a good kisser." She giggled.

Oh, no.

"Lucy, where's Jacob?"

"Tess, do you like my hair this way? Bobby says it's cute."

"Lucy, I'll be right back, okay?"

"Hey, I'm gonna sneak out tonight. You wanna stay over? I can get Bobby to meet us. He can bring that nice friend of his—Jack."

Oh, no.

I rushed down the hall to the nurse's station and met Jacob coming toward me with another doctor.

"What the hell's going on? She thinks we're in high school," I demanded.

He put his hands on both my arms to stop me crashing into him, I suppose. "Tess, this is Lucy's oncologist, Dr. Hightower. I called him when she developed such a high fever."

"So, it's an infection? Like before?" I relaxed a little. The devil you know is so much easier to deal with than the one you don't.

"Well, not exactly." Dr. Hightower burst my bubble. "This particular infection is a little rougher, I'm afraid."

"Oh?"

"In Lucy's weakened condition, it's very dangerous."

I looked at Jacob. His usually ruddy complexion was pasty white. "When her fever spiked this morning, I knew it wasn't normal. That's why I brought her in."

My hands began to tremble. "She had a fever last night, but it seemed low. We weren't concerned."

He grabbed my arms again, this time to steady me,

as I had begun to sway a little. "You couldn't have known, Tess. It's okay."

"I have to go back in now." I attempted a weak smile. "We're planning to sneak out tonight to meet some boys."

Jacob ventured a slight smile. "That's the fever talking. Humor her. It won't hurt. And I'll be in and out."

"Thanks," I said, then remembered the tiny blue box. "You left this at the house this morning. I thought you might want to have it for when she's more—present." I handed the box to him.

He turned it over in his hands slowly, sadly. "Thanks, I'll keep it till the time is right."

I nodded and went back into Lucy's room.

****

She died two days later.

She hadn't been strong enough to fend off the onslaught of the infection, and it had consumed her quickly.

The last conversation we had was about what we were going to wear to the prom we had attended thirty-two years earlier.

I didn't even get to say goodbye, so I wallowed in a tub of self-pitying tears for the next twelve hours before I pulled myself together enough to make the phone calls that would get the inevitable ball rolling.

What I hadn't anticipated was that my family would be there *for me*. Mom took over my house and fed the throngs who came to help or just stopped by to pay their respects. Donna made notes of all the flowers and food that poured in. The men sat around, watching football with no sound, taking care of Jacob, who was heart-breakingly bereft.

Whitney helped with the phone calls and held my hand through the painful meeting with the minister to plan the service that would remove Lucy from my life.

Edith flew in from the Hamptons, where she'd spent Christmas. Whitney and I met her at the funeral home. It didn't take long for her to create the chaos she was famous for. No, she didn't want red roses on the casket. "They're so—passé." No, she didn't want a viewing. "I'm sure she looks hideous. All that chemotherapy, the drugs." No, she didn't like the simple, beautiful white casket. "Where did that ghastly *thing* come from? Really, Tess, this is Lucy we're talking about. She needs something more…chic."

That did it. My dam of self-control broke, and the emotions spilled out all over Edith. "More chic? She's dead! And you weren't even here! She didn't need *chic*; she needed her *mother*! And if you had been here, you'd know that she was beautiful right up until the moment she died in my arms."

Whitney's breath caught in a sob.

Edith's mouth twitched at one corner. "Tess, Tess. While I appreciate all you've done for Lucy. This is my decision as her mother—her next of kin. I'll handle the arrangements from now on. Why don't you run along?" She looked at my wrinkled top and tear-stained face. "Go buy something suitable to wear to the funeral."

And then I was able to do what I had wanted to do since the moment I had met that horrible, sanctimonious, evil, mean woman. I was able to excise her from Lucy's life. "Edith, Lucy's instructions were for *me* to arrange her funeral without *your* help. She was quite explicit."

Edith stiffened. "That's outrageous. You can't just move in that way and take over. She's my daughter, after all. Certain conventions must be met for a Trevain funeral." She turned to the funeral director. "I can't allow this, I'm afraid. Please escort Ms. Thomason out."

The dour funeral director, having heard it all before, I'm sure, smiled. "Ms. Trevain, I'm so sorry, but Ms. Thomason is correct. Miss Lucy Trevain called last month, and she made her arrangements, purchased her casket, selected her flowers and music, and was very definite about her preferences and her desire to have Ms. Thomason carry out her wishes."

Clutching Whitney's hand, I turned to Edith and said, "So, Edith, I'm afraid it is you who need to leave. Perhaps *you* can find something suitable for the funeral. Lucy has requested that everyone wear bright colors to the service."

Watching Edith swish from the room was one of the happiest moments in my life.

Chapter Seventeen

Lucy's funeral was breathtaking. The chapel overflowed with friends and flowers. A cascade of red roses topped the elegant, white casket. A skirted table held her portrait, a flickering candle, and one single orchid from Jacob. Simple, sophisticated, beautiful, perfect…just like Lucy.

The gathering at my house afterward was less so. Enormous quantities of food had been brought in by neighbors, friends, and family. The makeshift tables were a jumble of casseroles, cakes, and crudités. Wine, tea, and soft drinks were everywhere. And so was I.

I tried to keep an eye on Jacob, but he was being well taken care of by everyone who had loved Lucy, and him, by osmosis.

Sam showed up long enough to express his condolences, then disappeared out the front door. That made me sad, but only for him.

It was Roger I searched the house for and found in the kitchen, replacing ice in buckets. I walked over to him, and he reached an arm around my shoulder. I instinctively leaned in. He hugged me tighter, and I relaxed into the temporary shelter of his strength.

"You okay?" he asked.

"Yes, so far. Just staying busy."

"I'm here for you," he said. I thought he emphasized the *you*, but it seemed unlikely. But when I looked up to say thank you, his gaze was so genuinely soft and concerned I decided it might be true.

We stood for a long moment looking at each other, our faces inches apart, gazes locked, breathing slowed, and just as I thought he might kiss me, there was a commotion in the living room. The moment was lost.

We made our way back into the living room as Edith Trevain breezed in.

I glued on my best fake smile. "Edith, so glad you came. May I take your coat?"

"No, thank you, I can't stay."

"May I get you a drink?"

Her haughty gaze swept the room and landed on one groaning table. "You should have asked. I would have catered."

"This is a Texas funeral. Everyone brings food. It's tradition."

"How quaint." She looked around again. "Where is the doctor?"

"I assume you mean Jacob," I said, wondering what she would want with him. "He's there." I motioned to where Jacob sat with my parents, balancing a plate of food on his lap, untouched.

Edith wafted over to him. "Dr. Volmer." She stood with her manicured hands folded protectively over her purse.

Jacob set his plate on a nearby table and stood to tower over her. "Hello, Mrs. Trevain. I'm so sorry about Lucy."

"As well you should be, given this is all your fault."

"I beg your pardon."

"Your obvious conflict of interest regarding my daughter clouded your judgment and led to substandard

271

care."

I stepped between them. "Edith, that couldn't be farther from the truth. Jacob was no longer Lucy's doctor. And it was he who realized she had an infection and got her to the hospital." As she began to sputter her objections, I moved in closer. "You're out of line here. This is no time for accusations. You're outnumbered."

Jacob spoke up. "I would be happy to discuss this with you at another time and place, Mrs. Trevain. Or you can contact my attorney."

Most of the family had circled around like a pack of wolves on an injured gazelle. Jack said, "Edith, let me walk you to your car."

She spun on her heel and started toward the door. But unable to leave without a last word, she turned back toward us and growled, "I think maybe you'll all be hearing from *my* attorney."

When she was gone, I sighed. "Well, at least Lucy doesn't have to put up with *her* any longer. I'm sorry, Jacob. You didn't deserve that."

Jacob shook his head. "It's okay, Tess. It happens sometimes. Although usually, it comes from a place of profound grief. Clearly, that's not the case here."

"Sadly, no," I said and poured myself a glass of wine.

****

Sensible Shoes
By Tess Thomason
I lost my best friend last week after a brief illness.
Next to my divorce, it's the worst thing that's ever happened to me. And if it hadn't been for my family, I don't think I could have survived. (Come to think of it, the same was true of the divorce, which was also a kind

of death.)

Coincidently, I am saying goodbye to my time at this newspaper, as well. Sylvia returns soon and Fashionista will once again regale you with all the tips on clothes and beauty you've been missing.

I will be moving on to a new adventure. I hope you will come along with me as I start my SensibleShoes.com blog. I will be continuing our conversation about those things that are funny and wise and poignant and that fourth thing I can never remember.

So, I will see you soon on the Internet. Until then, thank you for joining me on this journey. It wouldn't have been any fun without you.

****

New Year's Eve passed without incident. I had begged off all social engagements (invitations from my folks, the kids, Jack, and even Roger) and had hunkered down with Slider, a bottle of wine, and delivery from a local steakhouse.

To hell with Weight Magic. I was ready to eat my feelings.

On New Year's Day, I went to Lucy's apartment.

I had not ventured there since she died. I went alone, armed with trash bags and bins to begin the daunting chore of dismantling a person's life. I did not take the responsibility lightly.

But I wasn't ready for the onslaught of emotions that came with the opening of the front door. Lucy was everywhere. In every drawer, cabinet, nook, and cranny. I wept and laughed and wept again. I made it through the bedroom, lugged bags and boxes out to my car, and vowed to bring some help next time. Not just to manage the overwhelming load but to ease the burden of decisions and the weight of grief.

Two days later, I received a call from a man who said he was Lucy's attorney. He needed me to come to the reading of her will.

I arrived at his office right behind Jacob, who greeted me with a warm hug.

We were led into the office of Jeremy Willingham, Esq, the Trevain family solicitor. The room was leathery and smelled of old cigars and older money. Jacob and I sat down in chairs across from a huge mahogany desk behind which sat a rotund man wearing a striped suit and pinky ring.

Unbidden, an image of Ruth Wiseman flashed before me. They would have made a lovely couple.

"I've brought you both in to hear the reading of the will of Lucy Trevain. She came to see me a month ago and made a few alterations to her will," Mr. Willingham said in a voice higher and softer than I would have thought possible. He had papers in front of him and began to read under his breath.

He stopped and looked up with a somewhat gleeful look in his eyes. "Ms. Trevain has made it very clear in her will that one million dollars is to be left to Jacob Volmer in hopes he will move to Washington and begin the practice about which he and Ms. Trevain talked."

"Further, the remainder of her estate, holdings, investments, cash, and personal effects goes to Tess Thomason, a sum valued at roughly five million dollars. I am to help Ms. Thomason with the transition and dispensation of the assets and will be retained at a fee of one-hundred-thousand dollars for one year."

The intake of breath from both Jacob and me was audible. I had known Lucy had money, a trust fund from her father, but *millions*? And leaving it to me? I was reeling.

Papers in hand, along with Willingham's card, I found myself with Jacob in the hallway.

He hugged me. "Tess, I'm so glad for you. This will change your life. Everyone's life around you. Lucy loved you so much. You were her entire family."

"And you, too," I said. "She loved you, too, Jacob. I'm so sorry you couldn't go to Washington together."

His smile was laced with sadness. "We were excited to start a new life there. But now, with this gift, she's told me it's okay to go on without her. It's the message I needed, I suppose."

"Well, life will be different for both of us, I guess." I paused, thinking about my friend. "I hope I can stay as grounded as she was."

"You will, I'm sure," he said, patting my shoulder. "It's why she left it to you. She knew you'd do the right things with it."

"It's quite a responsibility."

"Well, you have your family and friends to help you. I'll just be a phone call away. And there's Mr. Willingham, of course."

I laughed. "He's something, isn't he?"

Jacob laughed, too. "Reminded me of a mob boss."

We got on the elevator, rode down in silence, and stepped out into the January sun.

****

The next week was a whirlwind. I had finished cleaning out Lucy's apartment and terminated her lease but had put all her furnishings in storage to be dealt with at my leisure.

After learning about the inheritance, I met with a

financial advisor, and told the family about Lucy's gift. There were a lot of gaping expressions, and Paul had a number of financial suggestions, but everyone had assured me that any decisions I made would be the right ones.

Dozens of ideas roiled in my brain: donations to a number of charities I knew Lucy supported, including breast cancer research, or perhaps starting a foundation in her name.

Mr. Willingham was setting up an LLC for the blog but was moving at a snail's pace. Luckily, my retirement package from the paper would get me through a few months, and an advance on the inheritance made the package less important anyway.

The baby was due February fifteenth. Mark and Whitney had finally succumbed to peer pressure and their own curiosity and found out the baby was a girl, which set in motion a flurry of shopping, decorating, and planning.

Not the least of which was to choose a name. They decided on Lucy Teresa. My sweet friend would have been stunned by the gesture as I was stunned by the choice of Teresa, my seldom-used given name.

The planning also included scheduling family help after the baby came. Mark's mother claimed the first week, which Whitney wasn't thrilled about.

"Mom, I want you to be first!" she whined.

"I know, sweetie, but you're married now, and you will find that sharing events with both sides of the family is important. Anyway, you know you and I will have lots of time with Lucy. I will be right here. Even more, now that I'm working from home on the new blog."

It was true I was home more, but my schedule was

anything but open. It was populated with chunks of time set aside for writing and others for the business of writing. I had set up social media accounts, was working on a website, and looking into ways to monetize the blog.

I was settling into my new life.

The first Sunday after New Year's, we gathered at Mom and Dad's for lunch. The dishes were done, and everyone was scattered around the family room, some watching TV, others putting a puzzle together, the boys playing their newly returned video games, having served their time in fun-free prison.

Mom and I took our coffee into the living room.

I sighed. "It seems like a million years since my birthday party in September."

"A lot has happened since then. You know, Tess, you held it together through everything." She said it without looking at me as if it were a bit of an effort to compliment me.

"I felt like I was being swept along by the tide."

"I kept waiting for you to stumble, but you never did."

I don't think she meant for that to sting as much as it did. "Why would you think that?"

"Well, of my three children, you've always been the softest. The least confident. The weakest."

I laughed. "You sure know how to flatter a girl."

She laughed, too. "What I mean is that you are the most emotional, the most tender, the most vulnerable. None of those are bad things. But they can make you more hesitant, more afraid of risk, and more likely to be hurt."

"Paul and Lennie aren't afraid of the devil, and look where it got them. Paul almost lost his marriage because of his arrogance and need for control. And Lennie wanders the world alone and untethered with no one to love. But look at you!

"When the world and the people you love fell apart last fall, you opened your arms and scooped them all up and held them to you. You got us all through it."

I was crying now, and my mother uncharacteristically gathered me to her and held me tight, patting my hair. I didn't realize how much I needed her.

Then she quickly let me go, smoothed her skirt, and swiped at her eyes.

"Anyway, I'm proud of you and who you have become. Lennie said you are the Mother of Lions. I think she's right."

The Mother of Lions was way better than the Chicken. "I love that. I'm going to get that put on a T-shirt." I kissed my mother on her papery cheek. "Thanks, Mom. I love you."

We finished our coffee and went in to join the puzzle workers and movie watchers.

I felt as if the earth had shifted on its axis.

****

I walked into The White Tiger, armed with the last gift card from my birthday so long ago. Maybe I would get the silk blouse Roger had mentioned that first Saturday at the coffee shop. My new wealth and my new body certainly made a new wardrobe more obtainable, if not necessary.

Although I had made a plan that would require a few new items.

I browsed the racks, enjoying the feel of a cashmere sweater, the cold luxe of a gold bracelet, and the warmth of an imported, ankle-length coat. I had absolutely no idea what I wanted or even needed. I wished that Lucy were with me to guide my seldom-used fashion sense.

A saleswoman approached. "Can I help you?"

She spent the next two hours bringing one beautiful garment after another to my dressing room. And I tried them all on, choosing or discarding them based solely on how it made me feel when I looked in the full-length mirror.

Never had I been so selfishly indulgent. It was glorious.

At the counter, the saleswoman wrapped each piece in tissue, slipped them into the familiar The White Tiger bags, and tied the handles with ribbons. I walked out of the store with the makings of a new wardrobe, including a beautiful silk blouse and a very chic, black swimsuit.

All of it was a size smaller than I had worn in years, the result of four months of Weight Magic food, walking Slider every day, and carrying the weight of the world on my shoulders. Worry burns up a lot of calories.

Just ask my mother.

****

Mother of Lions
Tess Thomason
Back in September, I set off on a quest to spend four gift cards that implied I was hairy, fat, ugly, and unfashionable. Sadly, most of those things were true.

But since then, I have used those cards as stepping stones on a pathway to discovering my true self. Along the way, I experienced heartbreak, chaos, confusion, elation, broken relationships, and new, exciting ones.

I embraced loss. I stood my ground. I spoke my mind.

I became the Mother of Lions.

You can read it here on my T-shirt.

And on the name of this new blog. (The lawyers won't let me use the old name.)

So, I am embarking on a new adventure with this new blog.

It's actually the same old blog you're used to. I mean, I will still write to you about the things that matter to women: laundry, library books, family, friends. All those things that are nothing special and also everything that matters.

I hope you'll come along with me as we continue our journey of self-discovery.

I'd love your company.

****

I buckled my seatbelt and settled into the luxury of first class for the flight to Ft. Lauderdale. Tomorrow, I would board a luxurious cruise ship for seven glorious days of sun and sand, decadent food, and unbounded relaxation.

After the conversation with my mother, I decided to give myself a little reward for being the weakest of her children. A getaway to pamper myself before the baby came.

I decided to start small, with something to get my feet wet, so to speak. Since it was so last minute, I got a good deal on a one-week cruise to the Caribbean, even upgrading the flight to first class. It didn't occur to me later that it didn't matter if it were a good deal, and I wondered if I would ever get over the need to pinch pennies.

I had to hurry so I could be back in time for Lucy Teresa's birth. Although Mark's mom would be staying at the house first, Whitney had made it crystal clear I was to be there when she went to the hospital. What she didn't seem to know was I would not miss those first special moments for the world.

Sydney had left after New Year's for Ireland. I had gotten a few texts from him but was surprised to realize I wasn't too worried about him. He'd turn up eventually. If for no other reason than to pick up Bridget's dog, which was currently staying with Jack. I felt it was his turn to experience the little poopster.

I hadn't seen Roger since the funeral. When I asked about him, Jack told me he was traveling, working through locations for Habanera, and finalizing plans for the catering truck. I missed him more than I wanted to admit. He had been a comforting presence for me throughout the entire fall, and not seeing him had left a hole in my life that grew larger every day.

It might have been a hole in my *heart* if I had been willing to admit it. A big, cavernous hole left by all the lost and broken relationships that had been my life. A hole I had tried to fill with taking care of everyone but me. A hole I had secretly dreamed would be filled by Roger. But it was clear Roger was just a nice guy who, gay or not, wasn't that into me, judging by the radio silence I had been experiencing. And the idea I was in love with a man I would never have was one more loss I didn't want to deal with.

Maybe the trip would help me get over Roger. Maybe I would meet some dashing tycoon onboard. Someone who appreciated an older woman who wore comfortable shoes and enjoyed the occasional ice cream.

I sighed and settled into my seat as a parade of passengers filed past, but no one claimed the seat next to me. I smoothed my hands over the new top and pants I had bought at The White Tiger, closed my eyes, and leaned my head back, thinking about ice cream, when I heard a familiar voice.

"Excuse me, I think this is my seat."

My eyes snapped open, and I found myself staring at Roger, dressed impeccably in khakis and a blue polo shirt, putting his bag in the overhead compartment.

He didn't acknowledge me but sat down and busied himself with his seatbelt. Before I could even find my voice, the flight attendant asked us if we'd like a beverage. He answered easily, "We'll have two white wine spritzers."

"What are you doing here?" I squeaked.

"I'm flying to Ft. Lauderdale."

"That's so crazy. Me, too," I said, mouth agape. "Do you have business there?"

He laughed, that deep, rich sound I loved. "No, just pleasure, I hope."

"What do you…" I didn't finish because he took my face in his hands and kissed me like he meant it.

When he stopped, I took a breath and stuttered, "H-h-how—when—?"

"Ah, Tess, I've been trying to get you alone for months. Jack told me about the cruise. I decided if we were ever going to have a minute to ourselves to figure things out, I better get on that boat with you."

We were interrupted by the arrival of two drinks delivered by a grinning flight attendant.

"Figure out what?" I asked when she was gone.

"Figure out this," Roger whispered and kissed me again.

In that moment, the hole in my heart began to heal.

A word about the author...

Cindy Causey taught herself to type in the 8th grade because she couldn't write in her diary fast enough in longhand. A career as an advertising copywriter was the result. A fifteen-year stint as a copy chief at JCPenney Catalog qualified her to become Content Development Manager for JCPenney.com and then Internet Marketing Manager. After 20 years at JCPenney, Cindy retired in December, 2007, and started a multi-media production company, Dallas Media Center, with her husband, Scott..

After her first book, a non-fiction work called Cherish the Gift: a Congregational Guide to Earth Stewardship, was published, Cindy began writing fiction. She found her voice in romance, stories of the struggles two people endure on the road to happily ever-after.

Her first book, A Different Drum, was published in May 2009 by The Wild Rose Press. Cindy's second romance, A Hot Time in Texas, also with The Wild Rose Press, came out in August of 2009.

Scott passed away in 2019, and Cindy retired from the media business a few years later. She has continued writing and is excited about her latest published work for The Wild Rose Press, Sensible Shoes, coming out in 2024.

In addition to writing, Cindy enjoys digital scrapbooking, traveling, and spending time with her five grown children and four grandchildren. She would like to see the edges of the entire world from the deck of a cruise ship.

You can read more from Cindy on her blog, TheWidowWoman.com. www.cindycausey.com

Thank you for purchasing
this publication of The Wild Rose Press, Inc.

For questions or more information
contact us at
info@thewildrosepress.com.

The Wild Rose Press, Inc.
www.thewildrosepress.com